Most chil[...]ward to a
holiday i[...] the winter family
didn't want to go at all. For Rachel it meant giving up
her first real job as a dancer; for Tim it meant missing
the chance of being taught the piano by the great Jeremy
Caulder; and for Jane, the middle one, the difficult one
who didn't shine at anything in particular, it was worst of
all – she had to leave her dog, Chewing-gum, behind.
Yet they couldn't make a fuss, for their father had been
ill and needed to convalesce in the sunshine. When they
arrived, so many exciting things happened they forgot
their black moods of disappointment. Rachel met Posy
Fossil, now a famous ballerina, and her sister Pauline;
Tim found a piano; and Jane, who behaved rather badly
because she was missing Chewing-gum so much, had the
biggest adventure of all . . .

Noel Streatfeild's father was a Church of England vicar,
and she and her brother and sisters grew up in several
vicarages in the south of England. She draws on exact
memories of her own childhood for scenes in her books,
and her interest in stage children is a direct result of her
own career in the theatre.

NOEL STREATFEILD

THE PAINTED GARDEN

*

A Story of a Holiday in Hollywood

*

Illustrated by
SHIRLEY HUGHES

PUFFIN BOOKS

PUFFIN BOOKS

Published by the Penguin Group
27 Wrights Lane, London W8 5TZ, England
Viking Penguin Inc., 40 West 23rd Street, New York, New York 10010, USA
Penguin Books Australia Ltd, Ringwood, Victoria, Australia
Penguin Books Canada Ltd, 2801 John Street, Markham, Ontario, Canada L3R 1B4
Penguin Books (NZ) Ltd, 182–190 Wairau Road, Auckland 10, New Zealand

Penguin Books Ltd, Registered Offices: Harmondsworth, Middlesex, England

First published by Collins 1949
Published in Puffin Books in a revised edition 1961
15 17 19 20 18 16 14

Copyright 1949 by Noel Streatfeild
All rights reserved

Printed and bound in Great Britain by
Cox & Wyman Ltd, Reading
Set in Monotype Caslon

CONTENTS

FOREWORD

THIS is a story which is partly to do with the making of a film of THE SECRET GARDEN by Frances Hodgson Burnett. I could never have written this book without a great deal of help from a great many people, so I want to say 'Thank you'.

The first people I want to say 'Thank you' to are William Heinemann Ltd, the publishers in England of Frances Hodgson Burnett's books. They gave me leave to quote from THE SECRET GARDEN. 'Thank you very much, William Heinemann Ltd.'

There is a thing called copyright which belongs to the authors when they are alive, and is left to somebody when they are dead. Miss Frances Hodgson Burnett is dead, but the copyright belongs to Mrs Verity Burnett Chisholm. Permission was asked of Mrs Verity Burnett Chisholm for parts of THE SECRET GARDEN to be quoted and she too said, 'Yes, you may'. 'Thank you very much, Mrs Verity Burnett Chisholm.'

The Bee Bee Studios in this book are made up, and are not a bit like any studio in Hollywood, and everybody working at the studios is made up and is not a bit like any living person working at a real studio. But the Bee Bee Studios and the people working in them are as nearly like the real thing as I can get them, and the people I have to thank for that are the Publicity Department of Metro-Goldwyn-Mayer Studio. 'Thank you very much, Metro-Goldwyn-Mayer.'

The Painted Garden

CHAPTER I

THE LETTER

It was the first week of the autumn term. The Winter children sat round the dining-room table. They were supposed to be working. Actually there was not very much homework being done. Even Rachel, the eldest, who was twelve, and usually almost as conscientious about her homework as she was about her dancing practice – and that was saying a great deal – had not got her mind on her work. Tim, the youngest, who was eight, was not supposed to do any real homework, but was supposed to 'fill in the time usefully', which really meant anything except playing the piano, while the girls were doing their homework. On this evening he was drawing a picture of two cats meeting on the top of a brick wall, an inferior sort of drawing but one he sometimes did very well. Jane, the middle one, who was ten, never even on her best days worked at homework, or, in fact, at anything else. The worst thing about Jane, as Rachel often said, and so did those who taught her, was that she seemed to learn things without working. She did not know the things very well but she aggravated whoever was teaching her, because when they said, 'Jane, you're not attending. What have I just been saying?' she nearly always could reel off every word that had been said and looked smug after she had repeated them. The children's grandmothers, when they came to stay, said Jane had a difficult nature, or Jane was difficult to understand. Miss Bean, called by everybody Peaseblossom, who was part of the family, a friend of the children's mother, who had come to the house to give a hand when Rachel was born and had stayed on doing everything that nobody else wanted

to do ever since, said that Jane was all right if you took her
the right way. When she said that it made Jane's mother sigh
and say she was not always clever, she was afraid, at finding
the right way. Rachel and Tim did not exactly criticize Jane.
Sometimes they groaned and made expressive faces, but mostly
they just accepted her. There she was, with bad days, worse
days, and worser days, but one thing she hardly ever had was
a good day. The children's father, in the time before the accident, had called her his 'little millstone', because, he said, she
was a millstone round his neck which was bowing his back;
but the way he used to say that made everybody, including
Jane, laugh. You could see that though, like all the others, he
often found her terribly aggravating, he was very glad she
was there, millstone or not.

Rachel was trying to finish her algebra. Mathematics was

not her subject. Even when she was giving her whole attention to it she was not often able to get a right answer. Today, with not even a quarter of her mind on what she was doing, the answers she was getting would have disgraced the jury in *Alice in Wonderland*. You cannot work out the sort of problem which begins 'Let x equal the number . . .' when both ears are strained until they feel as long as a donkey's to hear little sounds that might tell you what is going on in the drawing-room overhead.

Jane was not even pretending to read her chapter on the Magna Carta. She never had cared for history, and what she called 'that old Barony bit' she hated worst of all. She was not pretty at the best of times; now, with her plaits untidy and a scowl on her face, she looked downright ugly. She felt a sort of emptiness inside which gave her a pressed feeling in front because she was frightened. Her ears were strained for sounds, just as Rachel's were strained, only whereas Rachel tried to work to keep her mind off her worries, Jane let her feelings out by kicking at the leg of the table.

Tim looked up reproachfully.

'It's not a very important drawing I'm doing, but this was a nearly perfect cat; now you've kicked the table and the tail has run all down into the brick wall.'

Rachel was in charge at homework. She knew, even if it was her duty to do so, it was no good telling Jane not to do something. Her voice showed she knew that what she was saying might just as well never have been said.

'Don't kick the table, Jane.'

Rachel was pretty, that sort of prettiness that nobody argues about. She was small and fair; her hair, unlike Jane's, curled, and, even more unlike Jane's, her plaits never got that hairs-standing-out-everywhere look. Even if Rachel got ink on her nose or had a cold she remained more or less pretty. Jane thought it was one of the meaner things about life that

Rachel should be pretty and Tim noticeable and she, in the middle, should be plain. There were so many things that Jane ranked as mean, and hoped to put right one day, that if she had written them out they would have filled a whole exercise book.

'Doesn't make any odds if I kick the table; nobody wants to see Tim's drawing and you'll get all the answers wrong whether I do or don't; you always do.'

This gloomy fact was so true that Rachel could not argue about it.

'You couldn't be more right, but you know I've got to do them. I mayn't do any practice until they're finished.'

Rachel's reasonableness was another thing that Jane found mean about life; she never felt reasonable herself.

'I couldn't think that any child wanted to practise dancing with its father ill upstairs and the doctor there deciding if he'll ever be well again.'

The words had been said. They flowed into the school-room like a door opening, letting in a cold wind. Until that moment the children had been trying to pretend to each other that nothing unusual was happening, that this was an ordinary day. Nobody wished more than Jane that she could take the words back. She had been glad of the pretending by the grown-ups and themselves there was nothing wrong, that one day things would come right, and life be as it had been before Dad's accident. Saying what she had said would not do any good; it just made everybody feel worse because they had to admit that there was something to fuss about. Angry with herself she got up and marched over to the window. It was raining; long, straight, grey lines of rain, falling relentlessly on London. The houses in Saxon Crescent were narrow and all alike and not very nice to look at at any time. When it was raining they looked simply awful. Now that the summer was nearly over there were not even flowers to be seen in the window-boxes, except some shabby, dirty geraniums at number four.

Rachel finished her last problem; it was wrong, but she had done it. She looked at Jane's back. She guessed that she had said what she had said because it was her way of being worried.

'He'll get better. It isn't as if he was properly ill, in bed with a temperature and medicines and all that. It's just a matter of time.'

Tim looked up from his drawing.

'Everybody's been saying it's only a matter of time ever since it happened, and that was last January, which was months and months ago.'

Rachel joined Jane at the window.

'If only it didn't have to be winter soon. Dad's heaps better when the sun shines.'

Jane thumbed the curtain with her fist; she wanted to hurt somebody, and Rachel was the easiest person to get at.

'We ought to live in the country; we would live in the country if it wasn't for our dear little ballerina, Rachel Winter, the child wonder.'

There was a pause. Rachel's inside felt as if it turned right over when people talked about living in the country, and there had been talk of it since Dad's accident. Of course, if it would cure Dad to go to the country, she would do her best to bear it, but it was something she could not think about, especially now when she had just had her twelfth birthday and Madame Fidolia was talking about auditions for Christmas pantomimes; besides, she had sense on her side. In a pantomime she might earn some money. Nobody tried to pretend that they did not need money now that Dad had been ill and unable to work for nearly nine months. She said at last:

'There's Tim's piano lessons as well as my dancing, and, actually, the sun doesn't shine in the country any more than it does in London; it's just that you see more of it because there are less houses and things.'

Tim sprawled across the table.

'It isn't often that I agree with Jane, but I do think

that's the most awful lie, if you don't mind my saying so. When I was evacuated to the country the sun shone almost every day.'

Rachel left the window and opened her attaché case, which was on the table, and took out her ballet shoes.

'You don't really remember, Tim; you spent most of being evacuated in a perambulator.'

This was true, but Tim did not like the fact that he was the youngest rubbed in. He said in his grandest voice:

'As a matter of fact, you see the sun rather better from a perambulator than you do standing up.'

Jane gave a squeak and peered sideways through the window pane up the street.

'Here's Peaseblossom and Chewing-gum. I bet the poor darling is terribly wet. I told Peaseblossom it wasn't fit for him to be out.'

Rachel tied on her shoes.

'If it comes to that it isn't fit for Peaseblossom either.'

Jane was still peering up the road.

'Oh, he is wet, the poor angel! His fur's sticking to him so tight he looks as though he hasn't got any. I'll have to rub him and rub him to get him dry.' She turned angrily to Rachel. 'That's like you to stand up for Peaseblossom, who's got a mackintosh and goloshes while poor little Chewing-gum has to walk along on his bare feet and nothing to cover him but his own fur.'

Rachel had tied on her shoes; now she raised herself on to her points.

'Don't forget to see you use his own towel; it's not the sort of day to have a row about using the bathroom one.'

Jane had opened the door. She was about to make a rude answer when voices were heard. Doctor Smith and their mother were talking at the bottom of the stairs. They were speaking quietly, but every word could be heard by the children.

16

'I know you're right,' their mother said, 'he mustn't spend this winter in England, but you know how difficult things are.'

Doctor Smith was always in a hurry and this made his voice have a permanent I-must-go note. All the same the children could hear he was trying to be kind.

'If only you could persuade him to get this bee out of his bonnet that he can't go alone.'

'It's going to be difficult; he was away so long in the war he feels he must be with me and the children.'

'But it's only a few months, and it might be the answer. It might cure him completely. Would he get on with that sister of his?'

'I don't know, I've never seen her; she married an American who died two or three years ago. John hasn't seen her since she was eighteen; I don't somehow see him going off to her on his own.'

Jane suddenly realized that, without meaning to, they were eavesdropping. She softly closed the door, but not before they heard Doctor Smith say:

'All the same, you must persuade him. I assure you another winter . . .'

The children looked at each other. Somehow, although they had been accustomed to being moved about during the war, that was years ago and they had almost forgotten it. They were used now to having a home and their father and mother with them. Tim spoke this thought out loud.

'Dad can't go away without us; all proper homes have a father and mother in them.'

Rachel said to Jane:

'That's Aunt Cora they were talking about, the one who offered to have you and me and Mum when London was bombed.'

Tim felt he was being cut out of relationship to Aunt Cora.

'She would have asked me too if I'd been born.'

Jane looked scornful.

'If we had gone to Aunt Cora you'd have been born after we'd got there, and that would have made you a citizen of the United States of America, and you wouldn't have been allowed to come back here after the war, which I often think would have been a good thing.'

Rachel guessed that Jane was only being nasty to Tim because feeling frightened inside at the thought of Dad going away made her have to be nasty to somebody.

'If Dad ought not to be in England this winter we'll simply have to persuade him to go away, but I do wonder who's going to pay; it must cost heaps and heaps of money to go to the United States. I do hope I get a job in pantomime, then I could help.'

Jane went out into the hall. She felt miserable. It was not only the talk of her father going away, but she hated it when Rachel talked about getting into a pantomime. It was not that she wanted to be able to dance, but she wished she was good at something. Nobody knew yet just how good Tim would turn out to be, but he was admitted to be unusually musical, and Rachel, if she went on as she was now, was sure to be a professional dancer; but here was she, good at nothing, unless you counted understanding dogs as something. She was sure that if only she had the chance she could earn a lot of money as a dog trainer, but at present she had only Chewing-gum, and though he was willing he was far from performing dog standard. Even though he had learnt to carry a newspaper he had never quite understood that he must not bite the paper to pieces.

Peaseblossom was sitting on a chair in the hall taking off her goloshes. She was that kind of woman who you could see had once been a splendid head of the school and captain of games. Even now expressions like 'Play the game, old thing' came to her naturally. The children's mother and she had been friends at school, mostly, the children's mother said, because she had not been good at anything, whereas Peaseblossom had been good at everything and was sorry for her. Peaseblossom had carried the being sorry into grown-up life. When she saw the children's mother struggling, not very effectively, to look after new-born Rachel, she gave up being a games mistress and took charge. 'You aren't fit to handle a baby and a house on your own, Bee, old thing,' she had said, 'better let me lend a hand. If we all pull together we'll manage splendidly.' She was quite right; they had managed splendidly. The children's mother was the gentle, rather spoiling, sort, and when their father had been away in the war the children might have grown up loathsome if Peaseblossom had not been there. Peaseblossom, though she was nice about it, believed in discipline. 'Rules are made to be kept.' 'No good saying a thing and not sticking to it.' 'Play up and play the game.' She looked up from her golosh at Jane's cross face.

'Quite true, Chewing-gum's sopping. Take him and give him a good rub down, but for goodness' sake use his own towel.'

Jane knelt down by Chewing-gum and felt his coat. He was a red cocker spaniel and usually a lovely autumn leaf colour, but now his fur was dark with water. He had been given to Jane by an American soldier who had left him behind when he went back to his own country. He had not had a name when he came to the children, for the soldier had just called him 'Pup', so Jane had christened him Chewing-gum because that was what the American soldier was always doing. She played with his wet ears.

'Did you see Doctor Smith, Peaseblossom?'

Peaseblossom gave Jane a quick look to see if she had heard anything.

'Yes, just leaving as I came in.'

'Where's Mum?'

'Up with your father in the drawing-room. Run along,

child, do, and dry that dog. Don't want a case of pneumonia in the house.'

Jane got up, but she still loitered. Peaseblossom would sooner or later know everything that was going on; she longed to think of a way to say to her, 'We heard about Aunt Cora, do go and find out if Dad's going away and, if you do find out anything, please tell us,' but she could not. It seemed difficult to say somehow, so, after a second or two, she called Chewing-gum.

'Come on, angel, come on, poor drowned dog. I'll rub you until you haven't a wet hair left.'

In the drawing-room Mr and Mrs Winter were standing together looking into the wet street.

'There's no harm done in writing to her, John, dear,' Bee Winter was saying. 'It must be lovely in California in the winter. Fancy! Oranges grow there! I believe it's never really cold.'

John scowled.

'What a place to live, Hollywood!'

'It's not Hollywood itself. You know the address is Santa Monica; she told you in one of her letters that her house was by the sea. If she had you to stay for two or three months it would just get you over the winter and then you might come back perfectly well.'

Though Bee did not mean her voice to sound pleading it was pleading on the last line. She could not help remembering John a year ago when he had been well. He was not always easy tempered because he was a writer and got angry with himself and everybody else when he could not write well, but he had been gay and excited about things, rushing into the room after a good day's work to tell her about it. Since the accident all that was gone. It was not his fault that a child had darted across the road to pick up a ball and had been killed. At the inquest John had been entirely exonerated; he had been driving slowly and carefully; it was the child, who had never been taught to cross a road properly, who was to blame, but that had made no difference to John; he had become ill from thinking about the dead child, so ill that he had what the doctor called a nervous breakdown, and when that got better he had lost faith in himself and decided he could never write again. The only thing which did him good was sunlight. Sometimes when the sun shone he would settle down at his typewriter and work away for an hour or two, then in would go the sun and he would slide back to his glooming mood saying, 'It's no good, Bee, I'm finished as a writer.' Bee knew that was not true, knew that if only he would go away, see new things, sit in the sun and give himself a chance, he was just as good a writer as he had ever been, but she also knew that if he did not get well soon she had got to say, 'Well, what are you going to do instead? There's this house to run; there's Rachel, Jane and Tim needing breakfast, dinner, lunch and tea, as well as new clothes because they're always growing out of them, and we've been living on our savings since January and they're nearly finished.' Thinking of these things she laid her face against John's shoulder.

'Just write to her, darling. Tell her what the doctor says. Write a nice long letter by air mail and see what happens. After all, if she invites you and you don't want to go you can always refuse the invitation; there's no harm done.'

John shivered. He was so tired and ill that even sitting down to write a letter made him feel worse, but he hated to refuse Bee anything. He gave her a lop-sided sort of smile.

'All right, I'll write to her if it'll please you, but I don't think she'll invite me, and if she did, I wouldn't go. I'm not leaving you and the children.'

Bee went to the writing-table; she laid out a piece of air mail paper.

'You write it now. I'll ask Peaseblossom not to take off her mackintosh, I'd like that letter to catch the six o'clock post.'

CHAPTER 2

THE IMPORTANT WEDNESDAY

WEDNESDAY started like an ordinary day. Rachel, as usual, flew out of the house five minutes before she need have started because she was so fond of her dancing school that she could not bear to waste time eating breakfast when she could be on her way to it. Jane and Tim went to the same school, and every day had the same sort of arguments before they started. This Wednesday was no exception. Bee said:

'Hurry up, darlings, and finish eating. You've only five minutes before you start.'

Jane immediately helped herself to another piece of bread and slowly spread jam on it.

'Yes, hurry up, Tim, I always have to wait for you.'

Tim had been just about to finish his milk, but at that insult he had put down his cup.

'That's the most monstrous lie. Yesterday me and Pease-blossom and Chewing-gum were standing at the gate, and standing at the gate so long that we didn't get to school until prayers were over, and both me and you got unpunctuality marks.'

Jane stuck her chin in the air.

'That was just once and only because Mum made me change my socks for so small a hole that anybody but Mum wouldn't have seen it; but almost every day I'm made late by you looking for your music and . . .'

Dad had seemed to be reading the paper. Now he looked up. His voice sounded as if it would very easily turn from a talking voice to an angry one.

'Shut up, kids. Scram.'

Peaseblossom took Jane and Tim to school. It was not far and they could have gone alone, but it was a habit which had never been dropped and had the advantage of giving Chewing-gum an early morning run. Jane ran on ahead with Chewing-gum. Tim walked beside Peaseblossom carrying his case of music. Usually they met the same people. The postman finishing his round, the dustmen and so on. This Wednesday, as they turned the school corner, coming towards them was the school music master, Mr Brown, and walking with him was another man. Tim liked Mr Brown better than anybody else he knew. Usually he would have run to meet him, but he did not like to as Mr Brown was not alone, so he just looked pleased. Mr Brown said something to his friend and when he got level with Tim he stopped.

'How are you? This is Mr Jeremy Caulder. If you weren't a little ignoramus you'd have heard of him.'

Mr Caulder shook hands with Tim.

'How do you do? I stayed with my godson here last night and he told me about you. You are fond of music, I hear.'

Tim was surprised that somebody who was as old as Mr Brown had a godfather. He had thought that stopped when you grew up, and Mr Brown must have been grown-up for years because he had said he would be thirty next birthday. Tim was so amazed about this that he almost forgot to answer Mr Caulder.

'Yes. Aren't you?'

Mr Brown laughed.

'Jeremy Caulder is one of the best piano players we have. He says I may bring you over to play to him this morning.'

Tim looked hopefully at Mr Caulder.

'Could I come at eleven? We do French then, which I simply hate.'

Mr Caulder seemed a nice reasonable sort of man. He said at once that eleven would suit splendidly. He and Mr Brown moved on. Tim wanted to move on too, but seeing Mr

Caulder seemed to have done something to Peaseblossom. She stared after him as if he were a blue elephant or something equally unusual. Jane came racing back with Chewing-gum.

'Come on, Tim, we'll be awfully late. What's up, Pease-blossom? That's only Mr Brown who teaches us piano and singing.'

Peaseblossom seemed to pull herself away from Mr Caulder's back like a person forcing themselves to wake up. Her voice was hushed with awe.

'That's Jeremy Caulder. I've heard him at the Albert Hall and often on the air. He wants Tim to play to him at eleven.'

Jane was not interested.

'More fool Mr Caulder. Do come on, Tim.'

Tim was not impressed either.

'All right, I'm coming; it's not my fault if Mr Brown stops and speaks. It would be awfully rude to walk on.'

Peaseblossom laid a hand on Tim's shoulder.

'This is your chance to show what you're made of. The family depends on you not to let down the side.'

Rachel arrived at the children's academy for dancing and stage training. As usual she went down to the changing-room for she had an hour's dancing class before she began lessons. The moment she opened the changing-room door she knew something tremendous was in the air. The other girls tried to tell her what it was, but as they all spoke at once she could not get the news straight at first; when she did get it straight she understood the excitement. At twelve o'clock a theatrical manager was coming to the school, bringing the man who arranged the dancing for his shows. He wanted six children for a big musical production. The top classes were to dance for him.

Rachel changed into her practice things. Her heart was beating so loud she thought she could hear it. She must get chosen, she must. It would be the most perfect thing that had ever happened to her, and simply marvellous happening now.

Imagine coming home and being able to say to Dad and Mum, 'I've got an engagement'. Mum wouldn't say much, but, of course, she'd feel less worried; who wouldn't? Somebody earning money just now would make all the difference. Her best friend, Caroline, came over to her.

'I bet you get chosen. You and, of course, Miriam and Sylvia, Frances, Audrey and Annette.'

The six were all small and considered in the school exceptionally promising. Quite honestly, that was the list Rachel would have picked, only she did not dare put herself so firmly on it as Caroline did, and there was always the chance the manager, or the man who arranged the dances, liked Caroline, and that took one of the rest of them out. Caroline was promising all right, but nobody could call her pretty; in fact she was plain. Rachel put an arm round her.

'Counting you, with any luck we ought to be the ones he chooses; six of us to dance and one to understudy.' Inside herself she added, 'Oh, don't let me be the understudy, though that would be better than nothing.'

*

Tim brought his news home first. He had a letter about it for his father. Mr Jeremy Caulder would give him piano lessons. Not regularly because he was away a great deal playing at concerts, but whenever he was in London. Mr Brown, who wrote the letter, said Mr Caulder agreed with him that Tim was an unusually musical boy and ought to have a chance, and for the time being the lessons would be free.

Dad had been sitting looking terribly tired and interested in nothing when the letter came, but after he had read it he was quite different. He said he had often heard Mr Caulder play and if he thought Tim was worth teaching there might be more in Tim's strumming than met the ear. He was gay enough even to pretend to box with Tim, something he had not done for weeks.

On top of the Tim excitement Rachel rushed in. She was in such a state she poured out her story so fast that her words tripped up on each other.

'Mr Glinken came to see us dance and brought the most marvellous man with him; he called him Benny. Benny showed us afterwards some things we'd have to do. He's, Mr Glinken, I mean, not Benny, putting on a simply enormous musical play and I'm one of the six children. Real dancing we're doing. Madame Fidolia's no end bucked. He chose, Mr Glinken, I mean, not Benny, me, Miriam, Frances, Audrey, Annette and Sylvia and Caroline's going to understudy. That's the only awful part, they took simply ages choosing between Sylvia and Caroline and when they chose Sylvia, though I was the only one who saw, Caroline cried.'

Though the drawing-room was not very big and was full of furniture Rachel could not bear that the family should not have the thrill of seeing the sort of dances Benny was arranging. She did not bother to take off her coat and hat or change her shoes, but just as she was, and as well as she could, she showed them Benny's steps.

Peaseblossom glowed.

'Well, this is a day! Up the Winters! Tim to be trained by Mr Caulder himself and Rachel a real professional dancer. Our side's doing splendidly. I think this deserves a special tea. I'll see what I can find.'

Peaseblossom did not get as far as the kitchen. A few moments after she had left the room she was back. She was holding two letters, a dull looking, long typewritten envelope for herself and a letter with American stamps marked 'Air Mail' for John.

The children knew John had written to Aunt Cora and that Peaseblossom had posted it. They did not know Bee had put on enough stamps to send it by air. They had not expected Aunt Cora would answer for weeks. Because nothing more had been said about it, John's going to California had gone to the back of their minds. It was not a certain thing like Christmas or a birthday or the beginning of term, it was just a 'perhaps'. Now, looking at Dad's fingers opening the thin air mail envelope with Aunt Cora's name and address on the flap, they felt cold inside. Could Dad be going away? Going all the way to Aunt Cora? Aunt Cora, who was only partly real, like people are whom you have never seen but only heard about.

John straightened the letter. Bee leant on his shoulder and read it too. All down one page, all over the next, all down the next sheet and half-down the back page, and while they read the children's three pairs of eyes were fixed on them. At the end John gave a half-laugh, half-snort and pushed the letter back into its envelope.

'Silly fool of a woman! What does she think I'm going to do for money?'

Bee said quickly:

'That's not fair. You told her it was what the doctor ordered and that it wasn't likely you'd really do it because of leaving me and the children, and she answers by not only asking the whole lot of us but Peaseblossom as well. I call it marvellous of her.'

John looked at the children.

'How would you like to go to California for the winter?' The children looked startled. 'All right, don't worry, there isn't a chance of it. It would cost in fares about a thousand pounds and your father would be put to it just now to find a thousand pence. Let alone we'd have to carry a grand piano for Tim and . . .'

Peaseblossom made a choking sound. They turned to look at her. Her face, which was always red, was the colour of an over-ripe purple plum. She was holding out a crisp sheet of notepaper, as if, by looking at the back of the letter, they could read what it said. Bee ran to her.

'What is it, dear? Bad news?'

Peaseblossom struggled to get her breath, just as if she was getting it back after tea had gone down the wrong way.

'We can go. All of us. An old aunt has died that I never met. She's left me a thousand pounds.'

CHAPTER 3

WILL YOU? WON'T YOU?

TALK went on all the evening. First of all there was a terrific argument with Peaseblossom about spending her legacy on the family's fares to the United States. It did not matter what John and Bee said, Peaseblossom had made up her mind. All her life she had wanted to travel, but up to that Wednesday in September it had been just dim wanting, now with the coming of the letter with the news of her legacy she became like someone dying of thirst who sees water; nothing and nobody was going to stop her having what she wanted. To every argument John and Bee put forward she had answers. Why should she save the money? What for? Why shouldn't she spend it on the family? What fun would it be travelling alone? It was everybody going that made the journey so exciting. Besides, if she went anywhere alone she would have to live in hotels which would cost as much and more than all their fares put together, whereas staying with Aunt Cora she would be living free. Yes, of course she would be expected to work for her board and lodging but who supposed she wanted to be idle a whole winter? Had anybody ever heard of her ever wanting to be idle? A holiday was nice, of course, but she would have a real rest on the boat and the change would be a splendid holiday in itself. All right, if they must be so businesslike, the money spent on the family could be called a loan. If ever there was a safe investment it was the Winter family. In no time, in all that sun, John would be writing again and, even if he were not, there were Rachel and Tim bound to be famous and earn enormous incomes one day.

Rachel sat on a stool hugging her knees and trying to look cheerful. It was awful listening to Peaseblossom beating down John's and Bee's arguments one by one, and feeling your heart drop lower and lower and knowing if it was decided they would go she ought to look pleased about it. The worst part was that the only thing John and Bee seemed to see in the way of their going was Peaseblossom's money. Nobody seemed to notice her career was at stake. Here was she, only just old enough to have a licence to appear on the stage, and she was one of six picked to dance in a big London theatre, and her family, who ought to be bursting with pride, were discussing whisking her off to the other end of the world. The firmer Peaseblossom's arguments grew the more miserable Rachel became, and the more sorry for herself and the more difficult she found it to look cheerful. Her lips kept dropping at the corners and had to be forced upwards again. Towards the end of the Peaseblossom argument, when it was clear Peaseblossom was winning, an enormous lump kept coming into her throat, which had to be swallowed without making gulping noises, and her eyes, however hard she blinked, kept filling with tears, and in the end she had to use her fingers to support the droop of her lips.

Just before supper time Bee looked at John. She tried not to sound too pleased, eager and excited, but she did not succeed very well. She had not let John know how worried she had been since his accident, but she had been pretty desperate. There were three children to bring up and how was she to do that when their father had stopped earning a living? She had not had great hopes of persuading him to go to Aunt Cora by himself, and the idea of their all going had never entered her mind. Now it was as if a fairy had appeared and given her a wish and made it come true. Of course, if she had been given a wish it would have been for a magic carpet to carry them all to spend a winter in the sunshine. She could not help every word she said having a singing note behind it because being gloriously happy makes singing notes come in a voice whether you want them there or not.

'Well, John, we seem to have produced every argument we can. If Peaseblossom really wants to spend her money like that, I think we ought to let her.'

John was beginning to get a little excited. Not the sort of gay excited that he used to be so easily before the accident but more as if the fog of depression which covered him most days had been blown on by a wind and was less dense.

'Let's accept for the moment we're using Peaseblossom's money. Now what are we going to do about the children? There's this offer of Jeremy Caulder's; ought we to let Tim miss this chance?'

Rachel had to turn her head so that nobody should see her wipe her eyes. Tim indeed! The only thing that had happened to Tim was that somebody important had offered to give him lessons, while she had a professional engagement. She was to dance on a real stage, walk in through a stage door, which was something she had always longed to do, wear lovely clothes, do lovely dances. Oh, it was too mean!

Tim had been playing an imaginary grand piano through most of the Peaseblossom argument. When the conversation turned to himself he took his hands off his imaginary keyboard and got up. He sat on the arm of John's chair.

'That'll be all right, Dad.'

John put an arm round him.

'That's what you say now, but what are you going to say to me in ten years' time about the opportunity I'm letting you miss?'

Rachel had to turn away her face again and sweep some more tears out of her eyes. Opportunity Tim was missing! What about the opportunity she was missing?

Tim said:

'I shan't miss any opportunity. Mr Brown told me he didn't suppose Mr Caulder would be in London much for a bit. Somebody in America can give me lessons while I'm there.'

John gave Tim a friendly shake.

'Don't you be smug, young man. Why should any American pianist want to be bothered with a little boy who's only going to be his pupil for a few months?'

'And who would pay for the lessons even if we could find someone to teach you?' Bee broke in. 'Peaseblossom's money will mostly be used up and we can't expect Aunt Cora to do more than keep us.'

Tim refused to worry.

'Mr Brown won't mind, as long as I practise every day.'

Bee had suddenly seen Rachel's face. Oh, my goodness, she thought, how mean of us all, forgetting Rachel's great chance, but she mustn't let her father see how disappointed she is or he may refuse to go because of her. She got up and went over to Rachel. She knelt down by her and put her arms round her in such a way that Rachel's face was against her shoulder and so hidden from everybody. Before she spoke she whispered, 'Be brave, darling. Don't let Dad see how much you mind.' Out loud she said:

'We've forgotten our ballerina. Will you mind not dancing in this show and missing your lessons for six months?'

Answering was the most difficult thing Rachel had ever done. Bee being so nice had broken her control and she was really crying, but somehow she managed a fairly non-wobblish voice, and said the only thing she could think of:

'Foreign travel broadens the mind.'

Peaseblossom gave a quick look at what she could see of Rachel and broke in hurriedly:

'Quite right, and a broadened mind helps all art. We'll bring back better pupils for Madame Fidolia and Mr Caulder. Now everything's settled I'll get supper. Jane, it's your night to help.'

Jane had been sitting in a corner. She had Chewing-gum

32

on the piece of sheet he had to sit on when his toilet was done. She had combed him and brushed him until he shone like silk, then she had lain down beside him and listened with half an ear to the arguments. When first Tim and then Rachel came into the discussion she sat up. She hugged Chewing-gum against her. There they went as usual, talk, talk, talk about Rachel and Tim; nobody seemed to care what happened to her. Peaseblossom saying 'everything's settled' was the last straw. Jane's voice was shrill with anger.

'I suppose it doesn't interest anybody if Chewing-gum and I don't want to go to America.'

The three grown-ups laughed. Bee said:

'I'm afraid not, darling. It'll be good for you.'

Tim turned to his father.

'Can Chewing-gum come? A boy at school's poodle couldn't go to Paris because he'd have been put in quarantine when he came home.'

Bee caught her breath. Of course Chewing-gum couldn't come. She hadn't thought of that. Oh, dear, surely Jane would not be difficult! She could not leave Rachel, who was crying quite badly, so she held out a hand to Jane.

'We'll fix something very nice for Chewing-gum but he can't come because it's the law that he must go into quarantine for six months when we get back and he'd hate that, poor boy.'

Jane was appalled. No Chewing-gum! How could she go away and leave Chewing-gum? All this talk about Rachel's dancing and Tim's piano lessons and the most important thing nobody had mentioned. They were going away and leaving Chewing-gum behind, as if he were nothing. She got up and came into the middle of the room.

'You can all go to America if you like, but I'm stopping here. None of you seems to care what happens to Chewing-gum, but I do. Poor angel, you'd let him die in the snow and starve to death. All this talk about Rachel's dancing and Tim's piano and nobody cares that they're taking from me the only friend I ever had, the only person who really and truly loves me. Well, you can't do it; I won't go to America. I'll chain myself and Chewing-gum to something so you can't get us away. You're beasts, all of you, to have thought of trying to do it. Beasts! Beasts! Beasts!'

Jane was wound up. She had lots more to say, but Peaseblossom felt they had heard more than enough. She went over to Jane and shook her. She raised her voice so it could be heard above Jane's.

'That's quite enough. California or no California we mustn't get slack or let discipline slip. It's your night to help with supper.'

CHAPTER 4

PREPARATIONS

ONCE it was certain they were going to California the days seemed to rush by. From the Wednesday when it was decided they would go to the day they were to sail was really a fortnight, but to the children it did not feel a bit like fourteen days. It felt to Bee and Peaseblossom like a fortnight all right, and the most awful fortnight in the world. Every day was a scramble to get everything into it that was planned. There was the house to shut up, which meant putting things away, and packing all clothes that they were not taking with crystals so that moths would not eat them, and getting dust sheets out so that at the very last moment the furniture could be covered over. So much was put away or packed that in the last few days before they sailed no one had any clothes out except the things they were travelling in, and there were only just enough knives, forks, spoons, glass and china for each of them, and these were a queer mixed lot nobody had seen before. The last two days before they sailed there were not even enough blankets for the beds and instead they had to use their coats to cover them.

John was busy too. It was he who managed to get them all passages on the *Mauretania* – a very difficult thing to do at short notice. Once he had made up his mind they would go he could not rest until he knew exactly what day they were starting. On the Thursday after the great Wednesday he rushed out immediately after breakfast to visit the Cunard White Star Line and see what they could do. Nobody supposed they could do anything, and Bee's and Peaseblossom's breaths were knocked away when he dashed in again two hours later to say he had accommodation for four on the *Mauretania* for Wednesday week. One big outside cabin in the cabin class. Whoever had been going to travel in it had cancelled that very day and he had taken it at once for Peaseblossom and the children; he was still trying for a double cabin for himself and Bee but he did not think there was much hope so he was going to see if he could get two places on an aeroplane. It was not often, even when he was well, that Bee argued with John and she never had since the accident, but when she heard about the aeroplane she not only argued but blew up like the lid blowing off a kettle. What! Let her children go all the way to America without her! John must be mad! Anything might happen. They might get ill. They might be seasick. They might fall overboard. They might get lost on the dock in New York. Of course she trusted Peaseblossom, but she could not be expected to be everywhere at once, and John must be crazy to think for one moment she would agree to an arrangement of that sort. It was so extraordinary to hear Bee blowing up that John never mentioned the aeroplane again. How he did it nobody knew but two days later he came in proudly announcing that he had a two-berth cabin. The next thing was passports. The passports were out of date and the children had never been abroad, so they neither had passports of their own nor were they down on their parents' passports. There were forms to fill in, and photographs to be taken, and hours to be spent in the passport office and, later, hours in the American Embassy waiting for visas, but John managed it all without fussing everybody else more than could be helped. He was like a very good sheep dog getting his sheep along at a nice speed in the right direction, with only an occasional little sharp bark. Oddly enough, though he looked terribly tired, hurrying about seemed to do him good; he was sleeping better than he had since the accident. Best of all, when the tickets and the visa'd passports were in the house he labelled his portable typewriter and packed several packets of typing paper. None of the family had supposed he would take his typewriter; why should he when he kept saying he would never write again? But there it stood in the hall with a Cunard White Star label on it and a big W for Winter. Everybody kept looking at it out of the corner of their eyes, but nobody said anything about it; after all, it's easy to take a label off again.

The children had their own affairs to put in order. The most difficult affair was, of course, Chewing-gum. Jane stuck to what she had said. If Chewing-gum was not going neither would she. She made awful threats. They would have to carry her to the boat and she would scream all across the Atlantic. It was Doctor Smith who found the way out. He stopped on his round of visits on the Monday morning after the great Wednesday to ask if there was any news from Aunt Cora. He did not need to come far inside the house to see that there was, for Bee and Peaseblossom were packing in the hall. The children were at school and John at the passport office, but Bee and Peaseblossom were glad to sit down for a minute and tell him all about it.

'The only trouble,' Bee said, 'is Jane. She says she won't go without Chewing-gum.'

Peaseblossom broke out:

'Don't think we are paying any attention to her. She will, of course, do exactly as she's told, and be punished if she behaves badly.'

Bee went on:

'But we don't want anything to upset John, for he really does seem a little better. The other two are being splendidly helpful and it's particularly good of Rachel because she does not want to go away now, poor child, as she had just been engaged to dance in a musical show. Her very first professional engagement, it really is bad luck.'

Doctor Smith thought for a minute, then he made a clicking noise with his tongue and held up a finger.

'Let me have a talk with Jane. You've all got to have certificates that you were recently vaccinated, and that it took all right, before you can land in the United States. Lucky for you that I vaccinated you all this spring. You write a note asking me for certificates and get Jane to bring it round about four-thirty and wait for an answer.'

Jane and Chewing-gum turned up at teatime at Doctor Smith's house and were shown into his consulting room. He read the note just as if he did not know what was in it. Then he rang the bell.

'Your mother wants certificates to say I vaccinated you all. They will take time to write so I suggest you and I and Chewing-gum have some tea before I get to work on them.'

It was a good tea. Jane was surprised at the sort of tea Doctor Smith ate all by himself. Sandwiches, buns and even some ginger biscuits. He talked about Chewing-gum's food, health and coat until tea came, and it was only when Jane was eating a bun and Chewing-gum a sandwich that he mentioned America.

'Exciting business this, you all going off to California.'

Jane laid down her bun.

'The rest of the family may be going but I'm not. I'll chain myself to the furniture, and if they cut the chains I won't walk, they'll have to drag me, and I'll scream all the way. I'm not leaving Chewing-gum.'

Doctor Smith did not show any particular interest. He sipped his tea before he answered.

'I see. Then it's no good my saying what I was going to.'

Jane looked very don't-care-what-you-sayish.

'Not if it was to try and talk me round it isn't.'

'Not exactly. It was to ask you to lend Chewing-gum to me. Some shocking car thieves about. I was thinking of getting a dog but if I could have an old friend like Chewing-gum whom I could trust to stay with me it would be a great help.'

Inside her, though she tried not to believe it, Jane knew

38

she would not be allowed to stay behind, that she would be taken to America even if she did what she threatened and used chains and screamed. If she had to allow anyone to look after Chewing-gum instead of herself Doctor Smith's was a good idea. Staying with a doctor Chewing-gum's health would be properly attended to, and he would have the right things to eat. However, she could not give way all at once. She had made such a scene for so long that it felt quite odd to think of stopping making a scene.

'Would you wait in a queue for horse meat?'

'Shouldn't have to. Patient of mine sells the stuff, he'll send round all I want.'

'He's used to walking, not driving all day in a car.'

'Always manage one good walk myself every day; shall enjoy Chewing-gum's company.'

'He's never been a watch-dog, he's not a biting sort of dog. I don't know how good he'd be at catching a thief.'

Doctor Smith gave Chewing-gum some tea in the slop-basin.

'Soon learn. I'll put a bone in the car with him. Any dog will bite anyone who comes near him when he's got a bone.'

Jane thought that clever.

'That's a very good idea. I'd be glad if he did learn to be a fierce watch-dog. I'd be glad if he learnt to do anything really well, because I hope to be a dog trainer when I grow up and judging by Chewing-gum I've got a lot to learn.' She lowered her voice. 'As a matter of fact he can carry a newspaper but he's still inclined to eat it.'

Doctor Smith nodded in the professional way he did when he came when anybody was ill and someone explained to him what sort of being ill it was.

'Ah! Must see if I can help the old fellow about that. Very good of you, Jane, if you trust him to me.'

Either because Doctor Smith was so nice, or because talking about leaving Chewing-gum was the beginning of leaving

39

him, Jane began to cry. She had been stubborn and angry since Wednesday but she had not cried; now, when the tears started, they seemed to have been holding back an absolute river of tears. Doctor Smith was perfect. He sat her on his knee and let her cry and cry, and only when at last she had reached the hiccough and shudder stage did he talk. He told her about the dog he had when he was a boy and how terrible it had been when he first went to a boarding school. How he had thought his dog would starve and die without him. How surprised he had been when he came home for the holidays. His father brought his dog to the station to meet him. The dog nearly had hysterics he was so pleased to see him, but when that was over he was surprised to find the dog looked splendid, and when he had remarked on this to his father his father had said, ''Course. Never make the mistake of thinking you're the only animal lover in the world, and never be such a fool as to get so tied up with an animal that you can't move without it. You'll be a nuisance to yourself and everybody else.' Doctor Smith said he had found that was a very sensible thing to have said, and he thought Jane would too. This going away for six months would be a useful way of getting used to leaving Chewing-gum if she had to, and to trusting him to someone else.

Jane reached home as the family were finishing tea. She marched in and gave Bee the envelope of certificates. Then she stuck her chin in the air and said in a proud, don't-you-dare-look-surprised voice:

'It may interest you to know I've decided to lend Chewing-gum to Doctor Smith while I'm in America. He needs a watch-dog for his car.'

Bee had written on the evening of the great Wednesday to Madame Fidolia, to the head of Jane's and Tim's school and to Mr Brown. The letter to Jane's and Tim's school was just a notification that the children would be leaving England; the letters to Madame Fidolia and Mr Brown said the same thing but as well were grateful and apologetic.

Rachel, knowing Madame Fidolia had been written to, did not tell her news to the other girls. She was quite sure Caroline would dance in the show in her place, but just in case somebody else was put in it seemed better to say nothing. It would be too awful to let poor Caroline hope again; she had not yet got over yesterday's audition. It was so awful, as she told Rachel, to have been nearly chosen and then to end up just an understudy. Rachel found it hard not to tell everybody her news. People kept coming up and congratulating her and every time that happened she had a lump in her throat. She was glad when she got a message to say Madame wanted to see her before she went home.

Madame Fidolia was sitting in an arm-chair with Bee's letter in her hand. To anyone who did not know her she was an odd-looking old lady. Her hair was dragged into a bun in the nape of her neck; she was wearing a dress so old-fashioned in shape it might have come out of a museum. Round her shoulders was a shawl kept in place by a large cameo brooch. Lying on the table beside her was a tall cane, which she always used when she walked. On her feet were pink ballet shoes. To Rachel there was nothing queer about her at all. Madame was not a person you could be fond of exactly, she was too grand for that, but she respected and admired her and was a little afraid of her. Madame no longer danced but she had been a very great dancer, and her arrival to watch a class sent a shiver down Rachel's spine. Madame could be patient but she was very critical. Rachel dreaded hearing Madame's stick tap on the floor, and her voice with its faintly foreign accent say, 'Precision, Rachel. Precision'. That afternoon Madame waited for Rachel to curtsy and say 'Madame'. Then she gave her a lovely smile.

'Come in, my child. This is disappointing news for you and for me.'

That was so like Madame. She would understand at once. Lots of people would think it simply marvellous luck going to California for the winter, but not Madame. She would know just how awful it was to have your first stage engagement snatched from you. Madame's understanding so well was a strain on Rachel's self-control. She felt tears smarting in her eyes and had to swallow before she could say:

'Yes, Madame.'

Madame did not seem to notice Rachel was upset.

'But we must be sensible about it. A winter in the sunshine will be very good for your health. Nor are your chances much affected. I, of course, telephoned Mr Glinken the moment I got your mother's letter, and I explained about you. He asked which you were and when I described you he said, "Oh, it would be that one, but you tell her from me to work hard while she's away, and not to let Hollywood discover her and I may have something for her when she comes back." '

Rachel could hardly believe she had really heard what Madame had said. Mr Glinken remembered her! Mr Glinken thought he might have something for her when she got back! She felt so gay it was quite difficult to keep from giving a pleased skip. She clasped her hands and said on a gasping breath:

'Oh, Madame!'

Madame nodded.

'Nice, isn't it? We'll keep him up to that when you get home. In the meantime your disappointment is great news for your friend, Caroline, and whoever I put to take Caroline's place as understudy, so you can look upon this Californian trip not as a misfortune but as the great adventure which it really is. Now, about your dancing lessons . . .'

Rachel dropped from happiness to despair.

'I shan't be able to have any. Aunt Cora, that we're staying with, can't be expected to do more than keep us; she couldn't be expected to pay for classes.'

Madame nodded again.

'I quite understand that. Indeed your mother says as much in this letter. She says that to save trouble and expense Miss Bean, who is travelling with you, will be teaching your school work; she asks for a report on your work and a list of the books that will be needed. Fortunately I can arrange about dancing lessons. Let me have your Californian address and I will ask my old pupil, Posy Fossil, to look after you.'

Posy Fossil was a legend in the school. There had never been a dancer to touch her. When she was quite a little girl she had marched in at the stage door of a theatre where the famous Czechoslovakian dancer Manoff's company was performing, and insisted on Manoff himself seeing her dance. He had seen her and when he returned to Czechoslovakia Posy, with her old nurse, went too and became his pupil. Everybody knew that Posy was dancing on the films and that she had a sister who was a film star. To Rachel, that she was to meet the fabulous Posy was like being told she was to meet Cinderella.

'Posy Fossil!'

'Yes. I don't know what she can arrange as she is out of pictures now and working hard. Manoff is forming his company again and she is his star; but do not worry, my child, Posy will look after you. Now run along and send Caroline to me.'

Rachel curtsied, murmured 'Madame' and left the room. Outside the door she stood still for a moment to get things straight. Thoughts poured in on her making her so happy and excited she felt as if she might burst with being pleased. California was going to be glorious. She was going to travel on a great line. She was going to a place where the sun always shone. She was to meet, actually meet, the wonderful Posy Fossil. Posy Fossil would arrange about her dancing lessons. It was just possible she might even attend a class taught by the great Manoff. Then, when she came back, Mr Glinken had said he might have something for her. It was all too much. She rushed round the school looking for Caroline. When she found her she flung her arms round her.

'Oh, I'm so happy and so are you going to be in a minute. Go to Madame, she wants to see you, but the second she's finished with you rush back here, I've got such marvellous things to tell you.'

Tim did not have a piano lesson with Mr Brown until the Friday. Because he was so excited about going to America he had not practised for two days. He knew Mr Brown would understand so he told him at once. Mr Brown did understand; he said if anything like that happened to him he wouldn't practise either.

'Has this aunt you're staying with got a piano?'

Tim thought that a stupid question.

'A piano! Every house has a piano.'

'On the contrary very few houses have pianos. Doesn't matter a bit that you're missing your lessons for a couple of terms, and Jeremy Caulder says it suits him better to start you at Easter as he'll be in London quite a lot then, but you must practise. What are you going to do about that if your aunt hasn't a piano?'

Tim could not believe he had an aunt so dead to decency that she could live without a piano, but even if she was as peculiar as all that everybody in America couldn't be queer. Somewhere there must be a piano. He sat down on the piano stool and, with one hand, made a brushing movement in the air, as if to brush Mr Brown's foolish fears away.

'Don't worry. I'll find a piano.'

Mr Brown laughed.

'All right, Tim, I'll leave it to you. I feel sure if there's a piano anywhere you will find it, but mind you do. If you come back without having practised I shall take you to a pond and drown you.'

CHAPTER 5

THEY ARE OFF

LIGHT had just begun to sneak through the curtains when Rachel opened her eyes. For a moment she was suspended half-way between being asleep and being awake. Then, with a jump, she sat up. This was going-away day. Since yesterday morning they had been saying 'By this time tomorrow we'll be driving to the station.' 'By this time tomorrow we'll be in Southampton.' 'By this time tomorrow we'll be on the *Mauretania*.' 'This is absolutely the last lunch we'll eat in this house. Imagine, tomorrow we'll eat it on the *Mauretania*.' Now it was tomorrow; the great day had arrived. Rachel got out of bed, pulled back the curtains and looked out. She let out a pleased 'Oh!' for it was a glorious morning. The sun was shining, making the already autumn-turned leaves on the two trees that could be seen from the window a glittering gold; the sky was a clear pale blue, a flawless poem of a morning, just the day to start to cross the Atlantic.

'What's it like?'

Jane was sitting up in her bed looking pale, tousled and cross. A hump under the eiderdown was Chewing-gum. As a rule he was not allowed on beds, but the night before Jane had said, 'Chewing-gum's sleeping with me tonight,' and nobody, not even Peaseblossom, had argued. In a house bulging with excitement Jane was the one sad person. She was so miserable that she had not been bad or rude for days. This was so noticeable it had made Tim say, 'I do miss Jane not being cross. I've nobody to fight with'. Rachel, turning as Jane spoke, felt a little of the gladness of the morning slipping out of the door. Poor Jane! Of course nobody liked leaving

46

Chewing-gum, but only Jane minded so terribly that she could not be thrilled by going away. Doctor Smith was coming to fetch Chewing-gum at breakfast-time; horrible for everybody seeing him go off in Doctor Smith's car, but simply ghastly for Jane, who loved Chewing-gum more than she loved her family. Rachel tried to cheer her up.

'It's a lovely day. No wind at all. I can see three lots of chimney smoke going straight into the air, and the leaves on the poplar trees aren't moving at all. I wouldn't think any of us could be seasick.'

Jane was not in the mood to like hearing good news.

'Some people don't need waves, they're just seasick.'

Peaseblossom came in just in time to hear this.

'Who's talking about seasickness? Your father's heard the seven o'clock weather forecast, it's splendid. Not a mention of a gale. Up you get, travellers. Fold your sheets and pillow cases and put them in the laundry basket in the kitchen. No rush and scramble, everything in order, and everything in time, that's our way.'

It was a funny morning, unlike any other. The boiler had been allowed to go out, so there was only cold water to wash in. It felt so queer packing each thing away as it was finished with, brushes, combs, washing things, pyjamas, nothing left about to show anybody had slept in the house. The house itself looked so packed away, all the furniture under dust sheets, it was as if it had shut its eyes and was saying, 'All right, you're off to California, well get on with it, let me have a nice sleep until you get back.'

A car stopped outside. Everybody tried not to look at Jane, but they all knew whose car it was. The front-door bell rang.

It was all over in a couple of minutes. Doctor Smith said he was in a terrible hurry. He picked up Chewing-gum's basket, which Jane had packed with his biscuits, a bottle of his medicine, his brush and comb, his special soap, his spare collar and lead, his water bowl, his rubber bone, his half-eaten

47

teddy bear and his rug. Jane knelt by Chewing-gum and clipped on his lead. She gave the lead to Doctor Smith, who very tactfully did not speak to her but to Chewing-gum.

'Come on, old man. You wouldn't believe what a bone I've got waiting for you in the car.'

The moment the front door shut behind Doctor Smith and Chewing-gum everybody began to run. The night suitcases had to come down and join the rest of the luggage in the hall. Jane was handed a wet dishcloth and told to give all the stick-on luggage labels a final dab. Tim was given the job of counting the luggage and seeing that the tie-on labels were all securely knotted. Rachel had to search the bedrooms to be sure everything was packed, and that nobody had packed the coats and hats they were travelling in. John went to the neighbours officially to say good-bye, but really to remind them once more that this was the day they were going away, and would they please keep an eye on the house to see it was not burgled. Bee and Peaseblossom rushed round the house doing all those last things that they had forgotten to do, or forgotten to ask Mrs Bones to do for them. Then the clock struck, John shouted, 'Hurry up, everybody, or the cars will be here.' They all rushed upstairs and put on their hats and coats, and only just in time for as they came down again the two cars Peaseblossom had hired stopped at the door.

They had a wonderful send-off. Every house in Saxon Crescent had somebody out to wave good-bye to them. There were extra people as well; the postman had loitered so that he could cheer. The newspaper boy had hurried through his round so that he could come back and see them off. Mrs Bones, her hat on one side, came tearing up the street to have what she called 'a last dekko' at them. Even the policeman who was sometimes on the corner was there that morning and he called out, 'Good luck'.

It hardly seemed possible that they really were safely on the boat-train. They were in a long railway carriage with tables in it, Peaseblossom and the children at one table, and John and Bee at another, which they shared with a Scottish couple who were going out to America to see their married daughter. It was so funny to look round the railway carriage and think that they would be seeing all the people in it for the next six days. That they were not the only people starting on a great adventure. The journey passed wonderfully quickly.

Just as it was beginning to be a bore Peaseblossom ordered coffee for them all, and, as a surprise, out of her case, she brought chocolate biscuits. Now that they had really started and, with all their luggage, were safely on the train, they found the appetites they had lost at breakfast had come back. Even Jane, who had not spoken at all but glared out of the window, ate three chocolate biscuits and seemed to enjoy them.

Southampton Docks was rather boring. A lot of standing

in queues and answering questions, but, just as it seemed as if the *Mauretania* must sail without them, John said, 'We're through. Come on, everybody.' They found themselves moving towards a sign marked 'Cabin Class Only', then up a gangway and there they were on board the *Mauretania*.

CHAPTER 6

THE 'MAURETANIA'

DAYS on land are like beads threaded on a string, big beads, little beads, gay beads for Christmas and birthdays; but days on a ship cannot go on the same string. They are different somehow and feel as if they need a special thread all to themselves. That is how the *Mauretania* felt to the Winters. As their feet touched the deck it was as if a door slammed, behind which were Saxon Crescent, Mrs Bones, Doctor Smith, everybody and everything that was life at home, even Chewinggum was behind that door. Six days ahead was another door which would open on America, but that was tight shut and they did not even think about what was on the other side of it.

Peaseblossom and the children had a cabin on one deck and John and Bee on another. The *Mauretania* seemed so big that Rachel felt a bit scared at seeing John and Bee leaving them. On a journey to the other side of the world it seemed safer not to be separated. A steward who had picked up most of their hand luggage saw her expression and understood at once.

'Don't you worry, you won't lose 'em, but by tomorrow they'll be lucky if they can find you when they want you. Never travelled with a child yet who didn't know the ship almost as well as I do before we was a day out.'

It was quite a walk to get to the cabin. Down two decks, along a passage, then down a tiny passage and there it was. It was the neatest place the children had ever seen. There were four bunks, two each side, two cupboards and shelves, two chests of drawers, a porthole with little curtains and a washbasin with hot and cold water. Of course the first important thing to decide was who should sleep where. Naturally all three children wanted the top bunks. After all, you can sleep on the floor any time, but it is something special to have a bed you have to climb to get into. Peaseblossom had to think quickly. She wanted to give Jane a top bunk because of Chewing-gum, but she did not want to say so as, obviously for the present, the less said about him the better. She decided to make a martyr of Rachel.

'I think we'll fix it by age. Rachel and I will have the lower bunks. We don't mind, Rachel dear, do we? It's all going to be such splendid fun.'

Rachel did mind and was just going to say so when there was a knock on the door and in came a steward in a white coat. He was carrying a long box and some telegrams. He was a cheerful man with a sunburnt face and very blue eyes.

'I'm your bedroom steward. Name of Williams. Which of you is Miss Bean?' When Peaseblossom had taken the box he looked at the telegrams. 'Miss Rachel Winter. Miss Jane Winter. Tim Winter.' He raised his eyebrows in a funny way. 'Would that be you three?'

No one had thought of people sending parcels and telegrams. After all, they were the ones who were having the luck to go away, so if any parcels and telegrams were being sent you would have thought they would have gone to people left behind. All the same, it was lovely to have them. Rachel's was from Madame Fidolia. 'Good luck dear from us all we shall miss you STOP Posy has cabled she will take care of you Madame.' Tim's was from Mr Brown. 'Have a good time but don't forget to practise Michael Brown.' Jane's was from Doctor Smith. 'Chewing-gum has been with me for an hour and has not yet looked up from his bone enjoy yourself love Smith.'

Rachel read her telegram out loud.

'Imagine Madame sending me a telegram! It's an awfully grand thing to have happened. Just fancy Posy Fossil having cabled about me, and her a star!'

Jane had climbed into the bunk over Rachel's to read her

telegram. It was so nice to think of Chewing-gum happily eating a bone that she spoke in quite her old way.

'I'm glad I'm not a dancer and have to feel humble as a worm whenever that Madame noticed me. Now listen to my telegram. This is a sensible telegram.'

Everybody was so glad to hear Jane being herself again and to think that Chewing-gum had settled down that they said nothing about her rude way of talking but agreed it was a glorious telegram. In fact Peaseblossom went on saying things about it so long that Tim, who had climbed up into his bunk, had to interrupt her.

'Everybody would think I hadn't had a telegram. Would you listen, please.'

They listened and Peaseblossom admired it very much.

'Splendid. Practice, that's the way. Mustn't let the side down.' She was undoing her box while she spoke and took out some carnations. She read the card and looked pleased. 'They're from a school friend and listen what she says. "Hope you have learnt to sing 'California Here I Come'."'

They had never heard of a song called that but somehow the line made them feel terribly gay and excited. Tim sang it to the tune of 'Good King Wenceslas'. 'California here I come, Cali-Cali-fornia. California here I come. Cali-Cali-fornia.' In a minute they were all joining in, even Peaseblossom. Tim knelt on his bunk and conducted. Between them they made such a noise that they did not hear a knock on the door, and were surprised to find the stewardess in the middle of the cabin; she was laughing.

'I came in to tell you I was your stewardess. My name is Miss Mann.'

They all said, 'How do you do?' Miss Mann was fat and cosy looking, just the sort of person, if you chose your stewardess, that you would choose. Peaseblossom was particularly glad to find such a friendly looking stewardess, because she knew there would be lots of things she would want to know.

53

'I'm afraid we were making rather a noise.'

Miss Mann laughed again.

'I gather you're going to California. My, I wish it was me.' She came over to Peaseblossom. 'Have you booked your sittings for meals? You'll want first sittings for the children, and, if I were you, I'd get some unpacking done; it's a good thing to get things shipshape before you start.'

Peaseblossom explained John would be seeing to the table bookings, but she thought unpacking was a good idea. She looked at the baggage.

'I think I'll do better on my own in this small space. You children run along and have a look round, and on the way go to your Mum and Dad's cabin and show them your telegrams.'

John and Bee's cabin was much smaller than the children's, and it had no porthole, but it was nice. Bee was alone in it unpacking. She was thrilled by the telegrams and sat down on the lower bunk and showed them all the telegrams that she and John had received. Almost everybody they knew seemed to have sent one, and as well there were five lots of flowers.

Rachel said, 'Aren't we grand suddenly! It's almost as if we'd become royalty.'

Tim, who had climbed up to the upper berth to see if it was as good as his own, shouted, 'One, two, three, all together,' and started, 'California here I come, Cali-Cali-fornia.' Rachel and Jane joined in at the top of their voices. Bee put her hands over her ears. 'Stop, darlings, we shall disturb everybody. Come down off there, Tim. Don't you want to see us sail? We shall be off in no time now. You'd better run up on the deck where you'll get a good view.'

The last person went ashore. The last gangway was pulled in. The last rope unhitched. There was a little gap between the *Mauretania* and the dock. People on the dockside waved and cheered. Hundreds of seagulls wheeled and cried. The gap widened. It was too big to jump across. It was too big to swim across. They were off.

*

The wind got up a bit in the night. It made the *Mauretania* roll. The roll was quite gentle and made the family sleep as if somebody was rocking their bunks for them. In the children's cabin they did not know it was morning until Miss Mann came in with orange juice and tea. She drew back the little curtains which were across the porthole and started on Tim.

'Wakey, wakey. Rise and shine. Show a leg.'

Tim blinked and sat up and, seeing who it was, felt pleased.

'Good morning. What did you say?'

'What they say in the navy. Wakey, wakey. Rise and shine. Show a leg.'

Jane leant out of her bunk to take her orange juice.

'Why do they say it?'

Peaseblossom had not moved nor had Rachel, so Miss Mann put a cup of tea beside Peaseblossom and orange juice beside Rachel. She shook a finger at Jane.

'I can see you're the "why" sort. Never ask me why anything in the mornings. I've all my passengers to call, and get to their baths. Now, when steward knocks to say your baths are ready, you're to run or you'll have everybody late for breakfast.'

The word breakfast made Jane and Tim hungry. The food on the *Mauretania* was too gorgeous to be believed. There was so much to choose from. Peaseblossom half sat up. She stretched out a hand for her tea. Then took it back again. She spoke in a much less brisk voice than usual.

'Good morning, dears.'

Jane hung out of her berth so that she could see Peaseblossom.

'Miss Mann says it's nearly breakfast-time.'

The word breakfast had an odd effect on Peaseblossom.

55

She gave a queer moan and turned over on her back and shut her eyes.

Jane made a face at Tim. Tim, curious to see what was going on underneath him, hung almost upside down.

'Are you ill, Peaseblossom?'

Peaseblossom spoke in a whisper.

'Not ill. Just a little tired.'

Rachel was awake and drinking her orange juice. She thought at first it was delicious. Then she was not sure. She put down the glass. Then she too rolled on her back and shut her eyes. Tim looked at Rachel in amazement.

'You can't be tired too. We've been asleep for hours and hours.'

Jane climbed out of bed. She looked pityingly at Peaseblossom and Rachel.

'They're not tired. They're seasick.'

It was unfair, Rachel thought, that she should feel the sea. Just her and Peaseblossom. Such heavenly things were happening on deck. There was a band. There were film shows. There was a game called Bingo, and the lounge steward said there would be horse racing, and when it happened Jane and Tim should each have a turn at shaking the dice. Jane and Tim had been down to see the engine-room and Tim had said good-morning to the captain and got a good-morning back, and had been invited to come on the bridge and see the Radar apparatus. They had all attended boat drill and Bee and John had been on a conducted tour through the kitchens. There were games on the deck, which Jane and Tim played all the time they were not eating or doing something else. While here was she, lying in her bunk, sometimes reading a little, but more often with her eyes shut, feeling all right when she was flat but simply terrible when she sat up.

On the second day out the wind dropped. The ship still rolled but not as much as she had done. Peaseblossom took advantage of feeling a little better to have a bath. She looked green and pale blue in stripes and staggered when she tried to walk, and had to be helped by Miss Mann, but it was her first bath and a great improvement. The door had only just closed on Peaseblossom when Williams came in. He looked so cheerful that he made Rachel feel better. He stood by her bunk smiling down at her.

'How are you getting along?'

Rachel looked ashamed.

'I've been seasick ever since the storm started.'

Williams laughed. 'Storm! Bless you, that wasn't a storm. Bit of a breeze I'd call it.'

'Oh, dear! Then I must be a very bad sailor.'

Williams laughed again.

'Don't you believe it. Half seasickness is habit, as you might say. You feel squeamish the first morning out, and who wouldn't, but later you settle to it, as it were. Get it into your head you feel queer and like as not we shan't see you on deck until we're seeing the Statue of Liberty. That's bad. I know how it is because I was a shocking sailor myself once.'

Rachel was amazed. Williams did not look as if he knew he was on the sea.

'Were you? How did you cure yourself?'

'Ah, that's my secret! Still, I think you're a nice young lady so I'll tell you. Strawberry ice.'

'Strawberry ice!'

'That's right. First moment I felt queer I got hold of a strawberry ice, a good big 'un. Never asked myself if I wanted it or if I didn't, down it slipped. That was the end. Five minutes later I was hungry as a hunter. There's nothing to touch it.'

'But if that's all anybody need do why doesn't everybody do it?'

''Cause most passengers give way.' Williams gave a good imitation of a seasick passenger. He made a pillow of his hands and rested his head against them. He closed his eyes and spoke in a whine. 'Don't talk about strawberry ices to me. I daren't touch a thing except lemon juice. How dare you suggest it, steward! My doctor said I was a martyr to seasickness and must just accept it.'

Rachel was enjoying talking to Williams so much that she was sitting up. She laughed out loud. She still felt peculiar but less peculiar.

'Do you suppose if I ate a strawberry ice I'd feel better?'

'I don't suppose nothing, I know it, and what's more, I'll bet you a tanner you'll never feel the sea again.'

Rachel knew the effect, if Williams was wrong, would be simply awful, but he made her feel brave.

'Get me a strawberry ice. I'll try it.'

Just before eleven o'clock a very pale Rachel came up on deck. Bee walked on one side of her and John on the other, but she did not need any help. Jane and Tim had a deck-chair with a leg rest all ready for her. She got on to it and shut her eyes, while Tim and Jane solicitously tucked a rug round her. Presently Rachel opened her eyes. There were people all round sitting on chairs, laughing and talking. The sky was blue, the sun shining. A solitary seagull was flying by the ship. She took a quick glance at the sea. It was dark green and navy blue, with gay white horses bobbing as far as the horizon. She took a deep breath and good, clear sea air filled her lungs, a lovely change after a stuffy cabin with a closed porthole.

A steward came down the line of chairs with a tray on which were cups. He stopped by Rachel.

'Chicken soup? Biscuits?'

'Chicken soup, please, and four biscuits.'

Poor Peaseblossom never really enjoyed the journey. She got up in the afternoon of that same day and each day afterwards, but her getting up was a dreary creep to a chair where she lay with her eyes shut. She never came down to a meal. Rachel told her about the strawberry ice and what it had done for her, but Peaseblossom behaved just as Williams had acted passengers behaving. She shut her eyes and shuddered and said, 'Please, dear, don't talk about it.'

Jane, who had not only got her spirits back but extra spirits to make up for having been miserable for so long, said, in a whisper loud enough for poor Peaseblossom to hear:

'It's all going to be such splendid fun.'

Peaseblossom was too depressed to say anything at hearing her words quoted against her, but she opened her eyes and gave Jane a look which said, 'You wait until I'm on dry land.'

*

Two nights before they landed there was a concert and both Rachel and Tim performed at it. After she got over feeling seasick Rachel had practised. She tried to find a corner where nobody would notice her, but anything makes news on a ship so that Rachel was a ballet student quickly got round, and when the concert was discussed, that Rachel would dance was taken as a matter of course. Bee groaned when she heard the news.

'Oh, darling, and I don't know where Peaseblossom packed your audition dress, and she can't look, she'll fall over if she tries to unpack. I wonder if it's in a box in the hold or in the baggage room. You couldn't dance in an ordinary frock, could you?'

Bee and John were lying in chairs side by side. Rachel sat down on the foot rest of Bee's between the two of them. She lowered her voice so the people near would not hear.

'The only thing I can dance is "m'audition".'

Every pupil of Madame Fidolia's when they were nearing their twelfth birthday, prepared material ready for auditions. Something to recite, something to sing and something to dance. These were called audition pieces, but the pupils always called them 'm'auditions', short for 'my audition pieces'. No pupils of Madame Fidolia's, once they were twelve, even if they went to the other end of the world, as Rachel was doing, would be without the music for their m'audition song and dance any more than they would forget the words of their recitation. John was lying in the next chair, apparently asleep, anyway, he did not seem to be listening to what Rachel and Bee were saying, but when Rachel used the word m'audition he opened one eye.

'You don't mean to tell me we've got to suffer "Cherry Ripe" in mid-Atlantic.'

John had been so gloomy and silent since the accident that Rachel had not known he knew how hard she had practised 'Cherry Ripe', for he had never before mentioned it.

'Did you hear me practising it?'

John opened the other eye and both were twinkling.

'Could anyone miss it? As for Viola's speech from *Twelfth Night*, I can say it for you. I know just where to breathe. I heard Peaseblossom reminding you. "Breathe there, dear".' He got up. 'I'm going to take a walk to get an appetite for lunch.'

Rachel looked after John in amazement.

'Dad sounds quite different.'

Bee too was gazing at John's back.

'Of course it's too early yet to say he's better, and it doesn't happen all the time, still it does seem as if there was a chance this holiday would work, but he isn't cured until he gets back to his writing. When we see him thumping at that typewriter, that's when we'll know he's well.' She lay back in her chair. 'But talking about Dad isn't getting us anywhere. What about this frock?'

Rachel tried to think helpfully. The audition dress was red crêpe-de-chine. It had been made out of an old evening dress of Peaseblossom's. It was so old that the crêpe-de-chine was cracking here and there, and there had been no thought of its being worn on the ship; it was much too precious. The clothes that had been left out for ship wear were jerseys, a pleated skirt, shorts and two summer frocks to change into in the evening. Both of these were cotton, one was green and the other blue.

'Nobody could feel like dancing in a cotton frock every-body had seen a person change into for the evening. Would it be rude to say I couldn't dance?'

'Disobliging, I think. I don't suppose there are many people on board who do things.'

John had been once round the deck. He stopped for a moment.

'Scrape her hair back and tie something on as an apron and turn her into Alice.'

As soon as John spoke Rachel and Bee saw he was right. With a ribbon round her hair and an apron tied over a cotton frock she could easily look like 'Alice in Wonderland'. Bee said: 'I'll make an apron out of something this afternoon, and you go and tell whoever's arranging the programme that your dance is called "Alice in Wonderland". If they announce it like that everybody will know who you are meant to be, even if you don't look much like it.'

Rachel got up. 'I'll go to the ironing-room this afternoon and press the blue frock. It'll have to be that one because there's more stuff in the skirt.'

Tim had practised every day. The day they sailed he knew there was a piano in the lounge and the next day, as if it was his own, he sat down to play on it. The lounge steward came hurrying over to him.

'Now then, young man, none of that; no strumming here.'

'I don't strum. I'm going to practise. I have to practise every day. I promised Mr Brown, who teaches me, I would.'

Tim had nice manners as a rule, and the lounge steward had already noticed him with approval as a child who would not be as much of a nuisance as some; but Tim changed when he was at a piano, or there was a piano in the room. He could be as difficult as Jane if anyone interrupted him when he wanted to play.

'Can't have every child in the boat practising; got the rest of the passengers to think about.'

Tim glanced round the lounge. Most of the passengers were on the deck. Those sitting about had not yet got their sea legs and had their eyes closed and anxious, suffering expressions on their faces.

'Them! I wouldn't miss my practice for them.' Tim struck a fine scornful chord to express his feelings.

Grown-up people who have no particular talent themselves are apt to think that talent in a child is miraculous. You have only to watch grown-up people watching children on a stage to know that they think quite simple dancing steps, a part acted or something played on an instrument too extraordinary, and to make it more extraordinary still they let themselves believe the child performer is about half the age it really is. The lounge steward was that sort of man. He looked at Tim's fingers and marvelled that they could find the notes at all, let alone make a big noise like that.

'You professional?'

'Of course not. I'm going to be, but not for ages.'

'Let's hear you play a piece.'

The lounge steward had a face and a voice which were just the sort of face and voice Tim liked best. There was a look and a sound about them as if, at any minute, there would be an enormous loud laugh coming. Besides, playing pieces was what Tim liked doing.

'Actually I'm supposed to do some special things first but I'll play my favourite tune for you.'

Tim, as Mr Brown and Jeremy Caulder had found out, was an unusually musical boy. Of course there were years of work ahead of him, but already, when he played, it was nice to listen. Even the passengers who had not got their sea legs opened their eyes and cheered up a little. The lounge steward leant on the piano and found himself forgetting where he was and was carried in his mind to the village in Hampshire where he lived and especially to his garden. He found himself thinking, 'Must pick the last of those tomatoes before the frost gets them.' It gave him quite a shock when Tim stopped playing and he found himself leaning on the piano in the cabin-class lounge.

'That was nice, what was it?'

'It's by Debussy. It's called "Jardin sous la pluie".'

'And what might that mean?'

'Mr Brown says that, turned into the English we speak, it means "Garden in the rain".'

The lounge steward blinked.

'Crikey, and that's just what it sounded like; as soon as you started I thought of my tomatoes.'

After that Tim practised as long as he liked, and, of course, when the concert was suggested, that Tim should play at it was taken for granted. To please his friend the lounge steward and himself, Tim said he would play 'Jardin sous la pluie'.

The concert would quite honestly not have been much of a success without Tim and Rachel, for the talent was poor. Tim was on in the first half of the programme, and everybody applauded so loudly that after he had bowed several times, which made the passengers laugh, he played as an encore Rachmaninoff's 'Prelude in G'. Rachel danced at the end of the programme. She could not use the stage, which was too small, so the audience moved their chairs back and she danced in the middle of the floor. They were that sort of audience who think that any dancing done on the point is much grander than any other dancing; in fact, that to be able to stand on your points at all is wonderful. Rachel looked nice as 'Alice'. Bee had brushed her hair back and tied a ribbon round it, and had made her an apron out of one of John's handkerchiefs. Her dance was quite short but arranged to show managers what she could do, so it was showy. The passengers were

63

enraptured and cheered as well as clapped. Rachel curtsied several times but when the clapping and cheering went on she hurried to Bee and John.

'What shall I do? I don't know another solo and I've no more music.'

John was pleased his children had pleased everybody, but he thought it was time the concert finished and they went to bed.

'Tell them so then, and thank them nicely.'

Rachel went back and curtsied again. Then she cleared her throat. She had never made a speech before so her voice squeaked rather.

'I'm afraid I can't do another dance. I haven't any more music and it's the only one I've practised.'

The audience clapped again and a voice shouted, 'Well, let's have the same dance.'

Rachel danced the dance again. It was not very good that time as she was excited and wobbled on her pirouettes and her arabesque, but the audience, who knew nothing about dancing, thought her wonderful and clapped louder than ever.

After 'God Save the King' had been played the passengers crowded round Bee and John and words like 'Wonderful' and 'Genius' buzzed about. Jane, who had been sitting between John and Bee for the concert, tried to get out of the crowd and off to bed, but it was difficult. Just as she reached the door she heard a woman say to a man, 'That child going out of the door is a sister, you know, but that one doesn't do anything.' The man answered, 'Queer having that plain kid with the other two so good-looking.'

When Jane reached the cabin, Rachel and Tim were telling Peaseblossom all about the concert.

'But it's so odd,' Rachel said. 'They clapped just as much when I danced worst.'

Jane shut the door and began to undress.

'That's what is known as an undiscriminating audience,

64

dear,' Peaseblossom said, 'but I feel sure our side did splend-idly.'

Rachel folded her apron.

'Tim bowed beautifully.'

Tim nodded.

'I thought that was rather good. It was copied from Sir Malcolm Sargent last Christmas when we went to the carols at the Albert Hall.'

Jane felt so miserable she would have liked to have cried, but she only cried over desperate things like leaving Chewing-gum behind. It would not have mattered what those silly fools said only it was true. She couldn't do anything, not anything at all, and she was the only plain Winter. She looked so sour that at last the others noticed. Peaseblossom said:

'What's the matter, dear?'

Jane was brushing her teeth. She took the brush out of her mouth.

'Nothing, it's just that I've already listened to that awful concert and I was not exactly enjoying hearing about it all over again.'

Peaseblossom was shocked. She had known that Jane had been getting out of hand ever since she had quoted 'It's all going to be such splendid fun'. She spoke in her usual voice and not the fade-away, gentle voice she had used ever since her first morning on board.

'Jane! That's a disgraceful way to talk! You're jealous. Jealousy is a horrible fault. We may not all be equally talented but we can all be equally nice people.'

Jane said no more. She climbed into her bunk with indignation sticking out all over her. She lay down and turned her face to the wall, and for the first time since the *Mauretania* had sailed missed Chewing-gum so much that it hurt. Chewing-gum, who thought her much the nicest of the family; who even thought her the best looking; who did not care a bit if she could dance or play the piano; who liked her just as she was with no alteration at all. 'I'll say exactly what I like,' she told herself. 'I don't mind being plain, and I don't mind not doing anything. I hate them all; I'll just be me whether they like it or not.'

*

The whole family, even Peaseblossom, were on deck to catch their first glimpse of the Statue of Liberty. After so long at sea it was thrilling to see land, and ships darting about. At first there was no sign of the statue. Then one of the crew held out a finger pointing. 'She lies there. You watch.' The statue was on an island. She was even bigger and more like herself than she looked in photographs. The man grinned at her affectionately. 'Looks a bit of all right, don't she, bless 'er? Now you look over there. Watch close.'

At first there was nothing to see, for where the man pointed was a bank of mist. What happened was like the end of the Sleeping Beauty's story. That part where the Prince fights his way through overhanging branches and cobwebs and sees a magic castle. The mist broke away as if it were overhanging branches and cobwebs and out of it came what seemed a magic castle. Pinkish in colour, an irregular outline stretching almost to the sky.

Awestruck, Rachel gasped:

'What's that?'

The man laughed.

'That! That's good old New York!'

CHAPTER 7

NEW YORK CITY

JOHN and Bee were met at the dockside by a man friend of Aunt Cora's. They were very glad to see him because he had dollars for them for, by the law of England, they might not change pounds into dollars, so if they had not met the man they would have had no money at all. The children, though they tried not to, had to look hard at the man because he was so exactly like a rich sort of American on the films. Somehow, in spite of films, they had expected Americans to look just like people at home. Aunt Cora's friend was rather short; he had a queer hat with more brim than an Englishman's hat, a lighter suit than men wore in London and the gayest tie the children had ever seen, and he was smoking a cigar. He was very welcoming, so welcoming that at first the children supposed he must be an old friend. When they found he was a stranger they decided that to be welcoming must be an American habit, and a very nice one, as it made the whole family stop feeling they were strangers in a strange land. After he had got over telling them how fine it was to see them, what a swell time they were going to have with Aunt Cora, who was just the nicest girl, and asking them how it felt to be in good old U.S.A., to which, luckily, he did not seem to expect an answer as they none of them knew yet, except Peaseblossom, who was glad of solid land of any sort, he became suddenly brisk and bustling. He said he would take them over to the railroad, where they could check their baggage, and turn the railway vouchers they had bought in England into railway tickets for California, and then he would show them round a bit and give them lunch. He said all this so obviously to John and Bee only, and was not including Peaseblossom or the children in his plans and invitations, that the only thing they could do was to separate. Bee said in a scared voice:

'We've none of us been in New York before. I suppose my family won't get lost.'

The man laughed.

'Why no. What these kids will like will be to go to the top of the Empire State Building and then to fill themselves up with ice cream sodas. Come along, you folks, we've a lot to fix.' On that he put one arm through John's and the other through Bee's and hurried them away.

Peaseblossom and the children looked after them feeling rather deserted. Rachel said:

'He's a friend of Aunt Cora's. Do you suppose Aunt Cora's that sort of person who thinks children never want to do the same things as their parents do?'

Peaseblossom tried to sound confident.

'Don't talk nonsense, dear. Naturally that nice friend of your aunt's doesn't want the whole lot of us hanging round. Besides, we'll manage splendidly on our own, won't we? Up the Winters!'

They would have managed perfectly if the effect of New York on Peaseblossom had not been to turn her from her competent self into something rather like a sheep in a narrow lane trying to go the opposite way to the rest of the flock. It was perhaps because she had eaten almost nothing for six days, still felt as if there was a roll under her feet and had legs which, because she had not used them much lately, seemed made of cotton wool. Everybody was kind and helpful and told them how to get out of the docks and which way to go when they were out, but Peaseblossom could not take in what she was told. She kept saying in an agitated way, 'I beg your pardon?' and even 'What?' which shocked the children, who had been told since they were babies that to say 'What?' was rude.

Worst of all, she behaved as though the directions were being given to her in another language, commenting on them to the children in loud whispers, which the people politely trying to help must have overheard. 'I can't make out a word he's saying.' 'It can't really be only a short ride, all docks are miles from the centre of a town.' 'Better ask somebody else. I don't think he knows where the Empire State Building is.'

The children, who had learned on board that in New York you did dock in the centre of the city, and that every citizen knew where the Empire State Building was, were so ashamed that at last they took control. Rachel gripped one of Peaseblossom's arms and Jane the other, and they hurried her out of the docks and across the road; but once there they forgot the directions they had been given and found it was difficult to get them again because nobody in New York walked slowly. Instead they moved at the same pace as in England men used when they were practising for a walking race. First one of the children and then another stepped forward to ask the way, saying politely, 'Excuse me,' but by the time they had got that out the person they had spoken to was almost out of sight and never knew they had been addressed. At last a man who was held up by the traffic lights noticed them and leant out of his car.

'You folks needing help?'

They all explained at once. He was a terribly kind man. He told them to get into his car and he would drive them to where they could get a street car. As they drove along he told them that he knew they came from Britain because of their British accents. This surprised the children, who had supposed that it was America which had an accent and not England, unless, of course, you were Scottish or Welsh or something like that, but they kept this thought to themselves. The man asked them how they liked being in America. That was difficult to answer as they had only been in the New York docks so far,

69

but they remembered their manners and said it was lovely. The man was most considerate; he put them down where he said the street car would stop, and that in the street car they had only to travel six blocks. He had been so kind that as he drove away they felt they had lost a friend.

A street car in America seemed to be a bus. The thing they had forgotten, and had not noticed when the man was driving them, was that traffic drove on the opposite side of the road to the way it did at home, so, in spite of the man having told them that they were at the right stop, they thought they must cross the road or they would go back the way they had come. Unfortunately they chose a moment to cross when a street car arrived, and the traffic lights turned to green. The driver leant out and shouted at them. None of them knew exactly what he had said but they recognized the sense, for angry bus-driver language is the same anywhere. They shot back on to the pavement knowing they had behaved stupidly. Even when they did grasp which street car to take they made a very silly entrance on to it, for they tried to get on to the back end, as they did at home, for they did not know there was no bus conductor, so passengers entered in front and paid the driver as they got in. Peaseblossom looked so flustered that Rachel said comfortingly:

'We couldn't know.'

Tim was indignant.

'If you ask me, American street cars are like tortoises; I mean, like you have to give a shut-up tortoise a buttercup each end to know which end's going to eat.'

Peaseblossom had always known the values of American money, and had carefully re-studied the subject before she left England, but by the time she was on the street car she was in that condition when people say 'I'll forget my own name next!' When the driver told her how many nickels he wanted she became deaf again, and repeated in an ever louder voice, 'I beg your pardon?' Fortunately John had given her a lot of small change and Jane had the good idea of taking her purse from her, tipping the money into her hand and letting the driver help himself. It worked all right, though the driver did not seem pleased, for he made international bus-driver noises.

Tim was surprised at this display of grumpiness in a country where everybody seemed so welcoming. As he sat down he whispered to Jane:

'It was because you didn't put the money in that slot machine the tickets came out of. Do you think I could go and tell him we aren't stupid really, it's only we've never seen one of those before?'

Jane was cross because, though she would not admit it, the driver being angry fussed her.

'Don't be a silly idiot; interrupting him when he's driving will make him hate us worse.'

To make up for the driver the people in the car could not have been kinder. Nearly all of them had expressions on their faces to show they thought seeing strangers get off street cars at the right place was the most important thing in life. Tim was so charmed by this that before they left the car he thanked everybody. 'Thank you all so much, you've been very kind', which seemed to cause quite a sensation for they got off to a hum of 'Isn't he cute!' 'Isn't he darling!' Tim looked after the departing street car with affection.

'Did you hear what those people said about me?'

Rachel looked at Peaseblossom. Neither of them said anything but they made faces which showed they hoped Tim was not going to be spoilt in America. Jane as usual spoke what she thought.

'You aren't cute and, goodness knows, nobody could call you darling.'

There would have been a quarrel but fighting their way through the half-running citizens of New York took up all their attention and breath.

The Empire State Building was a wonderful thrill to the children but not to Peaseblossom. What they called lifts, but they learned in America were called elevators, shot them up one hundred and two storeys. Peaseblossom's inside could not comfortably have stood a ride up two storeys; a hundred and two was nearly fatal. She arrived at the top looking green as grass and holding a handkerchief at the ready. Actually they got the best view when they came down one storey because there they could go outside and lean over a wall. The mist of the morning had gone and it was a marvellous sight. On the top of the highest building in the world the skyscrapers of New York ceased to tower above them; instead they seemed straining up to be as tall as the State Building. Away through the city wound the Hudson river, the ships on it looking from that height like toy ships made to float in a bath. They saw how neatly arranged the New York streets were, almost as neat as a chessboard; long roads stretching across the city and across them other roads east and west. They looked such little streets seen from a hundred and one storeys up, even the great Fifth Avenue seemed tiny, and the mass of traffic everywhere was so small it could have been built for gnomes. They would have stayed up there for twice as long as they did only Peaseblossom said it made her feel queer even to watch them hanging over, so in pity they had to take her down.

When they came out of the Empire State Building they remembered the other thing Aunt Cora's friend has said they would like. Ice cream sodas. Peaseblossom, though the sound of the words made her shudder, quite agreed that the children had been promised them. She looked round at the hurrying, swirling crowd.

'I must find a policeman. He will be sure to know somewhere nice.'

It took time but at last Peaseblossom found a policeman. At once she felt more at home than she had done since she arrived, for policemen always knew everything, never minded how many questions you asked and were never in a hurry. She went up to this one with a confident smile.

'Constable, could you tell me of a nice place to take these children to drink ice cream sodas?'

Peaseblossom waited for the brotherly smile, for the pause while the virtues of various places were considered, for the final advice, 'If I were you I'd take them to . . .' Nothing like that happened. The policeman never smiled, scarcely looked at Peaseblossom. He paused all right, but it was the pause of somebody marvelling why a stupid woman should bother him. Then he moved away; as he moved he said:

'Drug store opposite.'

Peaseblossom's faith in the United States of America quivered. What kind of a land was it where policemen were not everybody's friend and adviser?

'What a strange man! A drug store! Why should he think I want a chemist?'

The children did not say so because they too were thinking it was queer for a policeman to be unfriendly, but they could see why he thought it was probably a chemist Peaseblossom needed, for she was still the oddest colour.

Tim was thirsty and unwilling to wait longer for his drink. He knew now that in New York it was no good saying anything slowly as nobody heard you. He laid a hand on the arm of a passing lady.

'Where do we buy ice cream sodas, please?'

She was the nicest lady. People in America, except street car drivers and policemen, seemed, once they stopped hurrying, to have not only lots of time to help strangers, but all put on that special helpful-looking expression. The lady called Tim 'Honey' and said 'Surely' twice, and then showed them the same drug store the policeman had shown them. She laughed when she saw Peaseblossom's surprised face and said it was clear they hadn't been over long, and she remembered being just as mixed up when she first visited Europe. She explained

that a drug store in America was not the same thing as a chemist in England; it sold drugs all right, but everything else as well, including ice cream sodas.

The drug store was beautiful. All down one side was a counter with men behind it in white coats. A most friendly man mixed their drinks. When he heard that none of them had ever tasted an ice cream soda he could hardly believe it, but it made him full of advice. He thought they should all have different flavours so that they could taste each other's and see which they liked best. In the end Rachel had a strawberry, Jane a chocolate and Tim a raspberry. The man tried to persuade Peaseblossom to have one too, but when she explained about the sea and the Empire State Building he quite understood and said he had just the drink for her, and mixed her something which looked like fruit salts. He was obviously proud of the way he mixed his ice cream sodas, for he watched them drinking with a professional eye, and kept asking the children whether they were enjoying them. He could never have had more admiration.

'I wouldn't think,' Tim said, 'anybody living wouldn't like raspberry ice cream fuzzed up into a drink and then whipped cream on the top of that.'

'And straws to drink through,' Jane added.

Rachel was digging in her glass with her spoon.

'And there are strawberries at the bottom of mine.'

The salts, or whatever it was the man had given Peaseblossom, did her a lot of good. She made three loud hiccoughing sounds, but once those were over it seemed to be the end of her feeling peculiar, so much the end that for the first time for six days she was hungry.

'I don't know about you but I would be glad of something to eat.'

The rest of the time in New York seemed to fly away. They had a lovely lunch, then they went to the station in a taxi. The taxi-driver had been in England during the war and to begin with was full of chat. He told them what he thought about England, which was not all very complimentary, and asked them what they thought of New York. Peaseblossom and Rachel said politely it was lovely, but Tim told the man he thought it was a noisy town, for he had taken a dislike to the sirens screaming on the ambulances, fire engines and police cars, and Jane said that she didn't think much of the manners of policemen and street car drivers. The taxi man seemed surprised at there being anything to criticize and looked hurt and said no more.

As soon as they were out of the taxi Peaseblossom turned on Jane and Tim.

'How dreadfully rude you were!'

Jane thought this shockingly unjust.

75

'He told us what he didn't like about England.'

'Well, he's got a right to. He was over with us long enough to have an opinion, but you've only been in New York one day and you start to criticize. I'm ashamed of you.'

It took nothing to make Jane angry; Tim was usually fairly even tempered, but such apparent injustice was more than he could stand.

'If you think all the time I'm in America I'm going to be polite to people and say everything's perfect while they say what they like about England you're wrong. You couldn't make me.'

'I've always said what I think,' Jane said, 'and I'm not going to change just because I'm in America.'

Peaseblossom had a voice which she used only rarely, but when she did use it even Jane seldom disobeyed her.

'Be quiet, both of you! I'll talk to you about this another time.'

Bee and John were waiting with Aunt Cora's friend outside the gate that led to their departure platform. They could feel in a second that something was wrong, and if they had not felt it a glance would have told them. Jane looked at her most black-doggish. Tim's lips were sucked together and he was frowning. Rachel had a don't-get-me-to-take-sides expression. Peaseblossom had two bright pink patches on her cheekbones, always a bad sign. There was no opportunity to find out what was wrong, with Aunt Cora's friend there, and the great thing was to let him think the day had been enjoyed, whether it had or not, so John asked what they had done. Rachel answered, helped by Peaseblossom, and presently, as his temper wore off, Tim joined in. Jane said nothing at all. If Tim was weak enough to let Peaseblossom think she was forgiven, let him be, but not her; she would go on being angry until Peaseblossom apologized. Aunt Cora's friend was glad to hear what a good time they had enjoyed. Luckily Tim kept off the subject of policemen and street car drivers, so he thought that they had admired everything and everybody.

The train was just like a train on the pictures. A real American engine with a bell on the top and even a fender in front to push cows out of the way. The train was called the 'Twentieth Century Limited'. All the cars were pullmans and they too had names. Each car had little steps leading down to the platform and, best of all, at the bottom of each set of steps stood a smiling Negro porter. The children were so excited at finding they were to travel on what to them was a train in a film that all they could say was 'Oh!' Aunt Cora's friend came on to the train to see they were what he called 'fixed' all right. There were seats with room for two facing each other; each seat belonged to one person. Aunt Cora's friend showed them where presently the top bunks would come down, and told them that the porter would make up their beds when they were ready for them, and where he would fix curtains across so that each one of them at night would have a curtained place to themselves. Then he led them down the train and showed them the places where they would go to wash and dress, and where the diner was, and the club car, but he said after Chicago, where their through pullman would be fixed on to a train called 'The Chief', they ought to sit in the observation car because the scenery would really be something.

When they had waved good-bye to Aunt Cora's friend, John led the way back to their seats and sat down, and as he listened to the American train noise, which was quite different to English train noise, and saw their night luggage neatly stacked under their seats, and looked out of the window at New York slipping by, he said with more enthusiasm than they had heard in his voice since the accident:

'Isn't this fun!'

Jane was still very black-doggish and she was convinced she had a right to be. She had hoped John and Bee would ask her what was wrong so that she could tell the whole story, and in her mind she could hear them say, 'Well, Peaseblossom, I think Jane and Tim were right; if the taxi-driver gave his opinion of England there was no harm in their criticizing people and things in America' or something of that sort, which would squash Peaseblossom. As neither Bee nor John appeared to have noticed she was angry Jane had to open the subject herself.

'It would be more fun if people were allowed to say what they thought.'

Bee saw Jane felt she must tell her grievance or explode.

'What mayn't you say, darling?'

Jane explained. She was prompted by Tim who, now the whole story was repeated, was angry again.

While the story was pouring out in a very 'and then Tim said . . . and then I said . . .' way John seemed to be looking out of the window and not attending, but as Jane finished he turned round. He held out a hand to Tim and pulled him on to one knee; he put an arm round Jane and nodded to Rachel to sit opposite to him.

'Looks as though I ought to have had this talk on the boat. There's a thing we've got to remember every day, and every minute of the day from now on. We are foreigners.'

'Foreigners!' the children exclaimed. Rachel added, 'But the American soldiers weren't foreigners to us when they lived in England when there was a war.'

'Yes, they were, and I expect they felt it.'

Tim wriggled round on John's knee so that he could look at him. He did not feel he could expostulate well unless he could see his face.

'We can't be foreigners, we all speak the same language.'

'That's the snag. Just because we speak more or less the same language we forget we're foreign and expect Americans to behave and think like we do; actually we are just as foreign as if we were Dutch, French, Belgian or Swiss. Being foreigners

78

means we are staying in somebody else's house. When you stay with Aunt Cora you won't come down to breakfast and look at the food and say "We cook that better at home", or, when some plan's made, "I don't want to do that", and you won't criticize the way her furniture is arranged or what she says. You'll be in her house and you'll feel, as a guest feels, that what she does in it is her business.'

Jane was still looking very black-doggish.

'Do you mean that all the time we're staying here we've got to be visitors, and if somebody like that taxi-driver says things about us we can't say things back?'

'Well, he knew what he was talking about. He was in England for months probably, and got to know us well, but what's the point of you flying out about manners of policemen and street car drivers when you've only been in the country five minutes? It's not only rude, it's ignorant. I don't want to preach to you but it's common sense. Let's behave like visitors who hope to get asked again.'

There was a silence for a moment. The fact that they were now foreigners had surprised the children, for somehow they had not thought of themselves as that. It had been a shock to Tim and Jane to find that John sided with Peaseblossom in thinking they had been rude. Jane still wanted to argue. A holiday in which she was supposed to be on guest behaviour with everybody was not at all her idea of a nice time. She had, of course, known that they would be Aunt Cora's guests, with all the being polite that meant, but being the guests of everybody in America was too much.

'I think it's idiotic we can't say we don't like things if we don't.'

John was losing the gay mood in which he had come on the train. He looked tired.

'I can't help what you think, I'm telling you how we're going to behave. When we've been here a month or two it'll be different; we may be able to discuss ways of doing things,

79

but not the moment we arrive. Anybody who yaps about somebody else's country without knowing a thing about it looks a silly ass. You don't want to look that.'

Bee thought the lecture had gone on long enough. She was unwinding paper off a long, thin roll.

'Look what I bought for you all.' She held out a piece of music. It was a copy of 'California Here I Come'.

Tim had the music. The others leant over his shoulder. He read it through, then, very softly, he hummed the chorus. In tiny voices so as not to disturb the other passengers Rachel and Jane joined in:

> '*California here I come.*
> *Right back where I started from,*
> *Where bowers of flowers bloom in the sun*
>   *every morning at dawning.*
> *Birdies sing and everything.*
> *A sun-kissed maid said "Don't be late";*
> *That's why I can hardly wait.*
> *Open up that golden gate,*
> *California here I come.*'

They laughed at the words but singing them made a very gay feeling. After all, it was not just a song they were singing, they were really going to California. They were actually on their way.

A man across the aisle leant over.

'Sing up, folks. Let's all enjoy it.'

That was just what was needed; Americans seemed awfully nice on trains, not a bit stand-offish. Soon lots of people were joining in, including the coloured porter, and those who were not were laughing.

> '*Open up that golden gate,*
> *California here I come.*'

CHAPTER 8

THE SANTA FÉ TRAIL

THE children thought travelling in America was very grand. Such lots of things were given you for nothing. In every car there were jars of iced water with cardboard cups waiting for people to help themselves. In the club car there was a radio that anyone might turn on, great stacks of magazines for those who wanted to read and even free paper and envelopes at a desk in case you wanted to write a letter. Most miraculous of all the free things was something they discovered in the dining-car as they were finishing their breakfasts.

The train was due in early in Chicago. Peaseblossom, Bee and John had left the children to finish and had gone to make themselves tidy. The children were eating things called 'popovers' which they had not tasted before and thought too good to be eaten in a hurry. The man in charge of the dining-car came across to them.

'You going to the radio show?' Seeing that they did not know what he was talking about he explained. The train they were travelling on came in at one station, and the one their pullman was being attached to would leave quite a while later from another station. Of course you could stop in your car but no one ever did that, or you could spend the time sight-seeing in Chicago, but if you wanted a good time with no trouble to yourself you could get into a bus which would be waiting at the station; you would be driven to a theatre where you would be the guest of the people who were putting a radio show on the air. You would, of course, see the show but, as well, you would be invited to be part of it. When the show was over you would get back into the free bus and be driven to the station in time to catch your train for California.

The children had never seen a radio show, never been within miles of a chance of taking part in one, and it had been for years one of their ambitions, and not only theirs but Peaseblossom's and Bee's as well. How often at home had they said they wished they could see the people taking part in a wireless programme, but it was rather like saying they wished they could meet an Eskimo – it was not the sort of wish they supposed would come true. Now it was coming true. A glorious chance never to come again. Hardly waiting to thank the head of the dining-car they rushed up the train to tell Bee, Peaseblossom and John the gorgeous news.

While they had breakfast Joe, their pullman porter, had cleared away the beds. Their car was once more a day-time car; not a sign of bunks, sheets or curtains. Bee and Peaseblossom were sitting opposite each other on the seats which had been Bee's bed. They were talking to each other. As the children tore up Peaseblossom held up a hand.

'Quietly, dears. Your mother and I are discussing something.'

Bee smiled at them.

'Discussing you, as a matter of fact. We've got a nice wait in Chicago so I'm taking you two girls to have your hair washed, and Dad's taking Tim to have his cut, and Peaseblossom's going to try and find a valet service to press a dress for each of you girls. We think you look grubs and we don't want Aunt Cora to think she's taken in savages.'

'No indeed,' Peaseblossom agreed. 'First impressions are so important.'

The children listened and nudged each other. Hair dressing! Getting frocks pressed! Bee and Peaseblossom had not heard the news yet. Tim was so longing to tell them that he had to jump about to hold the words back, and when Peaseblossom finished they burst out of him.

'There won't be any of those things done in Chicago. You'll never guess what you are going to do.'

'And do it absolutely free,' Rachel added.

Jane sat down beside Peaseblossom.

'We'll give you three guesses, and I'll give you a hint. It's something that all of us except Dad have said for years and years we wanted to do.'

Bee shook her head.

'Whatever it is, darlings, I'm afraid we can't do it today.'

Rachel looked from Bee's face to Peaseblossom's, and knew in that quick way that thoughts sometimes come that this was going to be one of those chasms which divide children from grown-ups. It seemed inconceivable that anybody at any age could think having your hair washed or cut, or clothes pressed more important than being part of a wireless programme, but that was what Bee and Peaseblossom were going to think. Her face showed what she was thinking. Bee said:

'Don't look at me as if I was a particularly stupid animal you were watching at the zoo.'

Tim and Jane spoke at the same time.

'Go on, guess.'

Peaseblossom got up.

'It's no good our guessing, dears, we know what you're going to do and you ought to be getting ready, we'll be in Chicago quite soon now.'

Jane was exasperated.

'You might at least try and guess, but, as you can't, we'll tell you.'

Jane and Tim did the telling. Rachel knew it was no good, and knew too what a row there was going to be. It was a very bad row. At first Jane and Tim refused to believe that Bee and Peaseblossom had understood what they were being offered; when they grasped that they did understand and were turning the opportunity down they lost their tempers, even worse than they had over the taxi-driver.

'I wouldn't have thought,' Jane said, 'that there could be people alive who could be so stupid.'

'A chance in a lifetime missed for a haircut,' Tim raged.

'And all this talk about saving money,' Jane went on, 'and when we get the nicest treat we've ever had absolutely free you turn it down out of spite, for it can't be anything else.'

They would have said a lot more only at that moment John joined them.

'What's up?'

They all tried to tell him, but John said firmly, 'Shut up, kids.' Then he looked at Bee. Bee explained very fairly, leaving out the fact that both Jane and Tim had been rude, but John had seen their red faces and heard Jane's last remark. He hated undisciplined children who argued and were rude. He had suspected that with Peaseblossom in her bunk his family had got out of hand on the *Mauretania*, and, much as he hated them being out of hand anywhere, he particularly disliked it in a foreign country where people might judge all English children's behaviour by his children's, so he spoke more firmly than he felt, for actually his sympathy was with the children. He could think of no worse way of wasting their short time in Chicago than by titivating. He did not want to go to the radio show, but he did want to go to an art gallery which had pictures in it he had always longed to see, and he did not think it mattered a bit what they looked like when they met Aunt Cora, but he knew Bee and Peaseblossom; if they thought the family had to arrive looking tidy then that settled it, they would arrive looking tidy. He looked as stern as he could.

'You are the most pestiferous lot. Peaseblossom carts you across the world in a luxury liner, and you have what I understand was a good day in New York but you come on the train fighting, and the next morning here you are at it again. The trouble is you're getting out of hand, and that probably comes of being cooped up. As soon as the hair-do's are done with we'll take you somewhere and give you a good run.'

Jane and Tim still did not believe they were missing the radio show. Jane said, 'But, Dad, we've absolutely got to go.'

Tim nodded.

'Making us miss a thing like that for hair is the meanest thing I ever heard of.'

John was not allowing that tone of voice.

'The trouble is you are having too much and you're getting spoilt. One more word from any of you and you stay in the pullman, which is going into a siding for a couple of hours.'

The threat of the siding was too awful to contemplate. Without another word the children went off to tidy; but though they said no more in front of the grown-ups they could hardly wait to get out of earshot to speak their minds. They stood outside the women's dressing-room. Jane was almost stamping.

'Spoilt! It's them that's spoilt. Grown-up people always get their own way, and if that isn't spoiling I don't know what is.'

Tim stuck out his chin.

'I should think we're going to hate that Aunt Cora if she's the sort of aunt you've always got to dress up for. Oh, it is mean! Us on the wireless! Imagine!'

Rachel could have cried.

'It's all very well for you two to talk about meanness, but you did argue, and now Dad's going to think we're all spoilt.'

Jane looked at Tim.

'Did you hear that? Here was Rachel just as keen to go to the wireless show as us, and who fought to go? You and me, and now she's blaming us. I can't think how she came to be our sister.'

It was a pity the time in Chicago started badly because,

if not compared with being part of a wireless programme, it was a good morning. Bee took the children to an enormous store to have their hair done. A moving staircase took them to the hairdressing salon, and as it moved they had a grand view of all the other departments. They were very impressed by the length of the moving staircase, the size of everything and by what there was to buy in the store; so impressed that they travelled the whole distance in silence.

After their hair was finished Bee gave them ice cream sodas, which, apart from the pleasure of drinking them, raised the general tone of spirits, for though Bee did not say so they showed she was sorry about the radio show. Then they got into a taxi and went to the art gallery and picked up John, and from there drove to the shore of Lake Michigan. The lake was not like a lake; it was like a very big sea, with waves on it and a sandy beach of white, firm sand, the sort which is perfect for walking on. Bee told them to take off their shoes and socks and give them to her to look after, and have a run. The moment the children felt the sand under their feet they were mad, silly and gay. It was the first rush-about time they had had since they left England, and though they had not noticed it they needed stretching. To add to the niceness of the sand they found a live snake lying asleep by the water's edge. That snake coming on top of feeling so much better after running nearly cured them of minding about the radio show. It cured them enough for them to sing 'California Here I Come' in the taxi all the way to the railway station.

It was like coming home to find their own pullman and Joe, beaming and welcoming, waiting for them. He wanted to know about everything they had done just as if he was one of the family, and was as impressed by the snake as the children had been.

'That sho' was a mighty fine adventure.'

They were in plenty of time for the train so, on Joe's advice, they walked up the platform to look at their train from the outside. It really was a proud sight; gleaming pullmans, each one with a name of its own, and an enormous engine. The children decided that an American engine looked so unlike an English engine that if you didn't know it you would never think they were even distantly related. Coming back down the platform was like playing a game. The train was not really starting but there was a busy, fussy feeling as though it might, so they darted from one little set of steps guarded by a pullman porter to another, loitering at the bottom of the steps but running hard to the next ones, just in case the train decided to move.

After lunch the whole family went, as Aunt Cora's friend had advised, to the observation car. It was at the far end of the train and John had to lead the way, opening endless doors, and since the train was going quite fast they got a bit knocked about, but when they reached the observation car it was worth it. It was, in its way, the grandest part of a very grand train. It was glass, like sitting in a greenhouse. At the far end you could see what the car attendant called 'the track' running away behind them and out of the window was, first of all, a bit of the State of Illinois, then a piece of Missouri and then Kansas. It was when John said that they would pass through Kansas that the children got especially thrilled. The home of Dorothy in *The Wizard of Oz*. To be going to Kansas added a spice of danger to the journey, for in Kansas, as they knew from the book, storms of wind could get up in a second and blow down a whole house, and if a whole house what might not happen to a train?

Nothing did happen. It was queer how you settled down to live on a train almost the way you did on a boat. Things happened to time. Meals and washings and going to bed. The afternoon was long because there was no time when everybody moved into the dining-car to have tea. Americans did not seem to have tea. You could order it but it was not a real tea.

87

To make up for missing it they had Coca-Colas at half past four, which the children much preferred, and even Tim went to the diner for dinner. Dinners started very early on the train. Peaseblossom felt the first night on 'The Chief' was a good moment to make it clear that what happened on trains would not happen off them.

'This is only a treat for the train, mind you. As soon as we get to your aunt's it's a light supper on a tray for Jane and Tim as usual, and bed at six-thirty for Tim and seven for Jane.'

At the time she said this Jane and Tim had their mouths full of cream of chicken and rice and meals off trays seemed a long way off, so even Jane did not bother to argue.

In one night John got well. Not well in flashes, as he had done since he left England, but altogether his gay self. He was not writing but then he hardly could on a train, but he was in a writing mood. He came along to breakfast the first morning on 'The Chief', his eyes gay and shining and his hands full of guide books and maps. He stood at the end of their table.

'You know you all think you are sitting in a train, eating waffles, but you're wrong. Our family is travelling by wagon down the Santa Fé trail. Look, here's our wagon.' He held out a picture he had drawn. 'You see that man driving, that's me. You think we came out here on the *Mauretania* for a holiday. Wrong again. Over a hundred years wrong. We left England on a sailing ship in eighteen hundred and ten. We left because we wanted a new chance in a new world. We had a little money and some things we could sell, and we bought this wagon and these oxen.' He began to draw what, if he could have drawn better, might have been oxen. 'And we are going to a trader's post, which was founded in memory of St Francis of Assisi by some Spanish monks two hundred years ago. Two hundred years, mind you, before eighteen ten. The trading post is called Santa Fé.'

Before the accident that was the sort of game John had always played. It was only now that he had started that sort of game again that the children realized how much they had missed them. They stopped eating and gave advice.

Rachel said:

'Our oxen look rather thin, don't they?'

Tim took the drawing from his father.

'You don't look very well armed, Dad. We need guns.'

Jane took the drawing from Tim.

'Where are we?'

Bee leant across and took the drawing from Jane.

'At the moment we're out of sight having breakfast, but as soon as that's finished we'll all be seen walking beside our wagon.'

It was the best game John had ever invented. It needed far more than the little bit of paper the first drawing was on. It took up a whole table in the club car. They were all there in the dress of the early nineteenth century. Tim and John armed to the teeth. All sorts of things happened. An ox died and was buried at the side of the trail. Water was what they most needed and prizes were given to the first member of the family to spot the signs of a river. They thought there ought to be a dog with them and John, without seeming to remember that Chewing-gum had not been mentioned since they had started, drew a picture of him.

' 'Course old Chewing-gum's there. We're never going back, we wouldn't have left the old fellow behind. He'd be running like this behind the wagon.'

Jane was so deep in the game, so sure they were on foot on the trail, that seeing a drawing, or as good a drawing as John could do, of Chewing-gum did not make her think how far away he was. She just took it for granted he was there.

Towards sunset they pored over maps to decide where they would camp for the night. It was then that other people in the car joined in. They hung over the table arguing as to where would be the best place.

An old man opposite settled the argument. He pointed out of the window. The sun was setting in a blaze and ahead it was reflected in gold and crimson water.

'I guess you folks are glad to get a sight of that. You've come a mighty way and your oxen must be tired.'

It seemed dull to go to bed in a proper bunk after that and the children sensibly refused to do it. They were in upper bunks and had to lean out to talk to each other. Rachel, who had gone to bed at the same time as Jane, said:

'I hope Dad doesn't let the fire out. It'll keep animals away.'

Jane answered proudly:

'Isn't Chewing-gum there?'

Tim was half-asleep.

'Indians are more likely than animals, but don't worry, I've got my gun beside me.'

The next day the game went on and grew every minute more real and more exciting. There were the remains of Spanish mission houses along the trail. There were Mexican villages with odd, flat-roofed houses shining white in the sun, and chains of drying scarlet chillies hanging like garlands of flowers. There were Indians in beaded dresses with interesting brown, hook-nosed faces and straight black hair selling things at the stations. The country grew stranger and lonelier and wilder. The sun hotter and hotter. When they stopped at stations to take on ice for the air-conditioning and water the heat seemed to burn through them and made them different people from the Winters who had caught a boat-train in London less than two weeks ago. The air, when they got out at the stations, was unlike any air they had felt before. As they sniffed it in it made them excited without anything special to be excited about.

It had been so real travelling down the trail that when

they finished with the trail it was quite hard to get back to the twentieth century and remember it had been a game. John tore up the pictures.

'Well, there we are. We made it. We're going to trade in our oxen and see if we can get a bit of land and build ourselves a house.'

The old man opposite shook his head.

'Maybe. Most like you moved on. Not so long after you folks settled, gold was discovered in California.'

Gold in California! How lovely that sounded. Gold in California! California, where they would be tomorrow morning. The same idea came to the children at the same time. Tim conducted.

> *'California, here I come,*
> *Right back where I started from.'*

It was the same as on the first night out from New York. By the last line half the people in the car were joining in:

> *'Open up that golden gate,*
> *California here I come.'*

Everybody sang except Peaseblossom. She got up and, with a serious expression, went to have a look at the girls' pressed dresses, which Joe had hung up for her. Other people could sing 'Open up that golden gate', but she had remembered that tomorrow morning early they had to make a first impression on Aunt Cora.

CHAPTER 9

AUNT CORA

THE next morning life was just preparation for meeting Aunt Cora. Even Rachel's ears and nails were inspected and none of the children were allowed to do their own hair and, once dressed, were scarcely permitted to move. Breakfast, instead of being a pleasure, was one long fuss for fear they spilt something. After breakfast they had to sit with their hands folded in case they touched anything and got dirty. They had two sympathizers. John, who made a funny face to show he thought all this dressing-up tiresome but unavoidable, and Joe, who came over to the children. Jane sat on one seat and Tim and Rachel faced her on the other. He looked at their clean socks, at the girls' freshly pressed frocks, at Tim's spotless shirt and very brushed hair. His eyes twinkled and a huge grin cracked his nice dark face almost in half.

'Yo' Aunt Cora's sho' going to know yo's been fetched up right.'

The only thing which helped make the waiting time pass was the view from one window. The sky was startlingly blue. There were mountains. Most amazing of all, there were oranges and lemons growing on trees.

'Fancy us looking out of a train in October and seeing oranges growing,' Rachel marvelled. 'At home now the last leaves are blowing off the trees.'

For a moment they were back in Saxon Crescent. They saw it as it probably would look: dead leaves scratching dryly against each other in the wind, other leaves chasing each other up the street, perhaps a pale blue sky, more likely a grey sky and rain.

'Isn't it queer to think it's there and we're here?' Tim said.
Jane stared at the vivid sky.

'And won't it seem queer next year to think that this
time a year ago there was us looking at California?'

Aunt Cora was on the platform. She was just a little like
John but not a bit the children's idea of what a widowed aunt
ought to look like; in fact so unlike their idea of what any
aunt, widowed or not, ought to look like that they wished that
Joe had not told them he would be watching the meeting. Of
course Aunt Cora had married an American when she was
eighteen, but though they knew that fact it had not prepared
the children for an un-English looking and sounding aunt.
Aunt Cora was thin with bright golden hair; she was wearing
no hat and the most odd dress, a dress which seemed to Tim
and Jane like any fancy dress but to Rachel as if it belonged
to the first act of *Giselle*, for it had puffed sleeves and a peasanty
look. She had a whiney voice with a queer accent, neither
English nor American but half-way between. She was wearing
an American welcoming expression, and she said all the right
American welcoming things, only somehow, perhaps because
she was not an American, she did not sound or look sincere,
and the more welcoming her words and face tried to be the
more the whole family remembered how early she must have
got up to meet their train. She did the proper things, kissing
everybody, even Peaseblossom, and for each one had special
words. 'Bee! Why, isn't this too wonderful!' 'Miss Bean!
I'm surely glad to know you.' 'This must be Rachel, we'll
have to look after you or we'll be losing you to the movies.'
'You must be Jane. Poor little thing, she needs feeding up.'
'Tim! Quite a little man, isn't he?' After a lot more of this
she held John by the shoulders. 'John! Big brother John.'
John thought the welcome had gone on long enough. He said
in a very brisk that's-enough-of-that-voice:

'Fine seeing you, old girl. Oughtn't we to be doing
something about the luggage?'

Aunt Cora had borrowed a station wagon which held them all and the luggage. She drove very fast, talking in her funny, whiney voice to John. It was mostly asking about people in England and only John needed to attend, which was lucky because it gave the rest of them time to look around and there was such lots to see. Everything was unlike any place the children had been in before. Huge palm trees bordered the roads. There were no hedges or fences round the houses but each garden was open to what they called the pavement, but Aunt Cora, speaking to John, called the sidewalk. There were so many unusual plants and flowers about that Bee, who loved flowers, kept giving pleased squeaks.

'Oh, look, a plumbago hedge!' 'Oh, do look at that bougainvillaea!'

The town did not look a bit like Chicago or New York. There were no skyscrapers, and not many high buildings considering they were in America. Somehow, perhaps because it was so pretty under a royal blue sky with lovely mountains as a background, it did not look a real place, more like something on the stage or painted on a postcard.

Aunt Cora looked over her shoulder.

'We're just leaving Beverly Hills; at the end of this boulevard we're in Santa Monica.'

They were by the sea. There were sands, restaurants with big notices outside saying 'Sea food'. Houses built right up against the shore with steps leading down to the sands. A general gay seaside look everywhere. The children were thrilled.

'The sea! Look at the sea!'

Aunt Cora said, in a reproving way, as if the word 'sea' were insulting:

'You don't use the word 'sea' here. You say ocean.'

Peaseblossom hurried to cover the family's mistake.

'Of course we do. We just forgot the Pacific was an ocean, didn't we, dears?'

Aunt Cora had built her own house, or rather Aunt Cora's

husband, whom she called 'My dear Ed', had built it for her. It was at the far end of Santa Monica. A lovely house, long, low, white, with what the family called a veranda and she called a porch overlooking the sea. From the porch steps led down to the sand. The bedrooms were lovely. John and Bee had a big one with its own bathroom, and Tim had a dressing-room opening off it. The two girls and Pease-blossom had a big room and it had its own shower. Aunt Cora's room, which was too grand for words, had a bath-room, and there was another shower for Bella, Aunt Cora's old coloured cook-general. The number of bathrooms im-pressed the children very much, for in Saxon Crescent they had only one.

'I shouldn't think,' Rachel said, 'Buckingham Palace could have more.'

The first thing they did on arrival was to have another breakfast. Just as if she had known what they would like Bella had made popovers for them; as well there was the most amazing fruit. Blueberries, the size of gooseberries, served with thick cream. Purple figs. Little canteloupe melons cut in half and iced. Queer soft orange-coloured fruits called persimmons, and a whole bunch of bananas. There was a glass of chilled tomato juice, there was a cereal, there were eggs, bacon, and coffee and cream. Nobody was sure if in America it was the right thing to talk about food, but they simply had to. Aunt Cora looked in a sad way at the table.

'I always provide good food, but I scarcely touch it myself. I have to be so careful to keep my calories right.' She looked at herself and then disapprovingly at Peaseblossom, who had curves. 'That's how I keep my figure.'

Breakfast was served on the porch. While they were all admiring the food, without their noticing it Bella had come in from the back and was standing in the doorway. She was very fat but gay in a bright flowered overall, and her old face had a wide, pleased smile; it could not have smiled more if she had been welcoming her own relations. At Aunt Cora's words she gave a fat chuckle.

'Don' you listen to Miss Cora. You eat all yo's a mind to. Miss Cora don' eat no more'n a bird.'

Aunt Cora looked peevish.

'And Bella eats enough to keep a family and look at her!'

They looked at Bella. Just looking at her made them smile; she seemed so pleased about everything. Bella shook her head and gave another fat chuckle.

'Ah surely enjoy ma food, ah eat like a hawg, but ah ain't aiming to suffer from my nerves.'

Aunt Cora waited until Bella had shut the door and was out of earshot. Then she lowered her voice.

'I expect you'll think Bella very familiar, but she has been with me ever since I married and thinks herself one of the family. Sometimes I think she thinks it's she who owns the house. You want to keep her in her place or she'll be ordering you around.'

The family went on eating and said nothing. Inside they thought that they would not mind very much if Bella did order them around.

After breakfast the children were told to go on the beach while Bee, John and Peaseblossom unpacked. Only Jane went straight to the beach. Rachel and Tim had first to see about their special things.

Ever since they had arrived in America, between other excitements, Rachel had been saying inside her head, 'I'm going to see Posy Fossil.' 'Perhaps there'll be a letter from Posy Fossil.' 'On the very day I get to Aunt Cora's I might meet Posy Fossil.' The moment breakfast was over she had looked round the house. There had been no mention of letters so Posy Fossil had not written yet, but she might at any minute and, in the meantime, she must find a place to practise. It did not take long to find the place. The porch. It had a balustrade round it just the right height for a bar, and, being a porch, it was sticking out by itself so there would be nobody underneath to mind bumps. She was just trying out the balustrade from a practising angle when she heard Aunt Cora call up the stairs.

'Oh, John! Here's a packet of mail which came for you.'

Rachel stopped practising and listened. How perfect if Dad called out, 'Where's Rachel? There's one for her.' There was silence. Dad must be sorting the letters. Then she heard his voice. 'Good. News from home. Three for you, Bee, two for Peaseblossom and four for me.'

Bella came to clear the breakfast. She smiled when she saw Rachel.

'You enjoyed yo' breakfas'.'

This was clearly a statement and did not need answering. Rachel came over to the table and helped to stack the plates. Bella did not look the sort of person who would find it a nuisance answering questions.

'How often do posts come? I mean posts from people who live in California.'

'Miss Cora opens the mail box herself. Yo' was expecting a letter?'

'A letter or a message.'

Bella stopped, a pile of plates in one hand.

'Ah was remembering. Ah fetch Miss Cora to the telephone. There was a lady asking fo' you.'

Aunt Cora was in the living-room. Rachel peered round the door and looked at her. She was writing at a desk. She looked busy. Almost every day since they had known they were coming to California Peaseblossom had said something about their being as little trouble as possible to Aunt Cora. Interrupting a person who was writing was being a little trouble, but not a great deal of trouble, and if Posy Fossil had left a message it would be too frightful not to answer at once. Posy Fossil was important, she was the best dancer Madame had ever trained; she was a film star and going to star in Manoff's ballet. Rachel cleared her throat.

'Aunt Cora?'

Aunt Cora swung round. Her face, though all the welcoming had not worn off, looked as though she was hoping very much she was not going to be interrupted every time she sat down for five minutes.

'Yes, honey?'

'I asked Bella about letters and she said she thought there had been a telephone message for me.'

Aunt Cora looked vague. Then she nodded.

'That's quite right. A Miss Postle or Mossel called you up. She very kindly offered to fix you dancing lessons while you are here, but the studio was way over the far side of Sunset Boulevard, so I thanked her and said it couldn't be managed. I explained I was pleased to have you as my guests for the winter but that could not include my acting as chauffeur all over Los Angeles.' She gave a dismissing nod and went back to her writing.

Rachel rushed up to John and Bee's room. John was arranging a table as a desk. He was putting out his typewriter paper and reference books, and as he arranged them he whistled in a contented way through his teeth.

Bee was unpacking. She put an armload of John's clothes in Rachel's arms.

'Hang these in that cupboard, darling, only we mustn't call them cupboards any more, they are closets here.'

Rachel took the clothes but she did not move.

'Posy Fossil rang me up to ask me to dancing lessons and Aunt Cora told her I couldn't go; she said the studio was too far away.'

Bee pointed at the cupboard.

'Hang them up and don't look so distraught.'

'But I feel distraught; my learning dancing from Posy Fossil was just about the most important thing that ever happened to me.'

John stood back from his table to see how it looked.

'I don't think you need despair yet. I dare say there are

street cars, or we can borrow a bicycle; the great thing is not to rush your aunt for a day or two; after all, we've only been in the place about an hour.'

Rachel hung the clothes in the cupboard. Nobody could have a nicer father and mother than she had, but sometimes they were disappointing. It wouldn't seem possible that anybody could think that seeing Posy Fossil in a day or two would do. It was the sort of thing that ought to be done the very first minute. She said no more but she looked a lot.

Aunt Cora had no piano. Tim did not accept this strange fact without verifying it. He went into the kitchen and asked Bella; after all, the piano might just be away being repaired. Bella had a nice kitchen and seemed pleased to see him and, if the question of a piano had not been so urgent, he would have liked to have stayed and had a good look round. Bella was definite. She had looked after Miss Cora for years and there hadn't ever been a piano.

Tim went in search of Aunt Cora. He arrived just after Rachel had left. He did not make Rachel's polite entrance. He stalked in looking severe.

'Why haven't you a piano, Aunt Cora?'

Aunt Cora looked up from her letter. Her face lost more of its welcoming look. Another child! Really!

'Why don't you go play on the beach? I do hope you children aren't going to run in and out the whole time. My nerves won't stand it.'

Tim did not care what Aunt Cora's nerves would stand.

'I have to have a piano. I have to practise every day. I promised Mr Brown I would. How do you get a piano in America if you haven't got one? Can you hire one for me?'

Aunt Cora saw that Tim was going on talking about pianos until he had an answer. She laid down her pen.

'You can rent pianos in America but they cost money. You haven't money so you can't rent one.'

'I'll have pocket money I suppose, like I do in London.'

'I don't know from whom, unless you earn it.'

Tim was exasperated.

'Children don't earn pocket money, it comes from their fathers on Saturday mornings.'

Aunt Cora took up her pen in a very meaning way.

'In America it does not. You'll earn any you get here.'

Tim was quite prepared to start earning if that was the way to get a piano.

'How do I earn?'

'Will you stop asking questions. You make me so nervous. I don't know how children earn, I just know they earn. Now will you please run away, I'm busy.'

Jane loitered up the beach. It was a nice beach, and the sea looked perfect for bathing. There were lumps of a golden shade of seaweed floating on it like islands. It would be fun to swim out and bring some of the seaweed to shore. She walked slowly along the sand examining each house. She wondered if children lived in any of them; it would be nice if they did; with Rachel going to dancing with that Posy Fossil, and Tim practising, she would need people to play with. She thought all the houses very nice and gave marks to each according to her view of its merits. She was just turning back to find out what was keeping the others when she saw something which stopped her dead. She was in front of a white wooden house with brightly coloured flowers hanging from the porch and a very nice little garden, which would have got almost full marks only at the back of the lawn, fastened to his kennel by a chain, was a black spaniel. The spaniel seemed to be reasonably contented but Jane was not contented for him. What kind of people could live in a nice house like that, free to come and go as they liked, free to play in their own garden and run on the sand, and they kept their spaniel chained up like a prisoner? Without remembering any of the things she had been told about how to behave in a foreign country Jane marched up to the gate.

The gate was locked. Jane shook it, but it was a secure lock that would not come undone. She was planning to climb over it when what seemed to be the gardener came round from the front of the house. He did not notice Jane but fixed up a thing which revolved and sprayed out water. Jane let him fix it, then she called, 'Hallo'. The gardener looked up, nodded and said something Jane could not catch. She leant on the gate.

'Do you know it's awfully cruel to keep your dog chained up to his kennel like that?'

The gardener did not seem to have heard what she said, but he had caught the word dog. He smiled.

'Yeah, a fine dog house.'

Jane had never heard a kennel called a dog house before but she guessed what he meant.

'However nice it is he shouldn't be chained to it, poor boy.'

The man scratched his head. Then he came to the gate. He looked at Jane's angry face in wonderment.

'He gotta be chained.'

'Why?'

'If he's loose they'll take him.'

'Who will?'

'Cops.'

The gardener seemed to think the conversation was over. He took another look at the water to see it was spraying nicely and walked away.

Jane gave the gate another angry shake. She leant over to the dog.

'Poor boy! I don't believe a word he said. I think he made it all up. I shall ask Aunt Cora and if it's a lie I'll come and set you free myself.'

When Aunt Cora saw the third interrupter come in all signs of being a welcoming aunt left her. She looked what she felt, an aunt who had got up very early to meet relations; who felt she was being more noble than she could say in taking in the relations and, once they were in, wanted to see as little of the adults as possible and, of the children, nothing at all. Especially she did not want to see this child, whom she had noticed was the plain one, unlikely, therefore, to bring credit on an aunt.

'Well?'

Jane drew up a chair by Aunt Cora's desk.

'Do dogs in America have to be chained up?'

Well, really, said Aunt Cora's face! What next? The first child looked as though you had hit her when you said very reasonably you could not drive her daily to Sunset Boulevard for dancing lessons; the boy demanded a piano; now here was the ugly one pulling up a chair as if she had come to visit, asking about dog laws. It was too much.

'Yes, they do, I'm glad to say. I've never liked dogs and it prevents them running about.'

Jane eyed Aunt Cora with horror. Never liked dogs! What an aunt!

'Why do they have to be?'

'Hydrophobia, I expect. Now run along do and take the other two with you. Go play on the beach.'

The children held a meeting on the sands. They walked until they were out of earshot of the house. Then they sat. The sun blazed down warming them through and through. The sea made a lazy, lapping sound. Some sea birds of a new, interesting sort floated on the water; but for the three of them the day was a ruin.

'She said she thanked Posy Fossil and said my lessons couldn't be managed,' Rachel moaned. 'Oh, what will I do if Posy never rings up again!'

Tim threw a stone at an imaginary aunt.

'No piano, and not even ashamed.'

Jane rolled over on her face and kicked at the sand with her toes.

'That Dad could have a sister who could say "I've never liked dogs"! To think we are going to live with such an aunt six whole months!'

'And such a lovely place,' said Rachel, 'and Dad's put out his typewriter as if he was going to write again. If only Aunt Cora wasn't like that.'

Jane kicked the sand again.

'But she is like that, and she looked at me with a despising look.'

Tim hugged his knees and rested his chin on them.

'In America children don't have pocket money given them. They earn it, she said so.'

Jane looked superior.

'She, my boy, is the cat's mother.'

'Earn it?' asked Rachel. 'How?'

'I asked Bella. She said doing chores for the neighbours. I'm going to snoop at the neighbours this afternoon so I can see which would be the best to start on.'

Rachel turned to look at him.

'She wouldn't let you have a piano in her house if you did hire it.'

'Then I'll hire a place with a piano in it.'

'It will take a lot of money.'

'I'll earn it.'

Rachel felt respect. Here was she feeling just hopeless but Tim wasn't feeling hopeless, he meant to do something.

'If I can find how you do it I could earn too; I could earn fares to go to my dancing lessons; that is if Posy Fossil ever rings up again.'

Jane brushed some sand off her nose.

'Actually I'll be glad that Tim can't practise and you can't dance, it'll make it much nicer in the house for everybody else, but if it's to help you to get things that an aunt who's so low she doesn't like dogs won't let you have, then I'll earn money to help you. I vote we all start trying. Let's see which of us can earn first.'

CHAPTER 10

POSY FOSSIL

IT was not possible for the children to start earning the next day. Peaseblossom, in a conversation with Aunt Cora which, if Peaseblossom had not been a guest and Aunt Cora had not been a hostess, might have been an argument, found that it was going to be difficult to bring the children up in what she called 'regular ways'. Peaseblossom had planned a day of lessons, walks, meals and bedtime as nearly as possible the same as days in London. Of course there was no going to school because she was going to do the teaching, but otherwise there was to be little difference in their routine. Aunt Cora, in a roundabout way, showed her that this could not be. In her funny whiney voice, smiling as though she was saying nice things, she made it clear that Peaseblossom had been invited because house help was difficult and Bella getting old and not able to do much more than the cooking. This meant breakfast, lunch and dinner must be eaten at the same time by everybody, with no early suppers on trays and no schoolroom tea. In fact what Aunt Cora hoped was that now Peaseblossom was in the house she could what she called 'rest-up', and the house would run beautifully without her doing anything about it.

Peaseblossom did not mind a bit about the housework; she and Bee, with an occasional day from Mrs Bones, did everything in Saxon Crescent, but she did mind that while she was doing the housework there would be no lessons, and she did mind and had no intention of allowing Tim and Jane to sit up for evening dinner every night. However, she was tactful and did not say what she was thinking to Aunt Cora, but smiled and said that she was sure everything would work out splendidly.

By the next morning she had things arranged. Bee was delighted that Aunt Cora wanted help in the house; it was a way of repaying her kindness. She and Peaseblossom decided that they and the children would get the house done immediately after breakfast. That if they worked all out it should be finished by half past ten, except for extra polishings which Bee could do, and that the children could then get in two and a half hours' lessons. After lunch they could have a good walk and education at the same time, studying flowers, birds and places of interest. After tea there could be another hour's lessons or homework. Peaseblossom had got up very early and had a talk with Bella about meals. She found her most understanding. As long as she had not to prepare it she did not mind a bit Peaseblossom giving the children an English tea, and herself suggested they should eat it in the kitchen. Nor did she mind, though she thought it odd, serving cereal and fruit for the children's suppers. She did not say so in words but she managed, by the amused look in her eye, to suggest that she and Peaseblossom were conspirators planning strange goings-on behind Aunt Cora's back, which Peaseblossom, as a good guest, thought wrong but unavoidable under the circumstances.

It was the children who resented Peaseblossom's plannings. They were not domesticated. On Saturdays and Sundays and in the holidays they had helped clean the house at home, and they all had their days for helping to lay tables and wash up, but otherwise they did as little housework as they could and were glad of any excuse to get out of it. The very last thing they had expected in California was to find themselves doing more housework than they had ever done before. Even Rachel could not hide her thoughts; she pushed an electric polisher up and down the hall in a disinterested way with so sulky a face that Bee said:

'Hurry up, darling, and don't look so cross. We want to surprise Aunt Cora when she comes down.'

Rachel switched the electricity off the polisher.

'I don't care if she's surprised or not. I think it's very mean of her to expect us to clean her house. She ought to do it herself, not let us guests do it while she stays in bed.'

Bee was scandalized.

'Sssh! Don't let Peaseblossom hear you. That's a horrid and ungrateful way to talk.' She held up a finger. 'Listen, can you hear the typewriter? Dad's very first morning. Isn't that worth paying for by a little housework?'

'Not to me. As far as I can see we might just as well not be in California. Every minute of the day we're going to be doing something. I shan't even be able to get my proper practice in, and what's the good of it, anyway? I expect Aunt Cora's put Posy Fossil off for good, and if she has she's ruined my career.'

Bee laughed.

'Goose! Get on with that polishing. Your career shan't be ruined, I promise you. Dad and I will find a way.'

Jane was making beds with Peaseblossom. She looked and felt shockingly black-doggish. Peaseblossom noticed, of course, but Jane looking like that was no novelty and she did not ask what was wrong, which in any case she guessed. Instead she kept up a cheerful conversation and did not mind getting no answers. After a bit Jane could not keep her grievances to herself any longer.

'One would think visitors wouldn't be the ones to work.' She leant across the bed and lowered her voice to a dramatic whisper. 'I'm beginning to hate Aunt Cora.'

Peaseblossom used her finishing-a-conversation voice.

'I'm ashamed of you. Not another word. You are each as bad as the other. I shall speak to you all before lessons.'

Tim was in the kitchen cleaning the household shoes, a job he often did at home, and did not dislike except when it interfered with his piano practice. He was appalled at the arrangements for the day. When was he to start earning money to rent a piano? He scowled at Bee's shoe, which he was cleaning, and banged some polish on to it.

Bella shook her head.

'It don' do no good, honey, slappin' the polish on that way.'

Tim put down the shoe.

'I'm angry, Bella. Very angry. Everybody knows I have to practise every day. Everybody knows I promised Mr Brown, but they don't care a bit. If I was Peaseblossom and Dad and Mum I'd say the piano was the most important thing, and there'd be no lessons until it's rented. But they don't. I've talked to them all and they all say don't worry. But I do worry.'

Bella's old wrinkled face was kind but stern.

'Yo' hasn't no right to complain about yo's fambly. They's right to see yo's educated. It's a fine thing. In Georgia, where I was raised, I didn't get educated so good, but now my fambly they goes to college.'

'It's not that I don't want to be educated, and I don't mind cleaning shoes, but I must practise. I couldn't believe I had an aunt without a piano.'

'Yo's no call to go speaking that way of Miss Cora.' Bella's voice softened. 'Maybe I can help.'

Tim jumped up, scattering tins, polishers and shoes all over the kitchen.

'How, Bella? How?'

'Ah'm not tellin'. Yo finish yo's work and do good at yo's lessons and maybe I tell you somethin'.'

Lessons were on the porch. Before they started Pease-blossom closed the doors.

'I don't want to say any of this again, and I won't hear one word of argument from any of you. You are selfish little beasts. You know how long it is since your father worked, and he's started again this morning, and it's the first time since the accident your mother has looked really happy, but what do you three do? Since we arrived yesterday in this lovely place you've done nothing but grumble, Rachel about her dancing lessons, Tim about his piano, and you, Jane, about nothing at all. If you go on this way you're going to spoil the visit for everybody. I'm not having it. Today I'm warning you. You're probably tired after the journey, and I dare say upset by the change of air, but one more grumble and you go to bed. Children who behave as you've behaved must be ill, so I shall keep you in bed and dose you until I see that you are your old selves again. Now then, here are the lesson time-tables I have worked out for you.'

It was no good arguing. Peaseblossom always meant what she said, and she never punished as a punishment, but tried to find out why whoever it was, was doing what they were doing, and her punishments were supposed to be cures. She was only too capable of putting them all to bed, dosing them and feeding them on dull meals until they gave in, and then she would say she knew it was just rest and medicine they needed. It was insufferable. As they started working they exchanged looks which said as clearly as though words had been spoken, 'The meanness of her'.

The sun blazed down on the beach, the sea grew bluer and bluer and made an inviting, whispering noise. The children occasionally raised their eyes from their books and when they did it was hard to go on being angry. California was a very lovely place.

After they had been working an hour they heard Aunt Cora's voice. Again the children exchanged looks. So she had got up at last, had she, the lazy creature! She was calling to Bee.

'I'm going to market. You care to come?'

Market! That had a nice sound. That would be where all that gorgeous fruit was bought. If only Peaseblossom was not so strict about lessons they could go to the market too. Evidently Bee thought it would be fun because they heard her say something about a hat. Presently the front door shut.

Almost another hour went by. Then the front-door bell rang. Aunt Cora's front-door bell was not like a front-door bell in England; it made a chime like church bells. Even Peaseblossom listened to it. There were voices in the hall. Then Bella's heavy, soft-shoed feet came shuffling towards the porch. She beamed at Rachel, though she spoke to Peaseblossom.

'There's a Miss Fozzel askin' for Miss Rachel.'

Peaseblossom could be awfully nice. She said in a delighted voice:

'Oh, Rachel, dear, I'm so glad! I think your aunt is out so you could see her in the living-room.'

Rachel was suddenly shy.

'I wonder if I better change.'

She had on a shirt the colour of her eyes and grey shorts. Peaseblossom thought she looked nicely and suitably dressed and said so. Rachel flung her arms round her neck. She only said 'Darling Peaseblossom', but they all knew that what she meant was she was sorry she had been cross. She dashed out.

It is seldom people whom you have heard a lot about and seen pictures of look in real life like you thought they would look. Posy Fossil looked just as Rachel had imagined her. She was little and pretty in a way, but the most noticeable things about her were her hair, which was red gold and curly, and a sort of eagerness, as if life was too exciting to stand still for a minute. She was wearing a green shirt and slacks, which surprised Rachel, who had supposed that somebody as important as Posy Fossil would be a crêpe-de-chine and mink sort of person. She wanted to be respectful so, though it was difficult to do in shorts, she curtsied as she did at the academy to Madame.

Posy Fossil seemed to think the curtsy terribly funny. She laughed and caught hold of Rachel's hand and asked where they could go to talk. Rachel, feeling shy and self-conscious, led the way into the living-room, but once inside with the door shut she could not feel shy long. Posy, still laughing, swept a curtsy to the ground, and in the most reverent voice said 'Madame'.

'Fancy, I'd almost forgotten until I saw you do it.' She curtsied again. 'Madame. Mind you, everybody, even me, has to curtsy to Manoff. As we do it we say "Maître", only most of them think it's very silly so they do it like this.' She curtsied and said 'Maître', only it was not a respectful, humble 'Maître' but sort of I'll-do-it-if-I-must-but-I-think-it-ridiculous, which made Rachel laugh. Posy ran around the room examining everything.

'I spoke to Mrs Edward P. Beeson on the telephone.'

'Aunt Cora.'

Posy picked up a plant in a copper bowl from the writing-table. She came into the middle of the living-room. She did a little dance. It was made up of quick steps, but she danced as if she was too tired to lift her feet, and as she danced she kept opening her mouth in a hungry way at the plant then jerking her head back.

Rachel laughed so much she had to sit down. Really Posy was being very like Aunt Cora. She even made her feet look whiney, like Aunt Cora's voice, and you could see she was dieting and wished she wasn't by the way she looked at the plant.

'How did you know she was like that?'

Posy put the plant back on the writing-table.

'I felt her in my feet when she was telephoning. Go and get your shoes. I want to see where you've got to.'

Aunt Cora's living-room had a parquet floor so was perfect for dancing on. Rachel was surprised that she did not feel scared dancing in front of the great Posy Fossil, but she did not. Posy was not the sort of person you could be frightened of, she would have thought being shy of dancing in front of her showing off, whereas dancing as well as you could was a thing you did without thinking, like breathing. She rattled off strings of steps and Rachel listened and then danced them. Sometimes Posy danced the routine first to show what she wanted. Rachel did not get much right the first time but Posy kept saying, 'Do it again. Do it again', and by the end she was making a fair attempt at what Posy wanted. After about ten minutes Posy pulled Rachel down to sit beside her on the sofa.

'Yes. I could tell anywhere you were a pupil of Madame's. She's so thorough, and so strict about precision and arms.

You know about Manoff's ballet? You must come to a rehearsal; you can't believe how lovely some of his things are – well, I can't teach you often because I rehearse every day – I'll get Manoff to let you come to his Saturday mornings sometimes. He teaches them himself, but for regular work you better go to a woman called Donna. Madame Donna. She's good. I'll write it down for you.'

Rachel saw Posy was the sort of person who saw no difficulty in doing things. She had evidently forgotten what Aunt Cora had said about not being a chauffeur. Posy was getting a piece of paper and a pencil out of her bag. Rachel gently laid a hand over Posy's to stop her. Then, red in the face because nobody likes explaining the sort of difficulties she had to explain, she told Posy everything. About Aunt Cora and how good it was of her to have them at all, and John's accident, and the British Government's rules about money. Posy did not wait for Rachel to finish, she jumped to her feet.

'Where's the telephone?'

Rachel knew that using the telephone in somebody else's house was a thing you asked permission to do, but Posy Fossil was not a permission-asking person, so she led her to it, only hoping Aunt Cora and Bee would not come back from their shopping in the middle of the telephoning. Posy looked up a number in the telephone book, talking all the time.

'You're like my sister Pauline. When we were at Madame Fidolia's we never had any money and she always thought we couldn't do things. When Manoff saw me dance and said he would take me as his pupil Pauline tried to tell me I couldn't go to Czechoslovakia to learn from him. Imagine! Not learning from Manoff when he'd said he would take me! Of course I went.' She got her number and asked for Madame Donna.

Rachel listened in a mixture of admiration and awe to the conversation that followed.

Posy explained to Madame Donna about her and that she

had no money. There was a pause after that while Posy listened, looking bored and impatient, and then, unable to listen any more, she appeared to interrupt. She said that she knew that was how Madame Donna would feel and that of course she could not be expected to teach a child for nothing who would only be in the country six months and no lasting credit to her. That if the lessons were all it would not matter as Posy would see to it, but there was transport as well. What about *Pirouette*? Wasn't it true that she was providing most of the dancers? There was a lot of talk from the other end at that, which Posy interrupted with 'You can easily arrange it.' 'No harm in letting them see her.' 'Very pretty indeed', until finally, still holding the telephone, she began to dance. Then she said, 'She'll be there', and put the telephone down. Then she turned to Rachel. 'It's all fixed. Wait a minute.' She danced again the steps she had done at the telephone. 'I never can remember anything in my head, I have to remember it with my feet. The audition is at three, at the studio, but you are to be there at two so that Madame Donna can test you herself. You're to wear a tu-tu, which you won't have got, so pack your shoes and tights and I'll take you with me, and fit you into one of mine. Nana, our old nurse who lives with us, will alter it and take you to the audition, she's used to them.'

'An audition for what?'

Posy looked surprised that Rachel didn't know.

'That film they're making. *Pirouette*. It's got scenes in a theatre where a ballet's dancing. They'll want the girls they select on and off for three months. If they pick you, and I don't know why they shouldn't, you'll earn enough money to pay for taxis to your lessons, and you'll be working at the studios under the man who's arranging the dances, as well as Madame Donna.'

Rachel felt as if everything was going round. Her in a film! It was too gorgeous to be true. She clasped her hands, her eyes shining.

'Oh, Miss Fossil!'

Posy laughed.

'Don't call me Miss Fossil, nobody does. Now do go and get your tights and shoes. We haven't much time.'

Rachel was just going to dash upstairs when she remembered Peaseblossom and lessons. She raced to the porch. She was so excited that she couldn't speak clearly. It took Peaseblossom quite a moment or two to grasp what the excitement was about. When she did she got up.

'A film, dear? No wonder you're excited. Run up and pack your tights and shoes. I put the tights on that hat shelf. I'll have a word with Miss Fossil.'

Peaseblossom found Posy by the front door. She was dancing.

'This is very exciting news for Rachel. I don't suppose her parents will object to her being in a film if she gets the opportunity but her mother's out and I can't speak for her. I could ask her father but he's been ill and only just started working again, and it would be a mistake to interrupt him. I suppose attending the audition doesn't mean she has to take part in the film if her parents don't want her to.'

Posy stopped dancing.

'I wouldn't blame her mother for not wanting her to take part; I hate dancing in films myself; it hardly ever comes off and the director usually wants the most ghastly things done which never could happen in a ballet, but I don't think she need worry about this one. I believe it's real stuff, bar practice and that sort of thing. I've only suggested it as a way round the money difficulty. She'd have enough for taxis and things.'

Peaseblossom saw that Posy was not the sort of person to understand ordinary getting permission to do things. It would be easier to trust to Rachel's sense. She took down Posy's address and telephone number.

'We knew we were going to hear from you, of course. Rachel's talked of little else since Madame Fidolia promised to write to you, but I should like just to know where she is so that her mother could telephone to you if she wanted to.'

Posy was looking at Peaseblossom in a very interested way. Rachel would have guessed her feet were twitching to dance her.

'You'll have to meet my guardian and Nana. You three will agree about everything. It'll be lovely for Nana especially, she doesn't often find people in America who think the same way as she does.'

Rachel, changed into her blue cotton frock and wearing clean socks, came flying down the stairs with her tights in one hand and her ballet shoes in the other. Peaseblossom felt disgraced.

'Rachel! No paper! No string! You're letting the side down.'

Posy took the tights.

'Nana will pack them properly with a tu-tu of mine. So don't worry. Good-bye.'

Jane and Tim were listening to the excitement in the hall. This was a most extraordinary country they were in. A country where anything might happen. At one moment there was Rachel doing housework and lessons, with nothing but a rest and a walk to follow, and the next somebody rushed up in a car and took her to an audition for a film. Tim's annoyance about the piano disappeared. For him Rachel, from being his sister with no money at all, was a film star.

'She'll be able to rent me a music teacher as well as a piano.'

Jane was stabbing angrily with her pencil at the sum she was supposed to be doing. She did not grudge Rachel her luck but she wished just once luck would come to her. If only just once everybody, Mum, Dad, Rachel, Tim and Peaseblossom, looked at her with proud faces and said, 'It's Jane we have to think of. She's the one who's important.' She frowned at Tim severely.

'If you're going to use American words you should use them right. You rent pianos but not music teachers.' Then, because she was not at all sure that her statement was true, she hurried on, 'And if Rachel does get in a film she'll have to spend all she earns to dress in furs and diamonds like they do.'

Tim could not be crushed.

'It won't matter. I can do without her help. As a matter of fact I'm already making arrangements.'

Peaseblossom came back. Inside she was feeling a little anxious. She did hope it was all right letting Rachel go off with little Miss Fossil like that, but nothing of that sort showed in her face. She smiled at Jane and Tim.

'Our side's doing splendidly. Fancy, only here one day and Rachel at an audition! It'll be your turn next, Tim, and then we must arrange something special for you, Jane. Now, how are the sums going?'

Jane bit her pencil and scowled worse than usual.

'Arrange something for Jane!' That was how they all thought but let them wait. Some day she'd show them.

A PIANO AND A DOG

LUNCH was over. The children were supposed to read for half
an hour on their beds. Tim was reading *Treasure Island* for
the third time. He had just got to the place where blind Pew's
stick is heard tapping outside the inn when the door softly
opened and Bella waddled in, which, seeing where Tim's
mind was, made him jump. Bella put her finger to her lips
and nodded at the other door, which led to John and Bee's
bedroom, from behind which came the sound of John's
typewriter. She creaked down on the bed, which made it sag
over to one side. She spoke in a whisper.

'Ah has a friend works in a drug store . . .'

It was a long story as Bella told it. Her friend from the
drug store had been round that morning delivering bottles.
He had told Bella that she was right in thinking there was a
piano in the drug store. He also said his boss was a kind man
and he guessed if Tim asked him he would let him practise
on the piano at a time when customers weren't eating; then
Bella held up a warning finger.

'Miss Cora mustn't never know. She'll figure a drug store
is a trashy no-count place.'

Tim thanked Bella and watched her waddle out of the
room and close the door. He shut his book and sat up. He
could not imagine Bella's friend's drug store because the only
drug store he had seen was the one in New York. That had
not had a piano nor room for a piano. Then Bella had said
'eating'. In New York nobody had eaten anything in the
drug store, at least not when he was there. But Bella had said
there was a piano and that was enough. It drew him off his bed

as if it were a magnet. He listened to John's typewriter. Dad was sensible, he would be sure to understand about the piano and tell him to go along and try his luck, but interrupting Dad when he was writing was something they might not do; it was one of the really bad crimes, and, though it was months since Dad had written, Tim had not forgotten the awfulness of interrupting. He did not want a fuss and there would be a fuss if he went out alone when he was supposed to be taken for a nature walk. The right person to go to was Peaseblossom, but if he went to her she would be sure to say that they would take their walk in the drug store direction and she and Jane would come too. Tim did not want anybody with him; this was a matter between himself and the drug store boss. There was only one person who could help as Rachel was away at her audition. He slipped out of his room and moused along the passage to the girls' room. He listened outside the door. There was no talking so it sounded as if Jane were alone. He opened the door a crack and peered in.

Jane was alone. She was lying face downwards on her bed drawing. She was drawing an exceedingly fancy picture of herself in a circus ring, with Chewing-gum and six other dogs doing amazing feats round her. She did not draw at all well but she saw in her head how the drawings looked, so what her pencil achieved did not matter very much. She hated to be interrupted so she gave Tim one of her most disobliging frowns and said:

'You're supposed to be resting, my boy.'

Tim came in and closed the door, and in a whisper told what Bella had said.

'Aunt Cora's not to know because she'll think drug stores trashy no-count places.'

Jane got off her bed; she thought better walking about. She had never heard the expressions 'trashy' or 'no-count' before but she liked both.

'Which is just what I think of Aunt Cora. You go. I'll

119

do delaying action. I'll probably have to tell Peaseblossom in the end, but with any luck not till you've finished arranging about the piano with the drug store man.' Tim was going when Jane remembered that morning's conversation. 'And another time don't tell me in a loud voice you're making arrangements, because then you look a silly little boy when you have to come to me for help.'

Peaseblossom and Bee were lying on a rug on the sand. It was so lovely and hot that at first Bee was too contented to speak. Then she murmured:

'I feel too lucky to be real. In my wildest dreams I never thought of John starting to write the moment we got here.'

Peaseblossom would have liked to go on lying in the sun and doing nothing, but she had not come on the beach to enjoy herself but to talk about Rachel.

'I couldn't tell you before as Cora was there, but Rachel has not only gone to lunch with Miss Fossil. She's having an audition for a film.'

Bee sat up.

'Good gracious! For a film! But she can't act.'

'It's a dancing film I gather.'

'Bless the child! Is she excited?'

'Of course, who wouldn't be, but I wasn't sure what Cora would think.'

Bee thought about Cora.

'I think she'll approve. Oh, dear, I wish something like that would happen. The only thing that's wrong with this lovely, lovely place is our being poor relations. I don't believe even a saint could be a poor relation nicely.'

Peaseblossom glanced at her watch.

'I ought to go in and get Jane and Tim ready for their walk, but it's so lovely here I'll give myself another five minutes.'

Bee lay down again and gazed through her half-closed eyes at the blue, blue sky. She wriggled more comfortably into the rug and felt the hot sand, and listened half-asleep to the lap of the waves and the cries of sea birds. Then it suddenly struck her that Peaseblossom was very quiet. She sat up. Peaseblossom was asleep. 'Dear Peaseblossom! How good for her,' she thought. 'I'll go up and call the children; they can play on the sand instead of going for a walk.'

It was so easy. Jane had nothing to do. Bee came to her first and told her she was going on to fetch Tim, so all that Jane had to say was 'Don't bother, I'll fetch him.' Bee saw nothing queer in that and went back again to the beach and lay down on the rug beside Peaseblossom. When Jane came down the steps to the beach Bee was half-asleep. She did mutter, 'Where's Tim?' but all Jane had to do was to jerk her thumb at the house and Bee asked no more questions. 'And not even a lie,' thought Jane, 'for my thumb might just as well have been pointing at the drug store as anywhere.'

Jane ran up the beach to see how the poor tied-up spaniel was doing. This time the people who belonged to the house were at home, or at least what seemed to be the people belonging to the house. Two men were sitting smoking on the porch. Even before she got to the gate Jane heard the rumble of their voices. Evidently when the people were home their dog sat with them, for though his kennel was there the dog was not. Jane was glad for the dog that he was having a nice time, not tied up, but disappointed not to see him. It was sickening Aunt Cora had no dog, but no dog to know was unthinkable. Besides, she had plans about that spaniel. If Aunt Cora was right and it was usual for children in America to earn their pocket money, why couldn't she earn some taking that dog for a walk? She wondered what was the first step to becoming a professional dog walker. Did you go to the back door and ask to be hired, or did you write a letter to the dog's owner?

Jane was thinking so hard she was not noticing anything about her. From being engaged to take that spaniel for a daily walk it was no step to being engaged to take fifty dogs for

walks. She had an imaginary conversation with Peaseblossom.
'I'm sorry but I've no time to help with the house or do
lessons, I've my profession to think of. I've fifty dogs to take
for walks. After all, I'm paying for Rachel's dancing and
Tim's piano lessons.' It was as she thought of these satisfying
words that she saw a black shape down by the water. A black
shape which, as she moved towards it, became a spaniel eating
a fish. As she got closer her nose told her it was a very dead
fish.

Jane was angry. People like those men on the porch didn't
deserve to have a dog. One minute tying him up to his kennel
and the next letting him eat bad fish, which would certainly
make him sick and, as well, risking the poor boy going to the
police station because of being loose, and hydrophobia.

Jane did not know what it felt like to be afraid of a dog.
This one might be a stranger, and a stranger eating something
which, even if it was bad for him, he was enjoying, but that
meant nothing to her. She spoke to him severely.

'Bad, dirty boy! You'll be terribly sick, but it's not your
fault, poor angel.' In spite of furious growls she kicked what
was left of the rotten fish into the water. It was clear how the
dog had got out. He must have slipped his collar for he had
none on. Jane took her handkerchief out of her pocket and
tied it round the dog's neck. Her shorts had been Rachel's
and were too big for her at the waist and were kept tidy with a
belt. She took the belt off and put it through the handkerchief.
She spoke to him persuadingly: 'Come on, old boy. You'll
soon be being so sick it'll be nicer for you at home. Come on.
Come along, old man.' It was a slow start but presently the
spaniel began to like Jane's voice, and to trust her, and in the
end he was trotting along as if he had known her since he was
a puppy.

The two men were still on the porch talking and smoking.
Jane looked up at them and sniffed to herself. Selfish beasts,
lying up there not caring a bit about their dog! She was

going to shout to them when she saw the gate was ajar. So that was how the spaniel had got loose. Lazy brutes, they couldn't even shut their gate! She stalked in and, looking at her most cross, climbed the steps to the porch.

The two men sat up, looking surprised. Jane did not care how they looked.

'Some people don't deserve to have dogs. They fasten them up to' – she hesitated for the right words – 'dog houses. Then they leave their gates open so their dogs will eat bad fish and be sick, and' – she hesitated again – 'cops will get them because of hydrophobia.'

The dog made queer noises. One of the men got up. He was nice looking, tall and thin with dark hair and amused grey eyes.

'I guess you're right about his being sick. Come on, Hyde Park.' He picked the spaniel up and carried him down the stairs and out of sight.

Jane looked at the other man. He was older and fatter, with a large hooked nose and grey hair.

'Why's an American dog called Hyde Park?'

The man had evidently not been told as a child it was rude to stare. He stared so hard at Jane that she almost reminded him about manners.

'I believe he came from London as a pup. Bryan served there during the war. You're British, aren't you?'

Jane thought where she might come from unimportant while poor Hyde Park was being sick. She nodded.

'I should think he'll need medicine.'

'Bryan'll see after him. He's crazy on that dog. How old are you?'

'Ten. He's got a funny way of showing he's crazy on him.'

'Do you always frown? Can you smile?'

It was such a silly question that it made Jane laugh.

''Course everybody can. When my dog, Chewing-gum, got poisoned the vet said a white of egg would be good for him. Do you suppose a white of egg could be spared?'

'Sure.'

The man Bryan came up the steps, Jane swung round.

'How is he?'

'I've given him something to fix him.' He handed her the handkerchief and belt. 'Thank you for fetching him home. You fond of candy?'

The hooked-nosed man beckoned to Bryan.

'Not so fast. Come and sit a while.' He looked at Jane. 'What about a drink? I'm sure my friend here,' he looked at Mr Bryan, 'will fix you a Coca-Cola.'

Jane was delighted. If she stayed and drank a Coca-Cola it should be easy to ask about walks for Hyde Park. Perhaps the old man had a dog too who needed a professional dog walker. She thanked him and sat down on the top step.

Mr Bryan said, 'Sure', and went to fetch the Coca-Cola, but he too had taken to staring. Jane wondered if perhaps staring at strangers was polite in America.

The Coca-Cola was lovely. It was in a long glass with lots of lumps of ice in it. Jane took a big drink then, fortified, looked up at Mr Bryan.

'Who takes Hyde Park for walks?'

The old man said to Mr Bryan:

'You see what I'm thinking?'

Mr Bryan nodded.

'He doesn't get all that many, save maybe on a Sunday. How long have you been out here?'

'If you mean in California, one day; if you mean in America, five days. Dogs ought to walk every day.'

'Sure. Where you living?'

Jane thought they were the most curious people she had ever met. Such a lot of questions. However, they were nice and perhaps it was a good thing they should know about her, as Mr Bryan mightn't trust Hyde Park with a stranger. She told them about John's accident and Aunt Cora's invitation, and that the invitation was for food and keep and did not include dancing lessons and piano lessons, nor being a chauffeur all over Los Angeles.

'So of course we'll have to earn our pocket money, which Aunt Cora says children do in America.'

Both men said 'Sure' to that. The hooked-nosed man, who was staring more and more, asked what the family consisted of.

125

Jane told him. She gave good descriptions of Rachel and Tim, though she bragged a bit for she said Rachel was actually engaged to dance in the film.

Oddly enough neither man seemed impressed by that. Mr Bryan said:

'And you? What do you sparkle at?'

Jane longed to be able to say something, but there was nothing to say. While she had been talking she had looked cheerful, but at that question her face became its most black-doggish.

'If you want to know, absolutely nothing, and nobody need be despising because lots of people aren't good at anything special.'

The two men exchanged more looks. Mr Bryan said, apparently to nobody:

'Extraordinary.' Then he pulled one of Jane's plaits. 'How would you like to have a chance to show what you can do?'

Jane beamed.

'That's what I wanted you to say. I'm starting to be a professional dog walker. I'd like to start with Hyde Park.' The two men burst out laughing. Jane thought that was rude. She got up. 'There's nothing to laugh about. As a matter of fact it's about time somebody thought of poor Hyde Park.'

Mr Bryan stopped laughing.

'I'm sorry. Sure you can take Hyde Park walking. What kind of charge would you make?'

Jane was hazy about American money.

'Would one cent a day be too much?'

Mr Bryan got up. He looked questioningly at the other man.

'Too little, I think. Do you think I should visit her father to fix it?'

Jane thought that very grand.

'That would be a good idea, though perhaps you better see Mum. Dad doesn't like being disturbed if he's writing; both Mum and Peaseblossom understand American money.' She lowered her voice and spoke earnestly, 'But do be careful to ask Bella for Mr or Mrs Winter, otherwise you'll see Aunt Cora and that wouldn't be a good idea at all.'

Mr Bryan was writing in a notebook.

'Ask for Winter, say I've called about Miss Jane Winter. And your aunt's Mrs Edward Beeson. I know the house.' He closed the book. 'By the way, we haven't introduced ourselves and I think we should. May I introduce Mr Benjamin Bettelheimer.' The old man got up and bowed. 'And my name is Bryan J. Browne.'

Jane felt she ought to do or say something but she was not sure what. She gave a bow like the one Mr Bettelheimer had given to her and behaved like somebody leaving a party.

'Good-bye. Thank you very much for asking me.'

Mr Bryan J. Browne came with her to the bottom of the steps.

'Good-bye now, Jane Winter. I'll be seeing you.'

Jane ran back along the sands, and found Peaseblossom and Bee still asleep. She looked at them in amazement. How queer to go to sleep in the daytime! However, it was lucky for Tim. Given any luck he would get back from his drug store before they woke up. This was what happened for as Jane came in from the porch Tim came in at the front door. He closed the front door softly and let the catch down, for the door in Aunt Cora's house was supposed to be locked. He spoke in a whisper.

'Is there a row?'

'No. Peaseblossom and Mum have been asleep on the sand all the afternoon and I expect Dad's still working.'

'Where's Aunt Cora?'

Jane shrugged her shoulders.

'Don't know. She said at lunch she was going to rest-up; I expect that means bed again; she seems a very bed person.

Did you find a piano?' Jane thought she heard someone moving. She caught Tim by the arm. 'Let's go to your room. We shan't disturb Dad if we whisper.'

They sat on Tim's bed but Tim was so full of bounce because his afternoon had been successful that he found sitting still for long difficult.

'I found the drug store quite easily. It's back the way we came when we drove from the station. It's not a bit like that drug store in New York. It's got all sorts of slot machines like on a pier, and it's a place where you eat. Tables and all that.'

'Where was the piano?'

'In the middle on a sort of little platform thing. I came in and a man asked me what I wanted, and I said I wanted to see the boss, because I didn't know his name. The man shouted "There's a gentleman to see you, Tony," and Tony was the boss.'

'Was he nice?'

Tim was not going to have his story interrupted.

'He's brown and curly with a funny voice which isn't American. His name's Antonio, but he said everybody called him just Tony. I explained about the piano and at first he said no.' Tim got off the bed and gave an imitation of Tony saying no. '"I saya da no."' He ran his hands through his hair. '"I saya da no. I hav'a da customers."' Then I said I'd come when the customers weren't there. Then Mr Antonio's wife came from somewhere. She's fat and her hair's black and very untidy but she's nice; her name's Anna. She asked what I wanted and when she heard she laughed and said that the first thing was to hear me play. So I walked to the piano. It was very old and the dust came out as if you were emptying a carpet sweeper, and the notes were wobbly and yellow, and it wanted tuning, otherwise it was all right. They were the sort of people I thought would like a noise on a piano so I played Rachmaninoff's Prelude.'

'Did they like it?'

Tim was so pleased with himself that he fell back on the bed and turned a somersault.

'It was marvellous. Mrs Antonio cried and even Mr Antonio sort of sniffed, and they made sounds at each other in foreign, and did this.' Tim screwed up his face and threw up his eyes and hands. 'So then I made an arrangement. I'll go and practise for one hour in the morning after breakfast, and then I'll go back and play for the customers after lunch.' Jane made a startled sound. Tim stopped her. 'That isn't all. Mr Antonio will have the piano tuned, and he says the customers will give money and that's half for me and half for him.' Tim turned another ecstatic somersault.

Jane caught his legs as they came over and turned him the right way up.

'But, Tim, they won't let you. There's Peaseblossom's timetable, and I bet Aunt Cora won't like you playing in a drug store.'

Tim flicked his fingers to show scorn.

'They'll just have to like it. I'll call it all practice, which it is. I shan't say about playing to the customers. Dad and Mum wouldn't mind, but they might give in if Aunt Cora thought it trashy no-count.'

Jane was just starting to tell Tim about her afternoon when Rachel rushed in.

'Bella thought you were here. Where's everybody? Oh, I've had such a gorgeous, gorgeous day!'

The door leading into John and Bee's room opened. John came in laughing and looking exactly as he used to look before the accident.

'What's going on in here?'

They fell on him, each telling their own story. John sat on the bed. He pulled Jane between his knees and Tim sat one side of him and Rachel the other.

'Now, one at a time, and keep your voices down as your aunt's resting. Let's hear Rachel first.'

129

Rachel was incoherent with excitement. She had lunched with Posy Fossil, who had a most lovely house with a blue marble swimming pool in the garden. She had an old nurse called Nana, who had brought them up, and Nana had been heavenly and altered a lovely pale pink tu-tu of Posy's for her, and packed it and Rachel's shoes and tights in a box. There had been a gorgeous lunch and then Posy had to go to a rehearsal, so Nana had taken her in a taxi to Madame Donna's studio.

'You can't imagine how I felt. Other girls were coming in and they looked so grown-up and smart. Most of them wore the most lovely slacks; some of them had flowers in their hair; and me in this old frock, which isn't the sort Americans wear. Nana didn't care; she said the thing was to get changed as quickly as possible, and she took me into a dressing-room and dressed me and brushed and combed my hair. She said if she had half a crown for every audition she'd been to she'd be a rich woman. Then I went to Madame Donna.' Rachel shivered at the memory. 'Meeting her was much, much worse than meeting Madame Fidolia. She speaks American with a French accent and I couldn't understand her at first, and she shrugged her shoulders and looked round at the other girls to show what a worm she thought I was, and the other girls giggled. I felt terrible. I curtsied and called her "Madame" like I do Madame Fidolia. I hope it was right but she looked surprised. Then she asked me questions, which was the bit when I didn't understand, and made the girls giggle, and then I had to dance in front of all of them. Imagine!' Rachel got up. 'She gave directions very fast, much faster than I'm used to and then showed me steps I had to follow. Like this.' She began to demonstrate. John stopped her.

'Not here. You'll disturb your aunt.'

'Although I was always a bit behind Madame Donna seemed fairly pleased, for she said that what I knew I'd been taught thoroughly. Then she took me into her office, and told me that about fifty girls were wanted for a film called *Pirouette*, and that they were nearly all to be her pupils. That the man who was arranging the dances would see ordinary work going on and would choose the fifty for himself. That it was all wrong my pretending to be a pupil when I wasn't but to please Posy Fossil I was being allowed to, and then she took down your name and address, Dad, because if I'm engaged you have to see Madame Donna, and I warn you that'll be frightening for you.'

John did not seem to care.

'We can cross that bridge when we come to it. Did the man like you?'

'I don't know but the girls thought he did. He picked a lot of us out to do things alone. He asked me to do a few steps to show him how I moved, and I just did m'audition. The woman at the piano even knew the music. Oh, Dad, wouldn't it be too gorgeous if I was in a film! Imagine the glory!'

John looked at Tim.

'And what were you telling Jane you'd fixed? I heard the word piano fairly often.'

Tim told his story.

John was pleased.

'Good. I like you children to cope with things for yourselves.' He put his arm round Jane. 'What are we going to do about you while all this going on?'

Jane wriggled free from his arm. Her face was pink with triumph. It was so seldom she could say that anything was happening to her.

'As a matter of fact a man is coming to call. I told him not to interrupt you, but to see Mum. His name's Mr Bryan J. Browne, and he wants to engage me as a professional dog walker for his dog, Hyde Park. Oh, Dad, a lovely dog! A black spaniel. As a matter of fact I've plans for being dog walker to lots of dogs, perhaps fifty.'

John gave her hair an affectionate ruffle.

'What an enterprising family I've got. I shall tell Bella to fetch me at once when Mr Bryan J. Browne calls. If my daughter is going to become a professional dog walker to fifty dogs I think I ought to see the business begins on a proper financial basis.'

CHAPTER 12

THE CALLER

PEASEBLOSSOM's plans for a good organized day were changed. Not definite changing, with somebody saying 'This won't happen', or 'That won't happen', but as if the day was chipped at with a penknife until it was a quite different shape.

It was obvious if Rachel was perhaps to dance in a film she must work. So that was good-bye to her helping with the housework. Instead, as soon as breakfast was cleared, she changed her shoes and got in an hour's exercises on the porch. It was not so easy about Tim because Bee was nervous of the children being out alone in America. She could not forget that once there had been gangsters and kidnappings. What made it more awkward was that Aunt Cora sided with her. She said that she believed there were still gangsters and kidnappers, and that they now lived round Los Angeles as there were the film stars who would pay not to be machine-gunned, and ransoms if they were kidnapped. John laughed and told them not to be silly; if there were gangsters or kidnappers about they were probably a sensible lot and would not waste their time on a boy whose parents could not pay even a dollar to ransom him, and what would they machine-gun him for?

'You haven't a piano, Cora, and old Tim's found this one for himself. I'm glad he has. I was afraid my family might look rather helpless against American kids.'

So every day after breakfast and after lunch Tim ran off to the drug store, and when he came back he told Bella about it.

'It's a funny piano, Bella; the notes slip sideways and some don't play properly, but I like it better than any other piano;

it's got a very singy voice, and it says words which I hear in my head.'

The person who got no advantage from the new time-table was Jane. Six days went by and Mr Bryan J. Browne had not called, so she was not a professional dog walker but was still a houseworker. It had been bad enough doing house-work when they all did it, but to be the only one, that was too much. Rachel exercising on the porch, Tim in his drug store and she making beds and dusting. The meanness of it ate into her and she looked black-doggish even when she was eating a banana split.

Aunt Cora, though her voice whined as much as ever, and she spent most of the day resting-up, began to take a better view of the Winters. Her house looked like a new pin, for both Bee and Peaseblossom were good at housework. Bella was in wonderful spirits; she had not been what Aunt Cora called 'mean' since the Winters had arrived. She smiled when she served meals and she sang when she cooked. Then the children were turning out better than Aunt Cora had hoped, or at least two of them were; Jane – whom she still called to herself the plain one – would always be a disaster, but the boy had fixed himself a piano, and Rachel might be going to be a credit. A niece in movies would be a social asset. Aunt Cora watched the post and listened for telephone bells almost as anxiously as Rachel did herself.

The afternoon plans changed too. John seemed to go sun mad. It happened the second day between breakfast and going to his typewriter. He came down to the beach with Bee, Peaseblossom and Aunt Cora for what he called a lungful of air. He looked at the sea, he looked at the mountains, then he looked at the sky. His face when he turned it to Bee was like a face shining in a sunset.

'It's too much. The sun here isn't like any other sun. It's a golden haze which covers everything. Peaseblossom, tear up your old timetable. Buy yourself a sunsuit and you and

134

Bee lie on the beach every afternoon. I'm going out with my children. Oh, they shall see the birds, flowers and sights all right but I'm taking them.'

Bee saw the last of being ill was gone from John for good. She was so happy her voice sang like Tim's piano.

'What about me? They're my children too. What about bathing? We ought to bathe every day.'

Aunt Cora gave a scream.

'In the fall, Bee! The water will be terrible.'

John put an arm round Aunt Cora and gave her a brotherly shake.

'Rubbish! Even in the fall, as you call it though you were brought up to say autumn, it will be a lot warmer than bathing in England in August, for the beach will be warm when we get out.' He saw Peaseblossom was looking head-girlish. 'Don't look worried, Peaseblossom. I shall go back to my typewriter after tea and then you can have the children to yourself for more lessons and can bring them up properly.'

Bee said:

'It's you who have made the journey here possible, Peaseblossom. Think how nice it will be for you to be free of us all every afternoon.'

Aunt Cora looked at Peaseblossom's curves.

'You could have a beach outfit of mine only you'd never get into it.'

Peaseblossom had seen American beach outfits and knew how little there was of them. She thought people of her age and Aunt Cora's age shouldn't wear them, but she was a guest so kept that thought to herself.

'It's very kind of you but those sketchy things are all very well for sylphs like you but I'd make the children laugh if I wore one.'

Posy Fossil was a person who expected everything to happen at once. Each day she rang up to know if Rachel had heard if

135

she was picked to dance in *Pirouette*. She sounded as if she were dancing with anxiety at the end of the telephone.

'Goodness, I do wish they'd hurry! This is such an awkward place to live in unless you have a car; there are no street cars that go anywhere anybody wants to go. I can't make plans for your lessons until I know if you can afford transport. I'm certain you're chosen and Madame Donna's certain too. She says they had their eye on you.'

Rachel tried not to be too hopeful but it was difficult with Posy so sure. It was lucky for her that Aunt Cora was interested too, because only Aunt Cora had the key to the post box and she would have left it unopened for hours if she had not had something exciting to open it for. Peaseblossom and Bee were excited too, only their minds were taken off Rachel by what was going to happen to them. People in America were very hospitable. Once Aunt Cora's friends knew her family had arrived safely they began giving parties for them. Bee started by worrying that John, who hated parties in England, would refuse to go, but being in America seemed to have changed that; the more invitations there were the more pleased John was. He said he couldn't meet too many Americans; it was a wonderful chance to get to know and understand them and he did not intend to miss a party.

'It's all very well for him,' Bee moaned to Peaseblossom, 'but I've nothing fit to wear. My skirts are too short and the fullness is in the wrong places, and look at American hats!'

Peaseblossom was quite happy. She had her old, well-cut coats and skirts; but Bee was not the coat and skirt type and her dresses did look shabby. Peaseblossom tried to be helpful.

'Couldn't you borrow something from Cora? She's cupboards full of clothes.'

Bee made a face.

'I couldn't ask her, we're taking enough from her as it is. It's lucky we've brought all the children's summer things with

136

us. They'll have to dress up for those return parties Cora's going to give.'

Rachel and Jane heard this conversation and it made Rachel even more anxious about the film.

'Oh, Jane, if only I could earn money! I'm so afraid of Aunt Cora's parties for we'll have to hand round. If Aunt Cora won't lend Mum a dress she won't bother about us, and

Mum doesn't know how awful we look beside American girls.' She looked at Jane and then at herself. 'These are our only shorts and yours don't fit and mine are patched. Our only party frocks are short and very old, and for cocktail parties, which is what Aunt Cora's going to give, I shouldn't wonder if we were made to wear our cottons. There couldn't be worse shame.'

'There's my dog-walking money. We could buy clothes with some of that,' Jane suggested.

Rachel did not point out that Mr Bryan J. Browne had

failed to call; Jane knew it only too well. She just made a vague sound that might have meant anything and walked away.

Bella was clearing breakfast when the telephone bell rang. Rachel was upstairs putting on her ballet shoes. Bella stood at the bottom of the stairs and shouted:

'The telephone, Miss Rachel; it's that Miss Fozzel.'

Rachel ran down the stairs. She could imagine Posy at the other end dancing up and down, her red curls bouncing. She knew the quick way she would say 'Have you heard yet?' and the explosive 'Oh!' when she said she had not. Oh, dear, if only, if only she could say 'Yes!' But this morning Posy's voice was different.

'I say, it's sickening but I'm afraid that film's off; at least Madame Donna thinks so. The man did like you but the fifty he's chosen are older and they're nearly all dark.' Rachel felt as if the sun had gone in. The hall was suddenly cold. It was awful to have hoped so much. Posy evidently could feel how Rachel felt. 'Don't worry, I'll fix up about your lessons somehow; it's just getting you there. I hate to go on raising your hopes but there is still just a chance, it's awfully small,

138

but the man who engaged the fifty girls did take your name and address. It wouldn't be for much but there are two or three days' work for a child dancer. Madame Donna thought he might be thinking of you for just that.'

Rachel tried to be thrilled at that little straw of hope, but she could hear Posy did not believe in it really. She had an awful lump in her throat and though she swallowed most of it there was enough left to get in the way, and her voice came out in miserable-sounding squeaks.

'Thank you so much for telephoning.'

Even over the telephone line Rachel could hear Posy's feet dancing a sort of frustrated foot exercise.

'Don't sound like that. I tell you what, spend a Sunday with us soon. I'll have made plans by then and my sister Pauline, who's been making personal appearances, will be home. We'll bathe in the swimming pool. I'll fetch you.'

It was a lovely invitation but Rachel was too downcast to be pleased about it. Too downcast to be thrilled at meeting Posy's sister, who was a film star. Too downcast to be pleased about the swimming pool. So downcast that she could hardly say thank you. She put down the receiver and swallowed and blinked. It was silly to cry, but if only the film could have happened!

While Rachel had been on the telephone the front-door bell had rung, and Bella had shown somebody into the living-room. Breathing heavily, because she hated stairs, she had fetched John.

'There's a gent'man called. Ah's put him in the living-room.'

John had been in the middle of a sentence and would ordinarily have hated to be interrupted, but he remembered his promise to Jane.

'Quite right, Bella, thank you. I expect it's the gentleman with the spaniel who's going to start Jane on the dog-walking career.'

As Rachel turned from the telephone, fighting her tears, John was standing in the living-room door. His visitor's voice came down the passage.

'I've come to see if your daughter may come up to the studio for a film test.'

Rachel's lump disappeared. Her tears dried. She felt that must-jump-over-something sort of happiness. The man had not forgotten her. He had chosen her for that child dancer. She could not wait for John to call her. She flew down the passage.

'Dad, I heard! Here I am!'

John put his arm round her.

'Here's the ballerina. This is Rachel.'

The man looked at Rachel very kindly. His nice grey eyes were sorry.

'But it's not Rachel I've come about. Maybe the maid didn't tell you my name. I'm Bryan J. Browne. I've called about Jane.'

CHAPTER 13

JANE CHOOSES

JANE was helping Peaseblossom turn out their bedroom. She was so gloomy she could not bother even to grumble. What a situation! Rachel downstairs practising, probably any minute out of the house altogether making that film. Tim rushing off almost before he finished his breakfast to his piano. Herself the house drudge. Slaving at the work the other two were let off doing; and no one seemed to see how awful her life was. No one cared how badly they treated her; but let them just wait. This very afternoon she would write a letter to that Mr Bryan J. Browne. He owed her the job of taking Hyde Park for walks; he had offered her a reward of candy for bringing him home and she hadn't taken it. Not that she needed a reward for taking Hyde Park home, poor boy; all the same, Mr Bryan J. Browne thought that she did, and he had got to go on thinking it and engage her properly as a dog walker, and say he wanted his dog exercised every day immediately after breakfast.

Peaseblossom was using the electric polisher and the noise it made cut out sounds from downstairs. Jane did not hear the chime of the front-door bells, nor Bella call John, nor John call Bee, and the first thing she knew that anything unusual was going on was when Rachel came in and told her she was wanted in the living-room.

Jane, delighted, dropped the furniture polisher she was using on the floor.

'Why?'

Rachel said in a voice which, if she had been thinking about her, Jane would have thought funny:

'It's your Mr Bryan J. Browne.'

Rachel was going on to tell Jane to give her hair a tidy as it was something important, but Jane did not wait. She shouted, 'Galosh! Galoosh!' and ran down the stairs.

Peaseblossom did not seem to notice that Jane had gone out of the room, she was attending to Rachel, who looked so wretched that all the brisk head-girlishness went out of her voice.

'What is it?'

Rachel tried to answer, but she couldn't. She felt she must get away somewhere quite by herself and cry and cry. She gave a gulp and ran out of the room and downstairs. In the hall she hesitated, looking round in a scared way as if she were a rabbit chased by dogs. Mr Bryan J. Browne's voice came from the living-room; Bella's voice, singing, came from the kitchen. Peaseblossom was in their bedroom. Where could she go to be alone? Her one chance was the porch. The table was pushed back to leave room for her dancing practice; nobody would look underneath it. Thankful for even that little privacy Rachel crawled out of sight, turned over on her face and cried dreadfully.

Jane rushed into the living-room; she was so pleased to see Mr Bryan J. Browne she forgot her manners and, without waiting to say 'How do you do?' exclaimed:

'I'm glad you've come at last. Is Hyde Park better?'

John was walking about, his hands in his pockets, looking worried. He came over to Jane and held her by the shoulders. His voice was serious, almost as if she had done something especially bad.

'Mr Browne hasn't come about Hyde Park. He wants to test you for a part in a film.'

Jane was so surprised her eyes grew round as oranges and her mouth opened and stayed open.

Mr Browne was sitting in an arm-chair smoking. He gave Jane a nod to show they were old friends. He said Hyde Park was fine and maybe Jane would take him walking in spite of the film. Then he said:

'Mrs Winter tells me you've read a book called *The Secret Garden* by Frances Hodgson Burnett, who wrote *Little Lord Fauntleroy.*'

Jane was still feeling surprised, but she knew she had read a lot of books for somebody of ten, and when you had as little to brag about as she had it was a pity to let a chance slip.

'Of course I have. I've read it lots of times. The first time was years and years ago.'

Mr Browne then explained. He was what was called in the movie industry a director, and Mr Benjamin Bettelheimer, whom she had met with him, was what was called a producer. Mr Benjamin Bettelheimer was the man who decided what movies people wanted to see, and bought the stories that were made into movies, and engaged the people to play in the movies. Every movie company had a name; Mr Benjamin Bettelheimer's company was called Bee Bee Films Incorporated, and Bee Bee Films, like every movie corporation, had people who were what was known as under contract to act for them. This meant that they were paid money for so many years to act in their movies. Bee Bee Films had three children under contract. David Doe . . .

Jane interrupted there. They did not often go to films, only as a very special treat, but they had been to a film last August for Rachel's birthday. It was about a circus and David Doe had been the boy star.

'That was the boy who saved the life of that pony and trained him and made him a circus horse.'

Mr Bryan J. Browne nodded.

'That boy's something out of this world. He can imitate any accent, and he's wonderful with animals and birds.'

Then he told Jane about the other children. There was a British boy called Maurice Tuesday who was Jane's age. He had been under contract for three years and was a big box-office draw. Mr Bryan J. Browne saw Jane did not know what that was, so he explained that it meant when people saw Maurice Tuesday was in a movie they paid to go and see the movie. Mr Bryan J. Browne did not say so but there was something about the way his eyes looked when he was explaining about Maurice Tuesday being a box-office draw which made Jane think he was surprised that people liked seeing him so much. The last child was Ursula Gidden. A wonderful little girl film star who had been under contract to Bee Bee Films Incorporated since she was four. To fit these three children Mr Benjamin Bettelheimer had planned to make a movie of *The Secret Garden*. Shooting should have started this next week.

Jane frowned in a puzzled way.

'Who's to be shot?'

Mr Bryan J. Browne laughed and said that was the word for making the picture. You said 'shooting' instead of 'photographing'. Everything was set. The garden was built. David Doe, who was to play Dickon, had been working with a coach at a British north country accent, and had a whole lot of wild creatures who would be in the picture tamed. He came up to the lot every day to feed them. Maurice Tuesday had been for a vacation as his mother thought he needed one before he played Colin, the boy hero, and little Ursula had been fitted for her dresses. Then, on the very morning of the day Jane brought Hyde Park home, Ursula had been rushed off for hospitalization. She had appendicitis. Mr Bryan J. Browne turned to John.

'I didn't see it right off. It was Benjamin Bettelheimer who saw Jane's possibilities. We had just decided to postpone production when in she walked. Chip on her shoulder, English accent, right age. Mistress Mary to the life.'

Jane at last began to understand.

'Do you mean I'm going to be Mary in *The Secret Garden*?'

'Maybe. We've got to test you first.'

'Why didn't you say so when I was there?'

'Been waiting for a report on little Ursula. We've heard now she's not to work for six months.'

The full meaning of what Mr Bryan J. Browne was saying sunk into Jane. He wanted her. The plain, ungifted one of the family. Not because he couldn't have Rachel or Tim, but because he wanted her. Mary, in the book, was about the most important person. If she was Mary she would be a film star. Then another side of the glory that had come to her filled her mind. The thing she most wanted in the world was coming true. She would be the one who was important, who earned money. She would pay for dancing lessons for Rachel and piano lessons for Tim. She would buy clothes for everybody so they didn't look poor relations at parties. Her eyes shone more and more as these thoughts pushed one another about in her head. Jane's eyes could shine as if there was a candle in each of them but they seldom did, in fact neither Bee nor John had ever seen such a shine in them before. John said:

'I can see you like the idea.'

Jane looked at him in scorn.

'Like it! Who wouldn't like to earn lots and lots of money and be a film star!'

Bryan J. Browne laughed.

'Not so fast, little pal. Playing a part in one picture mighty seldom makes a star. As for money, you won't see much of that. Uncle Sam takes care of children in the film industry.'

Bee, not knowing that money earning had been so discussed by the children, thought Jane sounded a very mercenary child. If it had been Rachel she would have only wanted to know about the work, and Tim would have asked questions about the piano; it was so like the general contrariness of Jane that she fixed on the two points that it would be hoped no child would mention.

'There's a lot of things to think about and money is the least important.'

Jane felt her parents were making a very poor show before nice Mr Bryan J. Browne.

'Mum! How can you say that!' She turned to Bryan J. Browne: 'We aren't allowed to criticize anything in America until we've been here long enough to know what we're talking about, but if I could criticize I would say that California seems to have less buses and street cars going to places where anybody wants to go than even a village in England has.'

Bryan J. Browne looked surprised.

'What would we use them for? Everybody has cars.'

Jane knew John was on the verge of interrupting so she hurried on:

'We haven't one. Aunt Cora has but she won't act as chauffeur all over Los Angeles, so poor Rachel can't go to dancing lessons on the far side of Sunset Boulevard.' Jane turned back to Bee. 'And we do need clothes, you know we do. You were terribly pleased when Rachel told you she's probably going to dance in that film, and it wasn't because of the dancing, which Posy Fossil says is bad in films, it was because she would earn money. Now, because it's me that's going to earn, you stop being pleased and say money's unimportant.'

John looked apologetically at Bryan J. Browne.

'I'm afraid Jane's inclined to speak her mind.'

Mr Bryan J. Browne smiled.

'Go right on, Jane. Mistress Mary in *The Secret Garden* looked most times like you look right now.'

John felt everything was going too fast. Though Jane was being her usual argumentative self she had very shining eyes, which was anything but usual. It was clear that she was only seeing the exciting rose pink side of her chance. John had done some writing for English film studios and knew there was a grey, sometimes black, side as well.

'Mr Browne wants you along to his house this afternoon

to go through the scenes you will have to learn for the test, which is to be tomorrow. Before we decide if you go for a test . . .'

Jane gave an all-over bounce.

'Of course I'm going.'

John stopped her.

'Not so fast. You've got to know what you're letting yourself in for. Mr Browne told you Uncle Sam looks after children in the film industry. Mr Browne told us what that means. If you make this test and do play the part of Mary you become somebody who is looked after, not by Peaseblossom, Mum and myself, but by people who carry out the laws of the United States of America. You work eight hours a day, which includes three hours' lessons, either in the Bee Bee studio school or with a teacher from that school in a schoolroom in the studio where *The Secret Garden* is being filmed. To get to the studio in time for lessons or work will mean leaving here soon after eight o'clock each morning, and you won't be home until your bedtime. No fun except on Sundays. You won't see all the lovely things I hope Rachel and Tim will see, and I think you're going to find it very hard work and very boring. It would be different if acting was something you wanted to do but you don't.' He turned to Mr Bryan J. Browne. 'Jane hopes to be a lady dog trainer later on.'

Mr Bryan J. Browne stopped smoking. He held out a hand to Jane and asked her to come to him. He said John was perfectly right. That it was hard work and he could not pretend there was any future in it. Bee Bee Films would not want another girl under contract as they had little Ursula, but he thought that Jane would enjoy working with David Doe. If she meant to be a dog trainer later on David could teach her a lot; he could train any animal; he wouldn't be surprised if David could train a gopher to jitterbug. Jane was just going to ask what a gopher was when he went on to say he could promise that if she played Mary something would be fixed about transport, for he could see that Santa Monica was an awkward place to live in if you had no car.

Jane listened first to John and then to Mr Bryan J. Browne, and the more she listened the more her eyes shone. As John was speaking she heard everybody talking at breakfast. 'Jane, dear, have you everything you want?' 'No, Tim, you must wait until Jane has helped herself, she'll be leaving for the film studio in half an hour.' People would run about. 'Has anybody cleaned Jane's sandals?' 'Don't bother Jane about anything, she must do just what she likes, she's so important.' In the evening when she came home she could see in her mind everybody, including Aunt Cora and Bella, standing outside the house looking humble and admiring. They would all ask questions but she would not answer. She would just sweep in and say, 'Don't bother me now. Bring me my supper,' and everybody would dash about trying to be the first to wait on her. When Mr Bryan J. Browne was talking she saw David Doe looking mysterious and whispering secrets to her; such terrific secrets that when she got back to London she had only to have a day or two with Chewing-gum and he would be so marvellous a performer she could get him into Bertram Mills' Circus the very next Christmas. On the final words about transport she felt as Cinderella must have felt when she first saw her coach, only Jane did not see a coach but the largest car in the world, with a uniformed chauffeur, and herself bowing out of the window.

John said:

'Well, Jane? Do you want to try for the part? This is a matter entirely for you to decide. Remember, if you get engaged to play Mary and don't like the work, there's no going back. You'll be slaving away at it practically all the time you're out here.'

Bee added:

'Dad says we've always let you children plan your own careers, Rachel her dancing and Tim his piano playing, and we must let you have a chance at this if you want it, but do think carefully, darling. It'll be terribly hard work for you've never had an acting lesson in your life, and you'll be shut up all day missing this glorious sunshine and all the nice times the others will get.'

Jane was still standing by Bryan J. Browne. She thought the talk about not playing Mary silly. Of course she would play her. Of course she would be good. Peaseblossom saying, 'We must arrange something special for you, Jane.' She'd show them! She'd surprise them all. She laid a hand on Mr Bryan J. Browne's arm.

'What time would you like me to come and see you this afternoon?'

CHAPTER 14

THE OTHER MR B

JANE felt so proud it showed all over her. It showed so much that Tim, who came rushing home from his piano practice at the moment when she was waving good-bye to Mr Bryan J. Browne, noticed.

'What's up? Who's that man?'

Jane spoke as if Tim had in his ignorance not recognized a world celebrity.

'That, my boy, is *the* Mr Browne.'

'*The* Mr Brown! That's not *the* Mr Brown. *The* Mr Brown is my Mr Brown. When anybody says Mr Brown they mean my Mr Brown. That one is just Mr Brown minor.'

'You don't know who you're talking about. Yours just teaches music, but mine is a . . .' Jane had to drop her proud voice for a moment to think what Mr Browne had said he was, 'a director in the movie industry.'

'Who cares! My Mr Brown is a director in the piano industry.'

Tim, feeling he had crushed the argument, marched past Jane into the house.

Jane could have stamped. How tiresome of Tim to fuss about his old Mr Brown instead of asking what her Mr Browne had come about. She followed him into the house.

'Would you like to know why he came?'

Tim was going upstairs to put away his music and to wash before lessons, which was a thing Peaseblossom was fussy about.

'I'm not interested. Anyway, I know. You've talked and talked about Hyde Park and all the money you will earn taking him for walks.'

Jane was so bursting to tell her news that she dropped her grand manner.

'He didn't come about Hyde Park. He came to see if I would be Mary in *The Secret Garden* in a film.'

'That girl in that book Peaseblossom read me when I had mumps? The one who made that awful boy walk?'

'That's the one. Colin, he's the awful boy, is being acted by an English boy called Maurice Tuesday, but Dickon – do you remember the one that played a pipe and trained squirrels and things? Well, he's being acted by that boy David Doe we saw in that film on Rachel's birthday.'

'The one who trained that pony for the circus?'

'Him.'

Tim thought Jane must be making her story up.

'And they want you to act with him? I bet they don't. Whatever for?'

'Because somebody called Ursula Gidden is having appendicitis.'

'But in all America they must be able to find somebody better than you.'

Jane put out her tongue and made the rudest possible face.

'If you want to know, I'm exactly what he and Mr Benjamin Bettelheimer wanted, so you needn't be hateful.'

Peaseblossom spoke from the top of the stairs.

'And you needn't put out your tongue, Jane. I think it must mean that your tongue needs air. Go and sit at the table on the porch with your tongue out, and keep it out for five minutes; perhaps by then it will have had all the air it requires and will never need to be put out at anybody again.'

It was never any good fighting Peaseblossom; if you argued things grew worse; it was always easiest to give way at the beginning; but Jane was seething with rage. What a way to treat somebody who by tomorrow might be a film star! Wait until she was. She would crush Peaseblossom. Sit with her tongue out indeed! The insult!

Peaseblossom came down the stairs where she could keep an eye on Jane's tongue. She spoke in a quiet voice to Tim so that Jane should not hear.

'You were rude, you know. I can hardly blame Jane for being rude back, though of course nobody should put out their tongue.'

'I didn't mean to be rude, but I just can't believe it. Why would anybody choose Jane?'

Peaseblossom had heard the news from Bee and was wondering just that herself. She had said 'Jane!' when she heard. 'Why Jane?' and she saw that Bee was bewildered too. You can't change the way you see people all in a minute. Jane was the difficult one. Jane was the inartistic one. Jane was the plain one. Jane was by far the quickest at lessons, but that seemed hardly a quality to make someone pick her out for a film. If it had been some tiny part Peaseblossom would have been amazed, but Mary in *The Secret Garden* could only be a leading part. She said in what she hoped was a not surprised tone:

'And why shouldn't they choose Jane? She's having a test tomorrow and if she's engaged we shall be very proud, shan't we? Up the Winters!'

'I'd be much prouder if she was dog walker to fifty dogs like she said she wanted to be. I should think she'd be simply awful in a film so we won't be proud at all.'

'That's enough, Tim. Go and wash and put away your music, we must start lessons. All this excitement has made us ten minutes late already.'

John had not gone back to his typewriter. He wanted to but instead he went to look for Rachel. He did not have to look far; the moment he reached the porch he heard a choking, hiccoughing noise under the table. He leant down.

'Come on, Rachel. Come for a walk. Jane's outside saying good-bye to Mr Browne and Tim's not back; let's get out quickly before any one catches us.' John put his arm through

Rachel's and tried to draw her down the steps. He thought she was trying not to go, for she was so incoherent with crying that he could not hear what she said. Then she held out a foot. 'Oh, the ballet shoes! Of course. Well, just come down the steps. We'll find a quiet spot.'

They found a nice little place. John let Rachel mop up and feel better, then he said:

'Bit of a knock-out, I know. You thought that they wanted you.'

In a surge all the things she had been thinking while she cried poured out of Rachel. It did not matter, now that he was well again, telling John what a blow it had been at first when she had missed being one of the six Benny had picked for Mr Glinken's musical production. She explained about Posy's telephone call. How it seemed the end of all hope that she was not chosen for *Pirouette*, especially as everybody had been so sure she would be.

'If you'd just heard you were not chosen why did you think Mr Browne had come about you?' Rachel explained about the faint hope of her being the child dancer. John was pleased. 'Well then, there's still a chance of that?'

Rachel's voice grew very small.

'I don't want three days' work if Jane's to be Mary in *The Secret Garden*.'

John lit a cigarette.

'Yet Jane's playing that part, if it comes off, might be a help all round. There's a lot of rules about any money Jane earns but Mr Browne said there would be some sort of salary for whoever looks after her at the studio; she has to have someone there. That might mean we could fix about your dancing lessons and getting you to them.'

Rachel's voice was hardly a whisper.

'I don't want things Jane earns for me.'

'That's a clear statement. It's not nice to be jealous but I can see that you might be just at first. Especially as, if we had stayed at home, you were to have been our family star, appearing in your first show, but I think you'll get over jealousy pretty fast. The public transport in this place seems to be awful; that's because everybody here owns cars, I suppose, and I've been worried how we were to get you to your classes, to watch Manoff's ballet at rehearsals if you got that chance and anything else that might turn up. If you danced in a film it would have been a money help but it's nothing in your life. You are, we hope, going to be a real dancer; I'm reckoning by the time you're eighteen to be sitting in Covent Garden watching you dance *The Sleeping Princess* and whatever that leading part is in *Swan Lake*. I shan't care, and you won't care that you were never one of fifty girls in a film called *Pirouette*. What we both shall care about is that in the six glorious months we spent in California you kept up your training; in fact got some things you never could have got at home, and as well turned the colour of a peach because of the sun.'

Rachel rubbed her cheek against John's shoulder.

'Oh, Dad, I do feel better, and I do see all that. Of course that film doesn't matter, but Jane's younger than me, and she's pretty awful now, imagine what she'll be like if she acts Mary.'

John laughed.

'Poor old Jane! I should think, if she gets this part, she's going to be sorry before she's through. Mr Browne was quite fair, he admits it'll be very hard work. I think if it had been either you or Tim that got a chance like that I would have wanted to say no without asking you. But it may do Jane good. I believe it does everybody good to be the one to shine now and again. So far any shining done in our family has been done by you and Tim.'

'But she won't shine. She can't act. She's bound to be terrible.'

'We shall see. I suppose these fellows in the film industry know what they're doing. I dare say we shall have to put up with a little grandeur from her at first if she gets the part, but she'll settle down. In the meantime you be nice about it. Now go up to your bedroom and get on with your dancing practice. I'll ask Peaseblossom to excuse you from lessons this morning.'

Peaseblossom took Jane to see Mr Bryan J. Browne that afternoon. Jane strutted along ahead of Peaseblossom feeling brushed up the wrong way. Nobody had done anything mean exactly but nobody had done anything right. There had been no proper admiration. Nobody had said 'How splendid! Of course I knew Jane was just the sort of person to be a film star.' Instead they had looked startled and unbelieving. Aunt Cora, who Jane had supposed would have been more pleased than anyone because she had been pleased about Rachel's chance to be one of fifty girls dancing in a film, was almost annoyed. She was a great admirer of Ursula Gidden, and knew somebody who was a friend of Ursula's parents, and knew all the hard work that had gone into making Ursula famous, and she thought it almost insulting to Ursula that a child who had never acted in her life, who had only been in California a week and was the plain, untalented one of the family, should even have a test for her part. Of course she had not said these things out loud, but she had half said them, and looked them, when she had said in her whiney voice:

'It won't happen. You've no idea, Jane, how these movie people go on. Every day you read stories of somebody who's been discovered. Often the movie company pay their expenses right across America just to make tests like this one you're to have tomorrow, but not once in a thousand times does anything come of it. I guess most of these so-called discoveries just get their railroad fare home, and nobody hears of them again. Now you take my advice, don't expect anything for you'll feel lower than a snake when they say you won't do. It's not to be hoped they'll use you, for that little Ursula Gidden is really something.'

Even Bella, angelic Bella, whom Jane liked more than she had liked anybody for ages, did not have much faith in a movie career. She shook her head and looked more as if Jane was going to have a tooth out than a test. She had a grandchild who had had a test for the 'Our Gang' films. The family had got so uppity about it that Bella could have slapped them. Then, when nothing came of it, they felt madder than hornets. Bella didn't want to see Miss Jane feeling that way.

John had teased Jane at lunch and called her 'the little film star', but it was only teasing; he had not meant it, and he had backed Tim about the name Brown. He said Jane's Mr Browne had an 'e' on his name, but both Browns sounded alike and Tim's Mr Brown had been there first, and any other Mr Browne would have to be called something else; he suggested Mr Film Browne.

If anybody was made a fuss of it had been Rachel. Peaseblossom, John and Bee had treated her as if it was her birthday. As well, though of course Jane wanted to go to see Mr Bryan J. Browne, Aunt Cora chose that afternoon to take everybody for a drive, and they had all sympathized with Peaseblossom because she could not go, but not with her. So one way and another it was a very black-doggish Jane who stumped up Mr Bryan J. Browne's porch steps.

Mr Bryan J. Browne had everything planned. A chair on his lawn and magazines waiting for Peaseblossom. He had even arranged to have afternoon tea served for her as he thought she would like it, though he said he never touched the stuff himself and he advised her, if she wanted hers to be drinkable, to supervise the making herself. Peaseblossom had already discovered that Bella's idea of the way to make tea was to drop a little bag of tea leaves into lukewarm water, so she laughed and said she would be glad to do that. Jane could see from Peaseblossom's expression that she approved of Mr Bryan J. Browne.

Hyde Park gave Jane a fine welcome. He remembered her

at once and bounced over licking and barking. As soon as he settled down again Jane knelt beside him and examined him all over. She could not find a thing wrong; his coat was in lovely condition. Evidently he had got over the bad fish.

Mr Bryan J. Browne had a big book with a paper cover. He sat down and opened it and Jane saw that the pages inside were not printed like they would be in a book, but typed, like John's books and short stories before they were printed.

'I'm going to go over with you some short scenes I want you to learn by tomorrow. You a quick study?'

Jane had to think for a second what he meant, then she answered very fast because she wanted him to have a good opinion of her. She thought it lucky that the first thing he should ask if she could do was something that she could do, for it would have been terribly easy for him to ask about something she could not.

'Actually, very quick indeed.'

'Can you cry?'

'Cry! Whatever for?'

'You'll have to as Mary.'

'Why? Mary in *The Secret Garden* didn't cry, at least only in that bit at the beginning.'

Mr Bryan J. Browne laid the book on his knee and leant forward and caught hold of one of Jane's plaits.

'Stop looking at Hyde Park and look at me. Do you want to be Mary?'

'Yes.'

'Well, you won't if you argue about what Mary did and did not do. I'm the director of this picture and nobody, certainly not unknown little girls, argues with directors. If I say Mary cries, Mary will cry.'

'What's she going to cry about?'

'The first time she finds the garden. She looks round and she cries because it's so good to be inside at last, but though

157

she's crying her eyes shine through her tears. Do you think you could do that?'

'Mary wasn't the sort of silly fool who'd . . .' Jane remembered about arguing. 'I mean, getting into a garden you wanted to get into seems to me a funny thing to cry about.'

'What makes you cry?'

Jane remembered the last time she had cried. That day at Doctor Smith's when she had given in about leaving Chewing-gum behind. She did not like remembering about Chewing-gum so she said in a stuffy voice:

'I did about leaving Chewing-gum.'

Bryan J. Browne looked at Hyde Park.

'So would I, if I had to leave him any place.' He got up and held out a hand to Jane. 'Come over and see what you can do about this. Let's pretend here are the steps down into the garden. You come down the steps as if you are stepping straight into fairyland. You say in a whisper, "How still it is! How still!" Then you stand still and look round like this.' He looked round as if he were in a strange garden. 'Then you remember young Mrs Craven's story. How she fell out of that tree. You don't see Mrs Craven but as she comes into your mind she comes towards you . . .'

Jane was so shocked she had to interrupt.

'She couldn't do that. She was dead.'

'She is dead. It's her ghost who lives on in the garden. The ghost of the girl Archibald Craven loved.'

Jane scowled.

'Not in my book. There was only a robin in the garden.'

'In my picture young Mrs Craven's ghost is in the garden.'

'Then, if you don't mind my saying so, it'll be a very silly picture. Nobody who has read *The Secret Garden* will know who she is.'

'They will. I've two very lovely people playing Mr and Mrs Craven. The story opens with them way before Colin is born. We see her fall out of the tree, and we see him lock the garden and bury the key. It's young Mrs Craven's love for her son, little Colin, that puts the idea into Mary's head to bring Colin to the garden.'

Jane looked at her most black-doggish. She bit her lips together to stop herself from arguing, but it was no good.

'Very well, Mr Bryan J. Browne. That's how it's going to be, but if you don't mind my saying so, whatever story it is, it's not the one in the book called *The Secret Garden*.'

Mr Bryan J. Browne laughed.

'Perhaps not, but make up your mind it's the picture I am going to make; and must you call me by my full name? Wouldn't just Mr Browne do?'

'No. As a matter of fact that's a thing I'm very angry about.' Jane explained about Tim's Mr Brown. 'Dad sided with Tim although you're much the more important Mr Browne. Dad says I could call you Mr Film Browne, but I think My-Mr Browne would be better, if you don't mind.'

My-Mr Browne said 'Fine', but his mind was back to his script.

'Now, let's get on without any more arguments. As you feel Mrs Craven beside you that's when your eyes fill with tears. She kisses you. You look up, still crying but with your eyes shining, and you say, "Robin, your wing brushed my cheek. It was as if you kissed me." You look up at the robin, and you say, "No wonder it's so still." Then you clasp your hands and whisper, "I'm the first person who has spoken in this garden for ten years." Now, let's see how you shape.'

Jane at first shaped very badly indeed. She thought the line about it feeling as if the robin's wing had kissed her silly and she sounded as if she did, and though she made faces as if she were crying her eyes were not even damp. It was better when she remembered the words without prompting, but only a little, and there were still no tears, and not a sign of a shine in her eyes. Then, suddenly, just as she was pretending to step into the garden for the sixth time, My-Mr Browne said, 'Poor old Chewing-gum. I figure he's hungry, and lonely. It's tough on a dog to be lonely. He doesn't know what it's all about. He thinks maybe you've run out on him.' That did it. Since she had said good-bye to him Jane had tried to think of Chewing-gum as happy. Now here was Mr Browne saying all the dreadful things that could happen. It was too much; in a minute she was crying so hard that her nose was red and her eyes swollen. My-Mr Browne was nice; he said of course Chewing-gum was fine; that everybody had something that made them cry and Chewing-gum was evidently a sure fire way to set her off. Then he gave her a Pepsi-Cola, which was a thing she had never drunk before and which tasted very good. Then they started the little scene all over again. This time it went almost right. Having got upset about Chewing-gum the smallest whisk of a thought of his being lonely and the tears came. My-Mr Browne was pleased. He said if she acted Mary like that at the test tomorrow, and she had a face that photographed all right, maybe she had a chance.

The other scenes were easy. The first was the one where she stood by the boy Colin's bed and told him what she thought of him. She read the words from the script.

'You stop! You stop! I hate you! Everybody hates you! I wish everybody would run out of the house and let you scream yourself to death. You will scream yourself to death in a minute, and I wish you would.'

My-Mr Browne took the script back and told Jane to learn the words and say them exactly like that. Speaking that way she seemed to be a-doing of what came naturally. The third scene was Mary's first meeting with Dickon. My-Mr Browne said Dickon was sitting under a tree playing on his pipes and that all the wild creatures he was taming would be there. That what he wanted Jane to do was to look very interested, as if seeing tamed squirrels, rabbits and a robin was magic. This was so exactly what Jane felt that, though she had to imagine the creatures, nothing could have been easier. There were a few lines to say, but most of the words were spoken by Dickon. They went over the lines two or three times for what My-Mr Brown called inflections, but he seemed pleased and quite soon said that would do, but that he would try and get David to bring along some of his animals or the robin for the test, and then Jane would be grand.

They went to find Peaseblossom. She was just finishing her tea. She looked with rather an anxious face at My-Mr Browne. She did not say so but she was sure his afternoon had been wasted. It was still impossible for her to believe anyone was thinking seriously of Jane in a film.

My-Mr Browne gave Peaseblossom an envelope.

'These are the lines that Jane must know by tomorrow.' He smiled at Jane. 'A studio car will fetch you at nine.'

CHAPTER 15

THE PAINTED GARDEN

THE start for the Bee Bee studios was almost as grand as even Jane could wish. Bee was taking her, and although neither of them said so it was obvious that both Aunt Cora and Peaseblossom wished they had the chance. There was almost the fuss Jane had wished for about getting her ready, for, though nobody thought she would get the part of Mary, neither Bee nor Peaseblossom were going to have her disgracing them. It was not the sort of fussing Jane cared about as a rule, for it was of the 'Let me see your nails', 'Don't walk about without your shoes and socks or you'll make your feet dirty' variety; but there was just enough general hubbub on her account to give her an idea of how it felt to be important. 'Rachel, darling, would you lend those new brown hair ribbons for Jane? Hers are like bootlaces.' 'Tim, would you give one of those extra good polishes of yours to Jane's shoes.'

The person who really got in a flap was Bee. As John said, you would have thought it was she who was going to have the film test, not Jane. Bee said it was worse for her; it was possible they would dress Jane in other clothes, but she knew that she had to stop in her clothes all the time, and though John might think she looked all right she knew she had nothing suitable for visiting the Bee Bee studios, where she might run into glamorous stars on every corner. In the end she wore a hat of Aunt Cora's which was made of almost nothing but a big rose, her own black dress and shoes. Peaseblossom's new gloves and a pair of nylon stockings John had bought her in New York and were meant for best only.

Everybody came to the door to see them off. The studio

car was not any different from any other American car but it felt different. The driver was smiling and friendly, but the family could sense fetching people for tests was the sort of thing he did every day, and he was unimpressed by them. Bee and Jane were unimpressed by themselves. They got into the car, trying not to look self-conscious, but they felt it, and were both glad when they had turned the corner and left their waving family behind. They were probably imagining it but they thought the driver was thinking, 'Poor things! What a fuss about nothing!'

The Bee Bee studios were in Culver City. Long before they got there Jane and Bee could see the words Bee Bee Films Incorporated written on what seemed to be storage tanks which were built into the air. Close to, the studio looked rather like a prison. There were high walls all round the lot, guarded by a great many policemen and a great deal of barbed wire. The car stopped at gates with a policeman outside; evidently the policeman knew the driver by sight for he said nothing but let them drive in.

Jane had hoped that Mr Browne would be waiting for them; he was not but he had told somebody else to look after them. She was a nice woman who said her name was Miss Delaney, though everybody seemed to call her Dot. As they walked along they met all sorts of people, who smiled and said, 'How's my darling Dot?' or, as if it was amazing to meet her, 'Dot, honey!'

Inside the lot was like a town. Wide streets ran up and down, only instead of houses on each side that people lived in there were offices and studios. Cars and lorries drove up and down the streets, and there were even street cleaners with brooms. Miss Delaney showed Jane a long, low, white building standing back in a little garden, and said that was the Bee Bee school, where Jane would go for lessons if she got the part of Mary. Jane asked if that was where David Doe went to school and Miss Delaney said it was, that all the children under contract went there, Jane would meet David as soon as he came out of school, that the test scene with him would be shot after lunch so as not to interfere with his morning's lessons, as if he missed even a few minutes of his lessons between nine and twelve those minutes had to be made up in the afternoon, and that was the law.

Miss Delaney took Bee and Jane to a big place she called the wardrobe. Evidently they were expected. A woman in a white linen coat came and was introduced as Mrs Gates. She looked Jane over as if she could measure her by just looking at her, then said to Miss Delaney:

'Not far out. Of course Ursula's a bit bigger.' Jane was surprised to find Ursula was bigger than she was, for My-Mr Browne had spoken of her as little Ursula, but she had not time to say her thoughts out loud, for Mrs Gates led them over to a place where clothes were hanging under cellophane coverings. She threw back the cellophane. 'What would you like to wear, dear?'

Jane was thrilled. Of course she liked dressing up and this was dressing up in a big way. She had not thought of Mary in *The Secret Garden* having a great many clothes, but evidently she had. There were whole rows of frocks, and coats, and some nightdresses and a dressing-gown. The dresses were pretty, made of silks and muslins, not really what Jane thought suitable for a garden but then, of course, in those old days when *The Secret Garden* was written she supposed they probably did wear those sort of party clothes all the time. Mrs Gates said to Bee:

'Funny they look now, don't they? You wait till I show you the little petticoats and the frilled drawers that go with them. They're just darling.'

Jane chose, with advice from Mrs Gates and Miss Delaney, one of the plainer frocks. It was pink with very sticking out skirts. She was ashamed of the underclothes. Although the skirt of the dress was longer than her own, if she turned quickly the frilled pants showed, and although Miss Delaney said she thought they were cute Jane thought them awful. She was supposed to wear long black silk stockings and black shoes or button boots. Ursula's shoes and boots were too big and it was decided for the test Jane would wear her own shoes and socks. The dress needed a little altering and while this was being done, Miss Delaney took Jane and Bee to another place where there was a hairdresser. He was a man with a lot of black hair and very sparkling eyes. He stood away from Jane, looking at her with his head on one side, then he made pleased noises, pulled out a chair, gently pushed her into it, untied her plaits and started brushing and combing her hair and trying out different partings, in such a possessive way that Jane nearly asked him if he thought her head belonged to him.

Out again in one of the main streets of the lot Jane felt dreadfully self-conscious. Her hair was brushed out and tied with a bow, and the ends had been curled. A warm wind was blowing and, though she kept holding her skirt down, she was sure those dreadful pants were showing; but she was the only person who seemed to think her clothes queer, for though there were masses of people hurrying along nobody looked twice at her, and after a bit she saw why, for on a film lot it was more usual to be dressed up than not to be dressed up.

Mr Browne was waiting for them in a huge room with lots of little rooms opening off it. Each of the little rooms had one wall missing, for they opened straight into the big room. Mr Browne was sitting in one of these little rooms. The one he was in seemed to be a bedroom, for there was a very grand bed in it. They did not start on the test right away. Mr Browne took Jane round and showed her things. The place they were in was studio twelve, where most of the interior scenes of *The Secret Garden* were scheduled to be shot. The garden was in another studio. Mr Browne led Jane round and explained that what she had thought was a big room was a 'floor', that she would hear people say a picture was 'on the floor' and that meant it was being shot in a place like the one they were in. He explained that what she had thought were little rooms were really like scenes in a theatre. Each one was built to fit the scenes in the script. Most of them were rooms in Misselthwaite Manor. He showed her the script where it was written that the scene was in Colin's bedroom, and then he showed her the piece of room with the grand bed in it on which he had been sitting when they arrived, and told her that she was going to act one of her test scenes there and did she know which. What with her queer clothes and everything being so new and odd Jane had been feeling unlike herself, a sort of mustn't-speak-above-a-whisper sensation, but at that question her ordinary self began to come back.

'Of course. That's the scene where Colin's screaming and I tell him to stop.'

Although they would not use them in the tests Mr Browne showed Jane the sets which were Mary's rooms. The bedroom with a heavy old-fashioned bed and a fireplace with a great guard round it, and the nursery, just as described in the book, not a child's room but a grown-up person's room, with gloomy old pictures on the walls and heavy oak furniture. There was a window and Mr Browne asked if Jane thought she could imagine, if she looked out of it, that she was not in California with its hot sun baking everything, but looking at an English garden in winter. Jane thought and remembered the talk she, Tim and Rachel had in the train when they were looking at the orange trees, and Rachel had said that at home leaves would be blowing off the trees, and how in a second, in spite of the orange trees, they had all seen Saxon Crescent, so she said she thought she would, though she had never been to Yorkshire, but she expected English gardens in winter all looked alike.

Mr Browne asked if Jane would like to go over her lines before the test, and led the way to two chairs which were by themselves in a corner. Jane began to feel odd again the moment Mr Browne mentioned lines. A sort of worm-creeping-along-inside-her feeling. Mr Browne saw in her face how she felt for he laughed and said there was nothing to be scared of, as she would see for herself once they started, but he did want her to be sure of her lines, as forgetting them at the important moment was the sort of thing that would upset anybody.

Jane knew all the words perfectly; she had almost known them when she had come home with them the day before, and Peaseblossom had been hearing them off and on until the car came; but in the fuss of saying them at that moment she felt Mr Browne could not be trusted to remember what he had said, so she gabbled very fast both her lines and his directions.

'There's steps I come down looking as if it was fairyland and I say how still it is how still and look at the tree Mrs Craven fell out of and I remember . . .'

Mr Browne stopped her. He said he thought she should take a deep breath and start again, and that he would help by telling her what she was doing and all she had to do was to tell him what Mary said. This worked very well. Jane said every line in each scene perfectly, though with no expression at all, except a little in the scene by Colin's bed, which was the scene she really liked. When she had finished Mr Browne said they would go to the garden as she was ready for her test.

The garden was the queerest garden Jane could imagine. It was partly real and partly painted. It was a big garden with room to run about in like a real garden. There were paths everywhere and flower beds and some statues. It was not the garden which Mary first saw as a dead garden, but the beautifully kept garden to which Mr Craven had brought Mrs Craven when he first married her. The garden as it was when Mrs Craven fell out of a tree ten years before the story of Mary and Colin began. Mr Browne led Jane round the garden and showed her it was really another floor like the one in studio twelve. That all through it were places carefully built where different scenes took place. There was the door and the steps into the garden, not of course, the moss-covered steps Mary saw but the clean steps that must have been there when people ran up and down them every day. There was a funny mixture of real and unreal about the trees and plants. The trees seemed to be real growing in real earth, but the garden was full of rose trees and the roses were not real though they grew on real earth, nor were the little plants real, the pansies, delphiniums, larkspurs, lilies, pinks, poppies and all the other flowers that grew in the garden. Queerest of all was the grass, which looked just like grass until Jane got close to it and saw it was artificial, painted a good grass green. Except that you could walk about in it Jane felt the garden no more real than her toy farm at home, which lived in a box, but then, of course, the farm, sometimes when she had laid it all out, seemed real, and so perhaps the garden would in the same way. It was easier to understand a made-in-the-studio garden when she and Mr Browne came to the end of a path and found a different garden. That garden was not finished, for men were working on it. It was going to be a winter garden for the trees had no leaves, and the ground was a tangle of plants all wound together. Jane said:

'That's going to be the place where Mary scraped about and found bulbs trying to come through.'

To make the test there was a lot of getting ready. The distance between where Jane was to stand was measured, and great big cameras that moved about were pushed round, and a lot of people seemed gazing at Jane all at once, which she hated. Mr Browne saw how she felt. He came and sat beside her on the top step into the garden. He said some people could be themselves one minute and then imagine themselves into being somebody else the next, but he did not think Jane was that sort of person, that what she would be was Jane all the time trying to behave like somebody else. That he did not want her to try too much; he thought that Jane and Mary could behave very much alike and it was his job to try and use all the bits of Jane that were like Mary. Only in this scene Jane would have to think about Mary. If she did not there would be a piece of film showing Jane Winter walking into a garden, looking at it scornfully as if she was saying this isn't a real garden, just a painted one. Jane knew her words and knew what he wanted her to do, did she think she could try very hard to do it? This was a picture he very much wanted to direct, but he did not have the choice; Mr Bettelheimer and other important men in Bee Bee Films Incorporated had that. If she was wrong in this scene he was very much afraid Mr Bettelheimer would decide not to make the picture now and give him another one to direct, and though *The Secret Garden* would probably be made later on when little Ursula was well, it might be that he would be busy then and not be free to direct it, and having thought so much about it he would hate that. He was sure Jane would try hard, but he thought prizes were a help. If she was so good that Mr Bettelheimer and the other important men thought she might play Mary he would give her a prize. Had she a watch or would she like one?

Jane gazed at him, her eyes shining as if lamps were in them. A watch! Would she like a watch!

'Oh! A wrist-watch would be the grandest prize in the whole world.' Then suddenly as she said these words she thought of Chewing-gum. It was awful to say no to a watch. Her face showed how awful it was but she had to do it. 'There's something I want more than a watch. Something I made a secret vow I'd get somehow. A food parcel for Chewing-gum.'

Mr Browne looked at Jane in a funny way, then he pulled one of the curls the hairdresser had taken such trouble to make.

'That's a bargain. You get the part of Mary and Chewing-gum gets the best food parcel to be had in Los Angeles.' He made a face to show he was sorry he had to say this. 'We'll start shooting now; do what you can about those tears.'

A film studio in Hollywood was a difficult place in which to feel miserable about a dog in London, and nobody left Jane alone. First a woman in a white coat combed out her hair, then somebody else dabbed at her face with a piece of paper, and then Mr Browne brought up a fair girl in queer, old-fashioned clothes and introduced her. He said she was Betty, who was standing-in for Mrs Craven. Betty saw Jane did not understand what standing-in meant so she explained she was standing in the place of the girl who was going to act Mrs Craven. Then she laughed and said she guessed she looked pretty transparent as you couldn't be much less than a stand-in for a ghost.

Jane thought Betty looked nice but there were those awful tears.

'I do hope you won't think me rude if I don't talk much. You see, I'm trying to cry. If I do Mr Browne will buy a food parcel for my dog, Chewing-gum.'

'Well, isn't that just darling! I suppose your dog goes pretty hungry.'

'Not hungry exactly. He has horse. You don't eat horse much in America, do you? It's nice but you get tired of it. I think Chewing-gum does.'

Betty was looking at Jane intently as if she was thinking of something. Then she said, in a dreadfully grave voice:

'That's right. Must have variety. I don't think horse is healthy food. I wouldn't have my dog touch it. Specially packed tins of dog food she has. Sterilized, you know. I'm scared stiffer than a statue of germs. One germ and ...' Betty did not finish but shook her head in a very frightening way.

Jane was horror-struck. She knew lots of things might happen to Chewing-gum but that he might eat germs with his horse was a new danger.

'You mean a germ could kill him?'

'Faster than an atom bomb.'

A voice shouted, 'Quiet, everybody.' Lights blazed down on the garden. Mr Browne called, 'Come along, Jane. Open the door and come to the top of the steps.'

Jane was not actually crying but rather near it because Chewing-gum dead of a germ was dreadful to think of. She opened the door and came to the top step and looked down at the secret garden.

Film lights are queer things. They are very bright and very hot but as well, of course, they give special colour to everything. When Jane had walked round the garden with Mr Browne there were no bright lights; now that the lights were on the garden had changed. Jane found it was like opening a book on a painting of a lovely garden and suddenly finding she had the power to walk into it. She forgot about Chewing-gum but the tears that had nearly fallen were still in her eyes as she looked round entranced by the strangeness.

That was the only nice moment of making the test of that scene. Mr Browne and everybody were so slow, and Jane could not see why. There were the steps. There was Betty ready. There was even a toy robin ready in a tree; all she had to do was to come down the steps and say her lines, but the moment she had finished looking round the garden and before she had time to come down the steps Mr Browne said 'Cut', and all the bright lights were switched off, and more measuring happened, and somebody came and looked at Jane and dabbed at her face again with a piece of paper. It was even worse when they got to the place where she spoke. For no reason that Jane could discover Mr Browne made her say the words 'How still it is! How still!' four times, though she said them as nearly as she could the way he told her to the first time.

The bit with Betty was a little less tiresome, for Betty took

171

standing about doing nothing as something which had to happen, and seemed to expect to have to kiss Jane several times although she did it right the first time.

'It's so stupid doing everything so often,' Jane grumbled, 'and I hate having my face patted with that paper every time the lights go out.'

Betty laughed and said they would look pretty if it didn't happen. Under the hot lamps everybody perspired and needed wiping off.

Jane pulled down her pink skirts for she was still conscious of her frilled pants.

'Do lots of dogs die of germs?'

Betty's eyes twinkled.

'Got to cry any more?' Jane shook her head. 'Cheer up. Never knew a dog die that way. I was just trying to jerk a few tears so your dog gets his parcel.'

Suddenly the test in the garden was over. Jane wanted to find Betty to say good-bye because she liked her so much, but the woman in the white coat took her by the hand.

'Come along, dear. I want to change you.'

Almost before she knew what was happening Jane was dressed in a nightdress and dressing-gown, and was standing with a candle in her hand talking to a strange boy who was in Colin's bed. The boy was not Maurice Tuesday, because everybody called him Ted. Jane never found out who he was as every time Mr Browne said 'Cut' he got out of the bed and went and talked to one of the men who had something to do with the lights. When he was in bed he half sat up, as he was told to do, and looked at Jane, but nobody could have looked at anybody in a more bored way. Jane told Bee afterwards he looked at her with a fish-queue face and Bee said she knew exactly what she meant. Luckily it did not matter how Ted looked for Jane was fed-up and tired, and spat out her words at him to let off her feelings. Words spat out like that were just what Mr Browne wanted. After Jane had recited

them three times he laughed, and said, 'Two o'clock, boys.'
The lights went out. Everybody including Ted went away.
Mr Browne turned to Bee:

'Get her changed quickly. She's meeting David Doe in
the commissary.'

CHAPTER 16

DAVID DOE

THE commissary was what in England would be called a canteen, only there was much grander food than in an ordinary canteen. Miss Delaney had booked a table for five, and took Jane and Bee straight to it. Jane was given a menu with so many lovely things on it to choose from it would have been hard to make a choice even if she had her mind on it, but she had not, she had her mind on the door. What was he going to be like, this boy who tamed animals? Was he going to be friendly and sensible and explain exactly how training was done, so that she could make a skilled dog of Chewing-gum directly she got home?

Jane knew it was David the moment he and his father came in at the commissary door. She would have known it was him even if she had not seen him on the pictures, because he had the sort of face she was sure Dickon had in *The Secret Garden*. He had a great mop of dark-red hair, and queer wide-apart greenish eyes, and all over a sort of listening look birds and animals have, a look which makes you know that in one second, if they don't like the sound and smell of you, they will be out of sight quicker than you can feel a puff of wind.

David sat in the chair next to Jane, and Jane found that now she was actually meeting David, whom she could feel all over she was going to like, she had nothing to say. David was obviously not a person who talked much; he gave Jane a shy smile and then stared at the menu. Bee said:

'You must order your food, Jane, darling. You've only chosen clam chowder. What about fried chicken and ice cream to follow?'

Jane said thank you that would be lovely. Actually, she was so interested in David she would have said thank you if Bee had said 'What about slugs on toast, and grilled caterpillars to follow?'

Luckily Mr Doe was a man who liked talking and was very nice to listen to, for he had an attractive soft accent and enchanted Bee by calling her Ma'am, just the way you say Ma'am in England if you speak to the Queen or one of the Princesses. Prompted by Miss Delaney when he forgot the most interesting bits he told Bee the whole story of how David came to be in pictures.

Mr Doe had earned his living as a truck driver in the State of Missouri. He had two sons, Gardner and David, who went to the village school. From the time he was a baby every minute he was free David was off to the woods playing with the birds and wild creatures. The Bee Bee studios had a film unit which was travelling through all the States looking for people for some shorts they were making, who did unusual things. They chanced to come to David's village and there someone told them about David. They went off to the woods and found him playing on a pipe he had made to an audience of a rabbit and a chipmunk. The film unit took some pictures of him and his pets, and everybody thought that was the end of that, except that David's Ma hoped maybe the short would be shown some place near, where they could go and see it. Mr Doe could never tell Bee how surprised they all had been when one day a letter came from the Bee Bee studios asking him to bring David to Hollywood for a proper film test. Mr Doe went to his truck company and showed them the letter and they said he could have leave of absence, but he must just look on the trip to Hollywood as a wonderful holiday, for nothing would come of a film test; movie companies were always having people along for tests and nothing ever came of them. But as everybody knew now, the tests had been successful, and David was put under contract. Just at first Mrs Doe and Gardner stopped on in Missouri for they still thought nothing much would come of David's career in movies; it didn't seem likely somehow, and the studio had only taken David on as a speculation; they had no picture in mind for him. Then suddenly a book became a best-seller. It was the story of a boy who tamed a pony and got it a job in a circus; it was just the part for David. The company bought the book. David had a real wild pony and tamed it himself, and when the picture was first shown, which was a long time before the Winters saw it, David all in one night found himself famous.

Bee asked if the Does liked living in Hollywood. Mr Doe looked sort of homesick and said, Why, yes, Ma'am, they did. They were meeting lovely people, and they had a home in a nice neighbourhood not too far from the Bee Bee studios, but they did miss Missouri and he did miss his truck driving. David was not thirteen and quite soon maybe he would be giving up movie work, and when he did they would go right back to Missouri. Yes, Ma'am.

Bee asked what David was going to do if he gave up working in pictures, and Mr Doe said he kind of fancied a ranch, but at that, for the first time, David spoke. He had the same soft voice as his father only his words came slowly and gently, as if they were needing a little push to make them come out. It was not a ranch he wanted but land for a park. A place where any wild creature could live in peace, nobody hunting them, nobody stealing eggs, a place where they met human beings as friends.

Jane was puzzled by this ambition. If she was David she would not want that at all. She would like a private circus where all the birds and animals she had tamed could perform. Whole ballets of rabbits; squirrels as trapeze artists and, of course, the star of stars, Chewing-gum.

Immediately after lunch David went to the garden. He told Jane he had a robin and a squirrel for her test, and he was going to get them to feel at home while she was changing. Jane's Mr Browne took Jane back to the garden. He told her to walk in very quietly and when she found David to do exactly what he told her. That they would make the test as soon as David said he was ready.

David was sitting under a tree playing on queer, home-made-looking pipes. On his shoulder was a robin, and lolling against one of his feet a squirrel. He scarcely stopped playing when Jane arrived, but whispered 'Stand still'. Jane stood absolutely still. After a moment David stopped playing and said in an introducing way:

'This robin is called Mickey, and the squirrel is Bob. Mickey and Bob, this is Jane.' Then he played a few more notes and then whispered, 'I'm going to throw some food around you. While I play come nearer, but move soft.'

Jane was trembling. This was about the loveliest thing which had ever happened to her. This was magic. She crept inch by inch nearer to David, her eyes never leaving Bob and Mickey. Then something, perhaps a twig snapping or a stone slipping, made a disturbance. There was a flutter of wings, and a hoppity hop from Bob and they were both gone.

David was quite undisturbed. He still spoke in a whisper. 'Come a step nearer. That's right. Now I'm going to throw the food, then I'll play again and we'll see.'

David threw some nuts for Bob and crumbs for Mickey. Jane, scarcely daring to breathe, saw that one nut was almost touching her left foot, and a crumb was actually on the toe of her right shoe. She wished so hard it felt as if the wish must show coming out of her head. 'Oh, let Mickey trust me and take the crumb off my foot. Let Bob fetch that nearest nut.'

David was playing and at first nothing happened. Then from behind one of the rose bushes a pair of gay little eyes and a nervous nose came peeping. Then, with a couple of hops, Bob was in the open, picking up the nut farthest from Jane and nibbling it, and looking at her while he ate. Then there

was a flurry of wings and Mickey flew on to David's shoulder. David went on quietly playing, and Mickey, from the safety of his shoulder, studied Jane. She could see him thinking, 'Who is this girl? David seems to think she's all right. Shall I trust her?' Suddenly he made up his mind. He fluttered off David's shoulder, and, seeming wonderfully unfussed, began picking up his crumbs.

Jane held her breath. Although far away she could hear the dim hum of voices there seemed nobody in the studio but herself, David, Bob and Mickey. Bob's little teeth made a pleased chewing sound as he daintily picked up his nuts. There was only one left. The one near Jane's left foot. Would he trust her? Would he? Then suddenly he was there. For a second she felt his soft warm body against her foot. She looked down. He had skipped away to eat his nut, but not far, and while he ate it his eyes said, 'You'll do.' Suddenly Mickey was sitting on Jane's right toe. Jane was so proud she felt tight inside. 'They trust me,' she thought. 'Almost I believe they like me.'

Jane's Mr Browne's voice came from behind David.

'Grand. Can we get rolling?'

David did not stop playing; instead he nodded.

For Jane that part of the test was not a test at all, it was real. The garden was bathed not in artificial light but in real sunshine. It was not David sitting under a tree in a painted garden in Hollywood, but Dickon under a real tree in Yorkshire. He spoke with Dickon's Yorkshire accent.

'Don't tha' move. It'd flight 'em.'

Jane was not Jane, she was Mary, standing still as a rock. Of course she wouldn't move. It would be dreadful to flight Bob and Mickey.

David went on.

'I'm Dickon. I know th'art Miss Mary.'

Jane did not, of course, do anything to her face on purpose because she did not know how, but accidentally she was

179

looking just as Mary must have looked. Her eyes shining because for the first time she was being trusted by wild creatures. Jane would not have minded how long that test took but suddenly it was over. The cameras stopped turning, the lights were out and she was told to run along and get changed. David stayed where he was. He said he would wait and take Mickey and Bob back to where they lived a little later on.

Jane's Mr Browne seemed pleased; in fact everybody seemed pleased. He said:

'I shouldn't wonder if old Chewing-gum gets that parcel.'

It felt queer to be outside the studio riding home in the studio car. It felt queer to be just Jane Winter again.

Bee turned and looked at the storage tanks with Bee Bee Films Incorporated written across them.

'Well, it's been an exciting day, even if nothing comes of all those tests.'

Jane stuck her chin in the air.

'I think something will come. I thought I was very good.'

CHAPTER 17

SOMETHING FOR EVERYBODY

TIM was making money. Not a great deal, for the people who ate at the Antonios' drug store took somebody playing the piano as a thing that was part of the service, like iced water. Mr Antonio gave Tim a box to keep his money in, and he made counting the daily takings a ceremony. As soon as the last lunch eaters had left he would call out, 'Tim, you come'a here.' Tim would go into the office at the back. It had a red velvet tablecloth on the table, and red velvet curtains, and though red velvet was a little hot looking for California it gave a rich, royal air, and Tim liked it. There were artificial flowers on the table, roses of a kind only some of them were blue, which was unusual for roses; and, which was queer in an office, the walls were covered with religious pictures framed in shells. The best picture stood on a little platform with flowers in front of it. Altogether Tim thought the Antonios' office a nearly perfect room and very superior to any room at Aunt Cora's. Mr Antonio would open a purse and tip what was in it on to the red velvet tablecloth. He did the counting because Tim was slow at American money. Mrs Antonio would waddle in and stand at the end of the table making admiring sounds. When the count was good she would throw every bit of her that would throw, up into the air, eyebrows, hands, eyes and shoulders, and say in a gasping voice, 'Santa Maria! One dollar five!' or whatever the sum was.

On an afternoon soon after Jane's test the money counting ceremony was added to. The count was extraordinarily good, Tim's share was nearly a dollar. He was just going when Mr Antonio said:

'Tim, see what'a is here.' Like a conjuror bringing a rabbit out of nowhere he laid a parcel on the table. Tim looked first at Mrs Antonio and then at Mr Antonio. Yes, the parcel was for him. They were both smiling in so pleased a way that Tim, without knowing what was in the parcel, smiled too. He undid the string and pulled away the paper.

It was music; but what music! There were about fifty sheets of it and every one was the sort you could hear by putting a nickel in a machine called a juke box. Tim did not know what to say. The Antonios were so pleased and proud he could not hurt their feelings, but what would Mr Brown, and Mr Brown's grand friend Mr Jeremy Caulder, say if they knew he was playing that sort of music as part of his practice time? Tim had been able to feel he was not doing so badly because he was playing things Mr Brown had let him play, but that music!

Luckily Mr and Mrs Antonio thought Tim was silent because he was too pleased to speak. Mr Antonio winked at Mrs Antonio.

'We make'-a da surprise, Anna.'

Mrs Antonio, chuckling and shaking all over because any movement made her fat shake, said:

'What did I say, Tony! It is'a no good to make'a da same music every day. Now Tim play'a da new music and da patrons pay's da big money.'

Tim took the music home. He could not, of course, play it, but he could read it through and he could talk over the situation with Bella. He did not catch Bella alone until the evening. She was making what she called biscuits and the family called scones. She was nice to talk to because she knew the moment a person came into her kitchen whether they had come just to visit or to discuss something serious. She could see Tim's call was serious. She moved her cooking utensils and made room for him at the end of the table.

'What's on yo' mind, son?'

Tim undid the parcel and laid the sheets of music out so that Bella could read all their titles.

'This! Mr and Mrs Antonio want me to play this. They bought it as a present. I just simply couldn't tell you how Mr Brown hates this sort of music, at least almost all of it.'

Bella looked calm and undisturbed.

'Yo's earning money?'

'Yes. I don't know how much exactly, but I should think in English money it's almost a pound.'

Bella put her biscuits in the oven. She came back to the table. She shook her head at Tim. The trouble was he was not trusting enough. He was thinking he could decide the way things should be done, but the Lord had no time for that. There was the Lord sitting up in Heaven fairly worn out with folks asking for this thing and that thing, and He was not aiming to give them just what they asked in the way they asked it. He had seen Tim fixed right with a piano, but there had been no talk about music and maybe the Lord was not aiming to fix the music, or maybe He was aiming to fix it, and this was the music He would enjoy hearing Tim play.

Tim went to church every Sunday but he had not in England thought of the things he heard about on Sundays being mixed up with week-day matters like the Antonios' music, but Bella, whom he considered about the most sensible person he knew, thought they did mix, and he was willing to accept most of the things she believed in as true.

'Do you suppose, Bella, if I play all this music the Lord's aiming to fix me another piano? Perhaps even one in Aunt Cora's sitting-room.'

Bella looked solemn.

'Yo' can't tell. Yo' jus' relax, son, and don't trouble none. Yo'll see. The Lord may be fixin' Jane is to go into movies jus' so's you can have yo' piano.'

Bella was also a help to Rachel. Usually she was finishing clearing the breakfast when Rachel came to the porch for her dancing practice. To Bella anything that you wanted enough came, though, as she had told Tim, not always in the way you planned to have it.

'But what I really need, Bella,' Rachel explained, 'is that Aunt Cora thinks my dancing classes so important that she drives me to them every day, or lets Dad drive me. The classes are at five each day and all Saturday morning. That's rather a lot to ask, isn't it?'

Bella's old face cracked into one of her widest smiles.

'It's no good askin' the Lord for that. The Lord'll just look down an' say you should know Miss Cora better'n that. No, what I figure the Lord's aiming to do is to fix up a car for Mister Winter.'

After that each time when the front door-bell chimed Bella would say to any of the family within earshot that maybe it was the car for Rachel or the piano for Tim.

A few days after Jane's test the front-door bell chimed just after Tim had rushed off to his morning piano practice. Rachel was on the porch dancing. Jane was angrily helping Peaseblossom to clean the upstairs passage. Bee was polishing the downstairs passage. The bell ringer was Jane's Mr Browne. He looked awful, Bella thought. Terribly tired with rings half down his cheeks. He told Bella he would not come in, would she fetch Mr Winter.

Because Jane's Mr Browne would not come in they all heard what he said. Rachel came to the porch door. Bee leant on the polisher. Peaseblossom and Jane hung over the stairs. Bella stood holding the front door. Mr Browne sounded as if he was all in.

'She's got it. It's been a fight. We started on her tests twenty-four hours ago, and we went over them most of last night. It was me and Benjamin Bettelheimer against the rest. We won somehow. Will you come up to the studio this afternoon at half past two to sign the contract? You'll have to take it to the judge of the Supreme Court to be ratified. Our lawyer will instruct you about that. Jane has to go with you. As soon as the judge has given his O.K. Jane has to attend the studio school. You'll hear all about that this afternoon. So long. I'll be seeing you.' He was just going when he remembered something. He felt in his pocket for a piece of paper. 'That car you wanted. Friend of mine at this address is going to Europe. He says you can use his old Ford. If you'll go along to his place he'll hand it over.'

When the door shut behind Jane's Mr Browne there was silence all through the house. Jane could not move or say anything. She could only think over and over again, 'I'm going to be Mary. I'm going to be Mary. I shall see David, Bob and Mickey every day!' Peaseblossom thought, 'Good gracious! Jane! Bless the child, who could have guessed it! Quite a feather in the family cap. Up the Winters!' Rachel clasped her hands and whispered, 'I mustn't be jealous. I mustn't be hateful. I must just think how gorgeous it is about the car. But, oh dear, I wish it was me.' Bee, leaning on the polisher, thought, 'I'm sorry. John may be right and it's good for Jane to shine but I'm sure it's going to be terribly hard work, poor darling.' John, standing by the shut door, thought, 'Well, that's that. No going back now. I hope we're right to let her do it. We must wait and see.'

The silence was broken by Bella. She clasped her hands and rolled her eyes.

'A car! The Lord's sent a car! Nex' thing we know there'll be a piano standin' right in front of this door.'

Jane felt that the day should feel special, like a birthday. It did not. It went on in a dreadfully ordinary way. There was the excitement of John fetching the car. He took them all for a run as far as the Antonios' drug store to drop Tim for his after-lunch playing, but he did not say, 'We've got this car because of Jane's Mr Browne,' which was how they had got it, and having delivered Tim he drove straight back to Aunt Cora's, and turned them all out because he said he had to go to the Bee Bee studios. When Jane said she would go to the studios too, he said nonsense, she would soon be seeing more than she wanted to of the Bee Bee studios and she was to go for a good walk with the others and finish up with a bathe, and that he hoped to be back to bathe with them. Jane thought this was a very offhand way to treat a person who had just become most important, and she black-dogged for the rest of the afternoon. 'Never mind,' she told herself. 'When I get to the studio they'll almost bow they'll honour me so.'

Nobody noticed Jane's black-doggishness for they had other things to think of. First there was Aunt Cora. It was impossible to guess if things would please Aunt Cora or annoy her. Of course as she had taken them all in as her guests they wanted her to be pleased all the time, but that didn't happen. Jane was not the only one who had supposed Aunt Cora would be glad she was to be tested for Mary, as she had been so pleased Rachel was to try for *Pirouette*, but she had not been; she had been annoyed. Equally they all supposed she would be pleased about the car. She knew, though nobody said much about it, that the family were finding getting about difficult, and almost every day she said in her whiney voice that she knew they thought she was a meany about the car, but her poor dear Ed had always said it ruined a car if you let anyone else drive it but yourself. The person who wanted to drive it was John and he answered each time, 'That's all right, old thing', or something of the sort, but they all knew Aunt Cora was very car conscious, and thought they talked about her and her car behind her back, which was not true. So they supposed it would make her happy to hear she had not to bother about them any more because of the Ford. Not a bit of it. Aunt Cora, on hearing the news, had what she called one of her nervous spells. Her whiney voice rose to a squeak. She said John had been grumbling to the studio people about having no car. That people would say she had acted meanly, which was not true as her health would never stand acting as chauffeur all over Los Angeles. Her doctor was already saying if she did not rest-up more she would have a nervous breakdown. She would have gone on talking like that much longer only Bella came in and took her away to lie down. The children, though as guests they were silent, exchanged looks which said, 'What an aunt!' Bee and Peaseblossom were upset and worried and refused to believe Bella when she said it was just one of Miss Cora's turns and of no importance.

The other thing which, though the children did not know it, was worrying Bee and Peaseblossom was Jane's engagement. It was the law of the United States of America that a child's parent, guardian, teacher or whoever it was arranged should look after him or her, had to be with the child all the time he or she was on the studio lot. It was all right for the three hours of lessons because Jane would either be in the school or a teacher would go with her to the place where the picture was being made, or to have her dresses fitted or anything else she had to do, but that only covered three hours' lessons time and the moment Jane had done her three hours' lessons somebody else had to take charge of her. Who was that to be? It really meant somebody being at the studio from twelve to six every day, for a studio day for a child was eight hours, including the three hours' lessons but not including the time for lunch. Bee was the obvious person to go but that would mean John would never have Bee with him in the afternoons when he was not writing. Of course John would expect this but he would not enjoy his afternoons very much, and for him to enjoy himself and get well was the whole point of their coming to California. Peaseblossom was rather keen to look after Jane at the studio but, if she did, what about Rachel's and Tim's lessons?

'I suppose,' she suggested to Bee, 'you could teach them sometimes. Of course not mathematics or Latin, those never were your subjects, but you can speak fair French, and you were quite a dab at English literature.'

Bee groaned. She thought the future looked pretty bleak whichever way she looked at it. She would hate never to spend an afternoon with John, but she would hate almost worse teaching French and English literature because she had never been really good at either subject whatever Peaseblossom might say, and had done nothing about them for years.

'I hope it won't come to that; anyway, I'll start off by taking Jane and then we'll see.' Then she added: 'I'm sure John's right and it's good for Jane to have this chance to shine. But, oh, how I wish her Mr Browne had never seen her!'

Rachel too was wrapped up in worries. Tomorrow was Sunday. Posy Fossil had kept her word and invited her to spend the day. Since she had been in California she had been noticing American girls of her age. Not a great many came to this part of Santa Monica, but those who did come spent the day with neighbours, and Rachel had plenty of chance to look at them. Aunt Cora said girls of Rachel's age were called bobby-soxers, because they often wore short socks. Rachel saw the socks all right but it seemed to her the socks were the only thing that made them different from grown-ups, for they seemed to have the grandest and most lovely clothes. Sitting on the beach she had studied visiting girls carefully. They usually arrived in shirts and sort of three-quarter length slacks. A little later they changed into a sunsuit, which was a tiny little skirt and a brassiere. When they went into the water the sunsuit came off, leaving a smart skin-tight bathing suit. Often in the afternoon they put on frocks, the prettiest frocks sometimes like the peasanty one Aunt Cora had met them in at the station, but often like Rachel's and Jane's cottons, only just different and much smarter somehow. Looking at the girls Rachel saw it was not only the clothes but the way they wore them. In America girls seemed to be expected to look as nice as they possibly could and nobody thought of showing off. Rachel tried to think how she would look in a sunsuit, kicking her legs in the air, or sitting on the porch steps in a pretty frock with a gardenia behind one ear. She was sure Peaseblossom or Bee would say, 'If you are going to kick about like that you better go in and swim. You must need to work off your energy.' As for the gardenia, she would never risk it. She could just hear Peaseblossom's tone. 'Rachel! What is that nonsense? Come here and let me plait your hair tighter. We don't want people thinking we've a mad girl with us.' Nothing like that happened to American girls. All the other boys and girls took showing off as right and proper, and when the grown-ups appeared they had the pleased, proud faces all Americans seemed to put on as a matter of course when they looked at children or young girls and boys. Posy Fossil was terribly sensible and easy to talk to, and so was the old lady she called Nana, and just a cotton frock and her bathing dress in a bag would have done for them, but her sister Pauline, the film star, was going to be home and so was her guardian. Rachel hated to think of meeting a film star in an old cotton frock. If only she could arrive looking right, that would be something. Trudging along for the afternoon walk she turned over various ideas. She and Jane had very few Californian clothes. She might let down one of her cotton frocks, and brush her hair loose, and perhaps, just as she was ringing the Fossil doorbell, she would dare to put a flower in her hair. Or she would wear her old shorts and a clean shirt and take her tennis racket, trying to look as if she thought it was tennis she was asked for. If only, oh, if only she had a pair of those three-quarter length slacks how gorgeously right she would feel. Of course it was not likely Pauline Fossil would notice her, but if she did she just might suggest her for a part in a movie. Of course Dad was right and it would not matter a bit by the time she was fully trained if she had ever been in a film, but just now, however hard she fought, it mattered dreadfully. Nobody could like their younger sister, who had never worked at anything, who was always being bad about something, being given a lovely part like Mary. It was not exactly that she was jealous, it was more that she felt a worm, and going to the Fossils in a very childish cotton frock instead of dashing American clothes would only make her feel more wormish, especially if it meant Pauline Fossil never noticed her. Rachel glanced back at Bee and Peaseblossom. Was it any good appealing to them? There might still be time to do something. One look at Peaseblossom's and Bee's faces and she gave up that idea. It was a day when, however understanding they might be as a rule, Bee and Peaseblossom were not going to care about clothes. Rachel set her mouth almost in the way Jane usually set hers. Very well, then, she must manage something on her own.

Tim lagged far behind everybody else, singing at the top of his voice. He did not know the words of the Antonios' fifty songs but that did not matter as they were mostly silly and very like each other, and he preferred words he made up himself. It was clear the Antonios were right; even in one day the eaters had shown they liked that sort of music, for they had not only paid more but had bought him ice cream sodas and cokes as well. 'Oh, lovely California,' Tim sang, 'where the sun shines every day.' 'Oh, gorgeous California, where people pay money so the Lord can send me a piano.'

John did not get back from the Bee Bee studios in time for a bathe. It was getting late when he drove the Ford up to Aunt Cora's front door. He called to the family to come out and look at it once more before he put it beside Aunt Cora's in the garage. It was quite an old Ford but to him it was as beautiful as a new Rolls-Royce. He had been looking better and better every day since they arrived in California, but the car seemed to be the final thing to make him absolutely well. Almost more well and more gay than he had been before the accident.

'You always hear America called the land of the free,' he said; 'but I've learnt one of the things that makes them feel free. They never queue for street cars and buses, they all have cars. They're a car-minded race and to be without a car in America, or at least in the parts of it that are short of public transport, is like getting about on crutches at home. You can fix about your dancing lessons, Rachel. Here's your car and your chauffeur. Tim can be picked up at his drug store in the afternoons and we'll start our expeditions from there. We'll see everything. Do you know there's a place not so far off called Death Valley? What about that for an expedition!' He caught hold of Jane. 'And we've you to thank, bless you.'

John's gaiety was catching. Bee and Peaseblossom forgot Aunt Cora's nervous spell. Rachel, for the moment, stopped feeling a worm or caring about her clothes. Tim was so enthralled by the sound of Death Valley that he hopped round the car repeating the exciting words. Jane's black dog dropped off her shoulder. It was happening! It was coming true! She was the important one. 'We've you to thank, bless you.'

In California it did not get dark like it did in England. In England there was a soft greyishness which very slowly grew thicker until it was black night. In California the sun shone, then it flamed into a sunset, then it popped out of sight all in a matter of minutes. It happened then. One minute they were looking at the car, and the next John had to turn on its lights to drive it into the garage.

'I do like nights in California,' Rachel said. 'There are such a lot of stars.'

Tim was still hopping round saying 'Death Valley'. He stopped in the middle of a hop.

'What I like is that singing from all the trees as soon as it's dark. Bella says it's tree frogs.'

Jane took a deep breath.

'I like it all, and it likes me.'

That was a very Jane-ish remark, but nobody mentioned it. Instead Bee said:

'I'm glad, darling. I can't tell you how much I hope you'll go on feeling like that.'

CHAPTER 18

CLOTHES, INFLEXIONS AND
A PIANO

RACHEL's day with Posy Fossil made a great difference to
her. On Sunday morning as breakfast finished she decided
what to do about her clothes. She would rush up and put on
her m'audition dress, with her coat over it so that Peaseblossom and Bee did not notice what she had on. This worked
perfectly. Posy turned up to fetch her punctually at ten, and
Rachel rushed down to her. Peaseblossom smiled to see her so
pleased and excited and shamed her by congratulating her on
taking a coat. Bee kissed her and asked if she had her bathing
dress and ballet shoes, and nobody noticed her frock.

The drive to Posy's home was lovely because they talked
ballet all the way, and it was only when they were walking
across Posy's garden to the swimming pool that Rachel
remembered her frock, and then for the very opposite reason
she had supposed she would think of it. Posy's sister Pauline,
the film star, was lying on a chair in the sun. She got up when
she heard Posy's voice and came across the lawn to meet them.
One look and Rachel saw that what Pauline was wearing was
an almost exact copy of the cotton frock she had taken off as
unsuitable. Pauline was not a bit what Rachel had supposed
film stars were like. She was not as bouncy a person as Posy,
but just as easy to talk to; in fact the only thing about her
which was what Rachel had expected was that she was
beautiful. She kissed Rachel and told her the whole family
were thrilled to have her with them, as they all wanted to
know the latest news from England. Then she took her by the
arm and introduced her to their guardian, whom she called

Garnie, but most people in Hollywood called Aunt Sylvia and Rachel could too. The Fossils' old nurse, Nana, who had taken Rachel to the audition, was sitting by the swimming pool darning a pair of Posy's tights. She gave Rachel a friendly, welcoming smile and said she was sorry she had not got engaged for *Pirouette*, but when Rachel had been to as many auditions as she had she would know there was no accounting for the gentlemen who engaged people at auditions. As far as Nana could judge they had no more sense than newborn babies. Then came the moment Rachel dreaded. Nana said:

'Take off that hot coat, dear, and give it to me.'

It was no good hanging about taking the coat off. The heavenly Californian sunshine was beating down on the garden, and Rachel was beginning to feel like a pudding must feel when it's being boiled. She took off the coat. Her cheeks were pink with shame when she had to let them see that she was dressed for bathing and the garden in a red crêpe-de-chine dress, which was so old it was cracking here and there, and looked as if it was made of what it was – Peaseblossom's old evening dress. Aunt Sylvia gave Rachel a quick, surprised glance and Rachel could feel she was thinking, 'Funny, she does not look as if she would wear clothes like that on a Sunday morning.' Posy was practising dancing steps and not noticing what Rachel wore, but Pauline's face was half-amused, half-sympathetic. Nana was not a person who thought things and did not say them.

'Good gracious, child, what did your mother send you in that dress for? There's no audition today, you've come to play in the garden. Take it off and put on your bathing suit. Later I'll find you one of Posy's play suits.'

Rachel's cheeks grew redder. She wished a crack would come in the ground which she could slide through and disappear. She had never thought that the Fossil family would think Bee had let her wear that frock. She said in a whisper:

'Mum doesn't know I'm wearing this. It's m'audition dress.'

Pauline flung her arms round Rachel.

'I knew it! I knew it! Oh, Garnie, isn't she like us!'

After that the day became heaven. Aunt Sylvia, Nana, Pauline and Posy could not talk fast enough to tell Rachel about themselves when they had lived in London and went to Madame Fidolia's academy. Rachel had never imagined Pauline or Posy had been poor. She had thought of them as always being rich and successful, but they had been really poor once and had a dreadful struggle to go to auditions in the right clothes. Pauline said the minute Rachel took off her coat she knew from the look of it that she had on her m'audition dress, and that she guessed she was trying to wear the right clothes for California, for that was just what she would have done when she was Rachel's age. The Fossils' conversation was all of the 'Do you remember?' sort, and all the remembering was how frocks had been raised for special occasions. When at last they stopped remembering Rachel felt so at home that she found herself telling them not only about Jane acting the part of Mary but how she felt about it.

'Oh, don't I know!' Pauline said.

Posy, who was dancing, stopped dead at that.

'You don't. Petrova never could act at all, let alone have a part you wanted.'

Pauline explained to Rachel that she, Posy and a third sister, Petrova, were all adopted and only sisters because they had chosen to share the name of Fossil. That Petrova, the second eldest, had been at Madame Fidolia's and done a few things on the stage, but she had always hated it as she wanted to fly. How, during the war, she had been a ferry pilot, ferrying new aeroplanes from the factories to their air bases. That now she was working in the experimental part of an aeroplane factory.

Posy broke in there.

'She's inventing something that's going to put the name of Fossil into the history books. You'll see.'

Pauline nodded as if that was certain.

'But I know how you feel about Jane. Because I've felt like that about Posy.'

Posy stood on one leg holding the other over her head.

'Me! Why! You never wanted to dance.'

'I shouldn't think,' Rachel said, 'you'd ever feel left behind like I feel, because you've always been a success. You played *Alice in Wonderland* when you were twelve.'

Pauline was pulling off her dress, under which she had a bathing dress.

'Yes, but I've always wanted to be a great actress. I want to act Viola in *Twelfth Night*, and Portia, and Rosalind, oh, such hundreds of parts, and here I am making movies.'

'You were sweetly pretty in that last one,' Nana interrupted.

Pauline threw her frock on to a chair.

'Sweetly pretty just describes it.' She undid Rachel's frock. 'Put on your bathing dress, and thank your stars you haven't got the part of Mary, or been picked for *Pirouette*. You be like Posy – know what you want and scorn all the things that aren't part of what you want.'

Nana took the red crêpe-de-chine dress from Rachel.

'You have a nice bathe, dear, and later Posy can bring you up to her room. I'm going to look out a lot of things she'll never wear again that will come in nicely for you.'

Aunt Sylvia looked worried.

'What about your mother? Will she mind?'

Nana was moving towards the house with Rachel's things over her arm.

'Nonsense, Miss Sylvia, putting ideas like that in the child's head! You can send a nice note to Mrs Winter. It's all very well Pauline talking like that but nobody could like their younger sister picked out the way hers has been, no matter if they don't want to go on the pictures themselves. Never let the elder ones feel the younger ones are getting ahead of them has always been a rule in my nurseries. We can't do anything about the part of Mary, nor, as Pauline says, would we wish to, seeing Rachel's a dancer, but we can help about clothes. Nice things to wear will make you feel a lot better, won't they, dear?'

The clothes, and the fact that Posy gave her a present of three dancing lessons a week with Madame Donna, and that John could drive her to them, did make Rachel feel much better, and it was a good thing, for she had a lot to put up with in the next weeks. Jane and Jane's appointments seemed to be the only things anybody talked about. It was not that John, Bee or Peaseblossom wanted to make a fuss of Jane, but Jane was under contract to the Bee Bee studios, and as she was earning their money she had to do anything they wanted. As well she was a foreigner and, therefore, John felt, should be extra punctual and well behaved. On top of these things he had talked to lots of people up at the studio and knew that most of them thought letting Jane play Mary was a very risky thing to do. It would have been better to waste the money they had spent on preparing to film *The Secret Garden* than to make it with an unknown little girl whose only qualifications were that she had an English accent and looked exactly as Frances Hodgson Burnett had written that Mary looked.

Jane did not make life easy for Rachel. Rachel tried at first to be nice and talk about Jane's work, and in fact she was awfully interested in everything that happened at the studio, but Jane was simply awful. She nearly always answered to everything, 'It's no good telling you about that, you wouldn't understand.' Nobody could like that sort of thing from anybody, let alone from a younger sister. Many mornings and evenings when she and Jane were alone in their bedroom it was all Rachel could do not to hit her.

Tim did not see nearly as much of Jane as Rachel as he didn't have to share a bedroom with her, but the little he did see of her was enough.

'Jane was always terrible,' he grumbled to Rachel, 'but now I know the worst she ever was in England was only the beginning of worst. Since she's going to act that awful Mary she's nastier than I knew any person could be.'

Aunt Cora was the only person who found Jane improved. She still felt vaguely resentful that Jane should have Ursula Gidden's part, but from being 'the plain one', though she was still that, she had her uses as an object of interest. Soon after

Jane's contract was signed she gave her first cocktail party for the Winters, and she actually bought Jane a frock for it. It was yellow musliny stuff, with little frills at the shoulders instead of sleeves, and, to go with it, very short yellow socks and yellow shoes. To explain why she was dressing Jane up and nobody else she said in her whiney way:

'Your Mossel friends have given you plenty of clothes, Rachel, and Tim's all right, but Jane seems to have nothing to wear, and she should have now.' She said 'now' in such a way that it sounded as if acting Mary had made Jane into somebody new. Nobody argued with Aunt Cora, of course, for it was very good of her to buy a frock for anybody, but Rachel, putting on an old silk frock of Posy's, could not help thinking that the newness of Jane's frock was going to show rather. Bee said sadly to Peaseblossom that she did wish Cora thought the mother of a child acting Mary should look well dressed.

'I can't help it, Peaseblossom, but I do feel a drab against Cora's smart American friends.'

Jane behaved beautifully to Aunt Cora. She flung her arms round her and told her she was the nicest aunt in the world. Rachel and Tim thought this the final awfulness of Jane, seeing how she spoke about Aunt Cora as a rule, and gave very good imitations of people being sick to show how they felt, but that only made Jane worse and she kissed Aunt Cora again.

On the party night Jane was a person none of the family had ever seen before. Not a sign of black-doggishness, not a sign of being bored at handing round plates; instead she was all smiles and politeness. Aunt Cora had explained that well brought up American girls curtsied when they met people, and Jane even agreed to that. Rachel and Tim, standing about unnoticed, heard over and over again, 'This is my niece, Jane, who has taken over little Ursula Gidden's part in *The Secret Garden*.' Then they watched Jane curtsy and smile, and saw

Aunt Cora's friends look admiring and say she was cute and darling.

John, Bee and Peaseblossom were enjoying the party so much, for they found Aunt Cora's friends amusing and gay, that they had not much time to notice the children. Bee did say, 'Oh dear, do look at Jane playing up to Cora. She'll be dreadful tomorrow.' But John only laughed. 'Won't do Jane any harm; it's the only time I've seen her give a display of good manners; don't stop her for goodness' sake.'

The real reason why Jane was being so especially awful at home was a reason nobody guessed. She was absolutely miserable at the studio. Being Jane, instead of admitting she was miserable, she stuck her chin in the air, pretended everything was marvellous and behaved insufferably. Her hope that everybody at the Bee Bee studios would treat her like royalty could not have been further from what really happened. She was not used in the early scenes of the picture and so, at the moment, all she was was just another child going to school. There was a little grandeur when the police at the gates recognized her and John drove the car on to the lot without being questioned, but that was the end of grandeur. Nobody could make a person feel more ordinary and unimportant than the people Jane met for the rest of the day. There was Miss Barnabas, head teacher of the school. She did not think it was good for children, whether they were world famous or not, to be treated in the slightest degree differently to any child in any State school. She had a mixed collection of boys and girls in her school between the ages of eight and eighteen. Many of them had faces as well known as Princess Margaret's but that made no difference to Miss Barnabas. They were children attending a State school, and just because in the outside world they were stared at and asked for their autographs every time they moved, the more reason inside the school to keep the balance by treating them as super-ordinary pupils. Jane, whom nobody had ever heard of, really was a super-ordinary pupil, and to her great annoyance she was not even an especially bright one. In the Bee Bee studio school there were more teachers than in an ordinary school because, at any moment, somebody, whether they were leading parts or stand-ins, might be wanted on the set, and if that happened a teacher went with them. The three hours' lessons the laws of the United States insisted that every child working in movies should have, had to happen. So along came the teacher with lesson books, maps and all the rest of it, and a corner of the floor where the film was being shot was fixed up as a school-room, and to a minute the three hours' lessons were made up. On top of that most of the boys and girls under contract for leading parts were clever. Of all the thousands of children who came to Hollywood in the hope of getting into movies not one in thousands ever put a foot inside a studio, and not one in tens of thousands made a success, so it was no wonder that those who did were not just good at acting but outstanding all round. A boy like David Doe, though he seemed to be interested in very little but his creatures and his pipe, would really have shone in any school-room in the world. For one thing, between pictures his father took him travelling, and though what he looked for was wild creatures and the places where they lived, he picked up a lot of things as well. Jane was handicapped in some subjects, like history, because it was taught differently and from a different angle in the United States, but even without that she knew that she was going to have to work very hard to keep up. Unfortunately for Jane her way of trying to keep her end up when she felt it was down was to be truculent and unpleasant. Before she had been in the school a week Miss Barnabas was saying to the other teachers, 'Jane Winter seems badly raised', which would have scandalized Peaseblossom if she had heard it.

The other people Jane met were Mrs Gates in the wardrobe, and Miss Steiman, the coach. Fitting clothes is a trial. Standing still for ages while people stick pins into you is a bore for any child. Jane had never been used to it. She had almost always worn Rachel's cast-off frocks, and if she had anything new it was bought ready made. The large wardrobe for Mary had all to be what Mrs Gates called 'made over' for her, and making over seemed to Jane to take hours and hours, and she thought it all unnecessary, the dresses fitted well enough without altering as far as she could see. She did not say what she thought about the fittings, for there was something about the cool competence of Mrs Gates which kept her silent, but she looked at her most black-doggish, and her expression did not miss Mrs Gates. Several times she said to her workpeople, 'What a bad-tempered child that little Jane Winter looks,' and the workpeople sighed and said how different from dear little Ursula. Nobody actually said to Jane's face how different she was from dear little Ursula, but Ursula's name was always cropping up, at school, at fittings and at coachings. Ursula was loved by everybody it seemed. She was a sweet-tempered, nice-mannered, clever child, and though Jane had never seen her, she grew to hate her, and the more she thought about Ursula the higher her chin stuck in the air, and the more black-doggish she looked.

The worst trial of Jane's day was the time she spent with Miss Steiman. This happened every afternoon; Miss Steiman worked with Jane on her part. Every line that she had to say had to be said in a certain way, and to get it said in a certain way depended on what Miss Steiman called 'inflexions'. Every afternoon Jane heard 'Your inflexions, Jane!' 'Your inflexions!' The word inflexion made Jane furious. She could not see that if she said a line in the right tone it mattered if she got the right inflexion or not, and she fought Miss Steiman over every line. The truth was that Jane, who had never acted in her life, did not really understand what an inflexion was, and she did not try to learn. Every day poor Miss Steiman, who was a patient woman, said, 'I'd rather coach anybody else for twelve hours than spend half an hour with that little Jane Winter. That child just wears me out.'

The one nice part of Jane's day was the time spent with David Doe. David had Bob, Mickey, two more squirrels, a baby fox, a crow, a pheasant, seven rabbits and a pony in a kind of little zoo on the lot. Every afternoon Jane was taken by Bee to play with David and his creatures. Actually to play with the creatures so they got to know her was part of her work, but Jane did not know this and the time spent with David was perfect. They never talked much because David was busy. None of the birds or animals was allowed to be fed by anybody but him. So it was that when they saw him they connected him first with food and would fly or jump to him and nuzzle or peck in his pockets or at his hands. What Jane had to do was to be about every day so that they all got used to her and would treat David with the same confidence when Jane was there as they did when she was not. Actually better than that happened. Jane, so difficult with human beings, was a different person with birds and animals. She thought any sign of knowing her the biggest compliment that could be paid to anybody. She thought David absolutely perfect; a person who could make rabbits, squirrels and a crow sit round him as if he was one of themselves must be perfect, and David alone of everybody Jane was meeting liked her. He showed that he liked her by letting her do things which he allowed nobody else to do. He could not let her feed his creatures because it was necessary in the picture that it was only to Dickon that they came, but he put food on Jane and let her feel the gentle, trusting nibbles of a little rabbit taking a crisp lettuce off her foot, and the softness of the crow's feathers against her cheek as he took a tit-bit from her shoulder. Nobody saw Jane at such moments except David, for even Bee was not allowed in the zoo but had to wait outside. If Miss Barnabas, Mrs Gates or Miss Steiman had seen her then they would not have believed their eyes, for a gentle, shining-eyed Jane was not a person they had ever met.

One day Miss Steiman told Bee that *The Secret Garden* had reached the place where Mary came into the story. Jane would start working the next day. In the funny way things seemed to happen in California it was a day when there was news for everybody. So much so that tomorrow was to be Jane's first working day passed without any of the family being particularly interested. Rachel had a phone message from Posy Fossil. Manoff said she might attend a rehearsal. Everybody in England chose that day to write letters. A gentleman was taking an interest in Tim from the point of view of putting him into a radio show.

Peaseblossom had driven the Ford up to fetch Jane and Bee and knew none of the excitements. So when Jane strutted into the hall and announced 'They start filming me as Mary tomorrow', her words were drowned. Rachel danced up to Bee and flung her arms round her.

'Imagine! Tomorrow Monsieur Manoff will let me watch a rehearsal. Isn't it the most gorgeous thing that ever happened to anybody!'

Tim, who was playing his imaginary grand piano, stopped in the middle of a concerto.

'I may be going to play a piano on the radio. A man's coming to see Dad about it.'

The family gasped. On the radio! What a dream come true!

Aunt Cora clasped her head.

'Radio! This is too much. You know, John, when I invited you all I never thought of such things happening. I'm worn out with all this excitement.'

John laughed.

'Don't worry, old girl. You look upon us as you might look upon a snowstorm – just a passing affair. When we've gone you might miss us, you never know.'

CHAPTER 19

THE FIRST DAY'S SHOOTING

Mr Hiram P. Sneltzworther, who wanted Tim to play in a radio programme, came to call the next afternoon. He had a most beautiful car driven by a coloured chauffeur. Tim was just back from his drug store so while Mr Sneltzworther was talking to John and Aunt Cora he had a nice time examining the car. The chauffeur said it was the newest sort in the world. It just drove itself; all he had to do was to sit back. He was a very nice man; he said he guessed his gentleman would be quite a time, and he not only took Tim for a short drive but he let him work the car gadgets and see for himself that all he said was true, that the car even changed its own gears.

In Aunt Cora's living-room Mr Hiram P. Sneltzworther was doing a lot of talking. Mr Sneltzworther said he was a man who had made himself. He had started as a small boy selling newspapers, and today he was just about the most important dealer in second-hand cars, not only in California but in the whole of the United States. Surely John and Aunt Cora had heard of Hiram's Hour? Luckily Aunt Cora had, for in spite of being so rich and successful Mr Sneltzworther was the sort of person you would feel mean if you hurt. He had a round, babyish face, and rather babyish blue eyes peering out anxiously behind glasses. He wore what the Winters called Californian clothes, which meant an almost white suit, an unbelievably gay tie and a hat whose proper name was a fedora. John took refuge behind Aunt Cora's saying, 'Why, of course. Everybody knows Hiram's Hour,' and just grunted in a way which could have meant yes and could have meant no. Mr Sneltzworther said he never let himself rest. There was never a moment day or night when he was not looking for something new for Hiram's Hour. So when, because of running out of cigarettes outside the Antonios' store, he had happened to hear Tim play he had a brain wave.

'I can see him, Mr Winter. The hall packed with people. And junior sitting at a great big piano.'

Aunt Cora was very useful. She understood about radio shows in the United States, which were quite different from B.B.C. shows in England. In America private citizens owned the different radio networks, and people rented time on them to advertise what they had to sell, just as they rented space in papers and magazines. Mr Sneltzworther had an hour three times a week, when he advertised his second-hand cars. Most of this hour was spent amusing people or, of course, they would not listen to his programme, but in between amusing them he had people who performed what he called 'singing ads' about his cars. He thought Tim might be one of the amusing parts of the programme, playing something catchy and perhaps having a few cracks with the announcer. In America radio shows were things that anybody might appear in. Just as the Winters might have been part of the one in Chicago if they had not had their hair washed instead. All kinds of ordinary people who could do nothing at all were invited to appear on radio programmes, where they could win wonderful prizes. Children were quite often used, and Aunt Cora thought it would be very nice for Tim to work for Mr Sneltzworther. John could see Tim's stock had gone up with Aunt Cora because it was Mr Sneltzworther who wanted him for his famous Hiram's Hour. Aunt Cora was so pleased she was almost signing a contract for Tim when John stopped her. He said decisions of that sort he left to his children to decide, so he called Tim in. Luckily Tim and Mr Sneltzworther's chauffeur had just brought the car back to the front door, and though Tim was still sitting in it, that was a thing anybody might do.

Tim had not really understood what Mr Sneltzworther had been talking about when he spoke to him in the drug store and said he would like him on his radio programme. He had thought he meant a kind of children's hour, like the B.B.C. one at home, and though the Antonios, who had been enormously impressed, tried to explain what Hiram's Hour was, they had not succeeded very well.

'You make'a da big money, Tim,' Mr Antonio said.

Mrs Antonio had kissed him.

'You play'a da tune to sell'a da car.'

John placed Tim between his knees so that he would not fidget and therefore would take in exactly what he was being told. He explained as clearly as he could what Mr Sneltzworther wanted. When he had finished Tim thought for a minute and said nothing. Mr Sneltzworther thought Tim's saying nothing meant he was not appreciating the wonderful opportunity he was being given.

'My announcer's just the funniest man. I've heard folks say they laugh more at him than at Bob Hope. Then you just think of all you could buy with a few bucks . . .'

Tim swung round to face Mr Sneltzworther. He had never really doubted Bella, but his piano had been slow in coming, and, much as he liked the Antonios, a piano in somebody else's drug store was not the same as a piano in your own house. Bella had said he wasn't to trouble none, and he hadn't, but he had wondered a lot how the Lord was going to send his piano. He had quite seen why the Lord had fixed up with the Antonios about the drug store piano, because the Antonios were those sort of people with lots of Sunday pictures about, but Mr Sneltzworther was a real surprise. A man like him, so fat and so rich, with so big a car, it had never entered Tim's mind that he could be the person sent by the Lord to deliver a piano.

'Enough bucks to rent a piano?'

'If you go over big, to rent two or three pianos.'

Tim's face was scarlet. How pleased Bella would be! Even she had not thought of the Lord aiming to send more than one piano.

Aunt Cora, at Tim's 'Enough bucks to rent a piano', had given a kind of moan. Mr Sneltzworther's cheerful 'two or three pianos' was more than she could bear.

'Don't put ideas in the boy's head, Mr Sneltzworther. I have the most terrible nervous spells. Just living the way I do I'm all tuckered out, but a piano would prostrate me right away. Anyway, there's no place for one to stand.'

Tim paid no attention to Aunt Cora. The Lord had sent Mr Sneltzworther to provide a piano, and the Lord would fix where it should stand.

'I only want one piano, but if there's enough bucks I should like some music.'

John gave Tim an affectionate slap.

'Excuse my offspring sounding mercenary. They all understand that while they are over here any money they need for lessons and so on they've got to earn.'

Tim wanted to tell Bella about the piano. He said goodbye to Mr Sneltzworther, who looked admiringly after him.

'Quite a kid!'

Rachel was having the day of her life. Manoff was working his company in a new ballet. It was very difficult and technical, full of lifts and holding difficult positions. The dancers looked hot and sticky and had old towels or scarves round their necks to keep the sweat from trickling down their backs. They wore old black practice costumes, many of them darned, but to Rachel they were gods and goddesses. Pure beauty without a flaw. As for Posy, Rachel thought her movements so lovely they hurt. Posy was the only dancer she had seen who had the magic of greatness about her. When there was a pause in the rehearsal the final touch was given to her happiness. Monsieur Manoff himself spoke to her. He asked her how she found his ballet. Rachel was too shy to say much but she did stammer that it was lovely, and Posy quite perfect. Manoff smiled at that and kissed his fingers towards Posy's back.

'Such a one is born but once in a century. Each day I wake singing because I have the privilege to work with her.'

Jane was having a horrible day. It started all right. She found she had a dear little dressing-room with a yellow settee and painted yellow furniture. It was the custom to send flowers to the leading artists on their first day on a new picture, and Mr Bettelheimer had sent her a Victorian posy, and her Mr Browne a box of gardenias and a fat envelope. In the envelope was a typed list of dog foods. Every sort of delicacy a dog could fancy. Many of them such grand things that

Chewing-gum had never tasted them. On the bottom was written, 'Please mark anything Chewing-gum would like and let me have his address.'

That was the end of the niceness of the day. Shooting had been going on for some time on *The Secret Garden*. It had been a difficult picture to make, but everybody who had seen the beginning part of the picture run through was excited about it. The first part of the picture told the story of young Mr Craven bringing his bride to Misselthwaite Manor, a part which was hardly mentioned in the book. The scenes in Misselthwaite Manor had been written to show a big house as it must have been at the end of the nineteenth century, when there were what was known as 'stately homes of England'. Stately homes at that date had a very grand way of living indeed. There were lots of men servants and maid servants, and stables full of horses, and a coach-house full of carriages, and parties with everybody very grandly dressed, and masses more food and drink than anybody wanted being offered to the guests. There had been several scenes in the secret garden when it was a beautifully kept garden, looked after very carefully by the Cravens themselves, with advice from Ben Weatherstaff, one of the gardeners. There were scenes where young Mrs Craven sat on the branch of the apple tree that she loved, and she and Mr Craven talked about the son they hoped to have, and Mrs Craven said she was going to call him Colin. Because it was a film and you have to have what is known as suspense in a film, there was a sequence where Mrs Craven told Mr Craven's cousin, who was a doctor, about the boy she hoped to have. The cousin in the book was a poor man and a bit of a villain. In the film he was a villain in a big way. Nobody who saw the scene in the film where Mrs Craven told him about Colin could miss that he was almost spitting with rage, because if there was no Colin, some day he might be heir to all Mr Craven's money. Then they had shot the dreadful scene when the branch in the apple tree in the garden broke, and Mrs Craven was carried into the house, and the doctor sent for, who, of course, being the bad cousin, was not a bit sorry that she died. Then the awful sad scene where Mr Craven locked the secret garden and buried the key. Then the day before Jane started work there had been a scene in the library of Misselthwaite Manor, where Mr Craven had told his housekeeper, Mrs Medlock, that he was going abroad for a very long time; he could not bear to live in Misselthwaite Manor now that Mrs Craven was dead. Mrs Medlock had been surprised and asked about the baby, Colin, who had been born before Mrs Craven died. Mr Craven had looked more miserable than ever at that and said his doctor cousin doubted if Colin would live, but even if he did he would be a cripple. Then he got into one of his carriages and was driven very fast out of the gates of Misselthwaite Manor.

Though Jane did not know it, the evening before she started work all the important people in the Bee Bee studios, after seeing the picture run through, had said very nice things about it to her Mr Browne, especially they had said, 'If it goes on this way . . .' Mr Browne had smiled and looked confident and answered, 'Why not? We've David Doe and young Maurice Tuesday,' and all the important people had said, 'That's so,' and they had not said, what clearly they were thinking, 'But you haven't got Ursula Gidden'. Jane's Mr Browne had sighed and thought, 'How right they were, he had not,' and he held his thumbs and said over and over again, trying to make himself believe what he said by repeating it often enough, 'Jane will be all right. I know she'll be all right.'

Jane, because she had felt unimportant and had made herself disliked since she had been at school on the studio lot, had counted more than anyone could guess on how life would be once she started filming. Mary was an important part; everybody would treat her with respect, and Bee would

211

go home and say to Peaseblossom and the rest of the family, 'You can't imagine how important Jane is. They treat her like a queen.' She had thought too, 'And once I'm making the film that awful Miss Barnabas will be so humble she'll almost kneel, and Mrs Gates won't say, "Stand still", in that way she does, she'll say, "I'm so sorry to bother you, Jane, dear, about this fitting, but if you would be so kind as to spare me five minutes."'

As Mr Phelps, the assistant director, led Jane by the hand on to the set all the people who were making the pictures, Jane's Mr Browne, Mr Browne's secretary, the camera crew, the lighting men, who worked overhead on things called cat walks, the ground electricians, the sound control man, who spent his day in a thing very like a mobile coffee stall only with glass windows, the green men, who were in charge of especial effects in the garden, the script girl, who had to see to what was called continuity, the men and women from the wardrobe, the hairdresser and the still camera man, looked at her. They had kind, friendly expressions, but, of course, showed none of the respect Jane had hoped for, because there was nothing so far for them to respect. They were a hard-working team of men and women whose business was making films, and they were looking at an unknown little English girl, and hoping for everybody's sake that Mr Bryan J. Browne's big risk in letting her play the part of Mary was going to come off.

Jane found her Mr Browne in the middle of making a picture quite a different person from Mr Browne sitting on his porch. Making a picture to Mr Browne was something that used up every bit of him. When he was getting dressed or undressed, having a bath, eating, in fact all the time he was not asleep, he was living, not in the real world at all, but in the picture he was making. People were important to him only when they were part of making a scene, and he forgot they were alive at all when they were not part of a scene. When

Mr Phelps brought Jane on to the set Mr Browne wanted her, but he wanted her to be like a piece of plasticine that he could make into any shape he liked. He put his arm round her and showed her the set. He explained it was a railway carriage, and he was just going to tell her exactly how he wanted her to feel when Jane interrupted him. She thought he did not know Miss Steiman had gone over and over this scene, fussing about inflexions until she could have bitten her. She thought he did not know that Miss Steiman had told her the first shots of her were her talking to Mr Craven's housekeeper, Mrs Medlock, in a railway carriage. She supposed he did not know that Mrs Gates had said, 'For the railway carriage shots you wear the black pelisse and hat trimmed with crêpe and the black button boots.' She honestly thought she was saving him trouble by letting him know he was wasting his time telling her things she knew already.

'I know all this. I sit there and Mrs Medlock sits there, and we eat our lunch out of a basket and she tells me about my Uncle and I tell her about India.'

What Mr Browne would have liked to have done was to have taken Jane by the shoulders and given her a real good shake. So hard a shake she had no breath for a bit, and while she had no breath he could have told her exactly what he wanted, and how very glad he would be if she would do just as she was told, and only say the lines she was told to say and nothing else at all. However, Jane was not his to shake, so instead he kept his temper and beckoned Mr Phelps over and told him to introduce her to Annie, and see if she knew her lines. He would take the run through in a minute.

Mr Phelps was young and gay-looking. His mother had come from Ireland and Irish people never mind saying what they think, and they do not always mind if what they say is polite. Mr Phelps was very like his mother. He had a lot of black hair and he ran a hand through it and looked sternly at Jane.

'Will you hold your tongue now, and do what I'm telling you.'

Jane was angry and hurt. This was not the way she had expected things to be.

'Why's My-Mr Browne gone away? Why's he looking cross? I know what I've got to do and I only told him so.'

'Your Mr Browne, is it? Well, if you want to please your Mr Browne you'll not tell him anything. He'll tell you.'

'But why shouldn't I? I'm being Mary; it's an important part.'

Mr Phelps put back his head and roared with laughter.

'And it's the living, breathing image of Mary that you are.' Then he stopped laughing and looked stern again. 'Now look, I'm your friend. I want to help you. You get any nonsense out of your head about the importance of your part. Young Ursula Gidden, who's made more money for this company than you or I will ever see, is as simple a child as you would find in a walk across the world. Remember that, and maybe in a week or two's time, if you come to me and ask me nicely, I'll be telling you something which you'll be glad to know.'

A stout elderly woman with black hair came on to the set. She wore a full, long dress of purple, with a black cape trimmed with shining things, and a black bonnet with strings under her chin. She came straight up to Jane.

'Hallo, my dear. I'm Annie Street. I'm English too. Yorkshire, what's more.'

Jane liked the look of Annie Street.

'Are you being Mrs Medlock?'

'Yes, and you've got to hate me, so don't smile.' She turned to Mr Phelps. 'Can we have a run through?'

Considering she had never acted Jane did not find the first day's shooting very hard. Mary was a child who had been brought up in India where, in the days when *The Secret Garden* was written, Indian servants spoilt English children abominably

214

and allowed them to treat them in the rudest way. Jane's Mr Browne, having got over wanting to shake Jane, came back and worked hard on her. He was sure, from what he had seen of her, that Jane could be made to play the scenes with Mrs Medlock just right. What he did not know was what a help Mr Phelps was. In a moment when Mr Browne was talking to Annie Street he whispered:

'Get out of your head that's Annie Street. There must be somebody you'd like to be snubbing.'

Jane thought of cool, competent Mrs Gates. Mrs Gates in her white coat, looking at her as if she was less than a caterpillar.

'There is.'

'A he or a she?'

'A she.'

'Well, speak to her then and you'll do fine.'

Bee was, to her surprise, liking her first day in the studio. She had been scared that she would feel awkward and in the way with the actors and actresses. Actually there were not many actresses and actors about, for they were not needed in the railway sequences, but there was somebody who made Bee feel at home at once.

Jane had a stand-in. A girl called Shirley Norstrum. She was really stand-in to Ursula Gidden, but Ursula was growing faster than she was so she was just about right to stand-in for Jane. Shirley, when Jane came on the set, was doing lessons in the school-room made up in the corner of the studio. Shirley's work was to sit or stand in the places where Jane would have to sit or stand when the shooting took place, and on her the cameras, lights and all the rest of it got their positions. While Shirley stood-in for Jane, Jane could have her clothes changed, or finish her lessons or anything else she had to do, and when she came on to the set everything was ready for shooting. Stand-ins like Shirley were people who saved time in picture making. Like every other child who worked in pictures Shirley had to have someone in the studio to look after her, and that person was her mother. Mrs Norstrum was the perfect person for Bee to meet. Shirley had stood-in for Ursula ever since Ursula started in pictures, and as Ursula had begun when she was four so had Shirley. There was nothing at all about studio life Mrs Norstrum did not know. She did something else for Bee. Because Aunt Cora was rich and had rich friends Bee had begun to think that all Americans were rich, and could have all the lovely clothes they liked, and eat marvellous food every day. Mrs Norstrum's life was not a bit like that; it was much more like life as Bee knew it in England. The Norstrums' ancestors came originally from Sweden. Mr Norstrum had tried to get a lot of jobs before he came to Los Angeles and became what Mrs Norstrum called a soda jerker, which Bee gathered was a man in a drug store who mixed ice cream sodas and other drinks. Mrs Norstrum had no car, so to get Shirley to the studio on time she had to get up very early and take three different street cars. As well as looking after Shirley at the studio Mrs Norstrum had her housework and her shopping to do, and shopping was hard work, because many things to eat in America cost more money than people like the Norstrums could afford to pay.

Listening to Mrs Norstrum Bee felt more cosy and at home than she had felt since she arrived.

'Oh, dear, I'm glad I met you! I was so scared of coming here, but you'll tell me all the things I want to know, and give me a hint if Jane isn't doing the right things.'

Mrs Norstrum liked Bee and smiled, but inside she felt worried for her. Shirley, of course, went to the studio school. She had not spoken much to Jane but naturally she knew her, and she knew what everybody thought about her, and what Shirley had said was, 'That Jane Winter is surely a horrid girl.' So Mrs Norstrum, wanting to help and liking Bee, dared to give a hint.

'If Jane does her best, and runs to her lessons when she's

called, and plays quietly between shots with Shirley or Maurice or David and their stand-ins she'll do fine.'

At that moment there was a call for silence as a scene was being shot. Then Jane's voice could be heard answering Mrs Medlock:

'I shall not want to go poking about.'

Actually it was said exactly right, in a mixture of Jane's worst black-doggish and being grand moods. Although it was right it made Bee sigh. Somehow she could not see Jane running to her lessons, and playing quietly with the other children, and she wondered more than ever if she and John were right in letting her act in *The Secret Garden*.

CHAPTER 20

MAURICE TUESDAY

SHOOTING had been going on for several days when Jane first met Maurice Tuesday. His doctor had ordered him a vacation until he started his new picture, and as he had not been well Jane's Mr Browne put off his first scenes for as long as possible.

Jane's first meeting with Maurice was unlucky for it was Miss Barnabas who introduced him.

'Maurice is British too. You should get on wonderfully.'

Jane, though she had made no friends in the school, had managed to pick up what the boys and girls thought of Maurice and it was not complimentary. Actually Miss Barnabas was trying to be kind and helpful in putting Jane and Maurice together. She thought they were of one nationality and both difficult and might get on well together. Jane, hating the school, hating Miss Barnabas, bitterly disappointed about the way a person playing the important part of Mary was treated, too proud to tell her family she was miserable, jumped to the conclusion that when Miss Barnabas said that she and Maurice should get on wonderfully what she meant was 'You are just as bad as Maurice, whom nobody likes', which quite honestly Miss Barnabas might have meant only she did not. So straight away, without bothering to find out what he was like, Jane shut her lips tight together and thought, 'We won't get on wonderfully. I'm going to hate him. I know I am.'

Maurice was a startlingly good-looking boy. He had fair hair and huge blue-grey eyes which he could, with no trouble at all, fill with tears. He had been brought to America by his mother as a refugee from London during the Second World

War. Even before he acted in pictures Mrs Tuesday thought Maurice the most wonderful boy in the world. She had always been that sort of mother who repeats things she thinks funny her child has said in front of the child, so of course in no time Maurice began to say things just to have them repeated. When Maurice got a film contract and then became famous his mother knew that all she had thought about the wonderfulness of him was true, and at last other people had found it out. She thought he was so precious he ought not to mix with ordinary children. She hated his going to the studio school and only gave in because, in spite of all the money he earned for them, the studio talked about cancelling his contract if she insisted on his having a private tutor, which was an arrangement the law seldom allowed. The truth was the Bee Bee studio company knew that if Maurice had a tutor he would never do any lessons, for his mother spoilt him so he had only to say he didn't want to do something and he didn't have to do it.

After two hours' lessons a call came for Maurice and Jane to go to the studio. As they had still an hour's lessons to do a teacher took them over. She walked behind, talking to Maurice's mother, and Jane and Maurice were sent on ahead. They just eyed each other at first, like two dogs who have a fight in mind. Then Maurice said, in the grandest, most aggravating voice:

'Wonderful chance for you playing Mary.'

Jane quickly turned over in her mind rude answers.

'Thank goodness I'm not you, having to act that sissy Colin.'

Maurice truly thought Jane incredibly ignorant.

'That's in the book. Of course he's quite different in the film script. My public wouldn't let me play an unattractive part.'

Jane felt like a kettle when it's boiling and the lid's about to blow out. Maurice was the very top of annoyingness, and the most annoying thing about him was that he was being grand in the way she had always wanted to be herself. Her voice was rude, even for Jane.

'Your public! Who are they? We never heard of you before, but we had heard of David Doe.' Out of the corner of her eye Jane saw Maurice didn't like that so she added, 'My-Mr Browne said about David, "That boy's something out of this world." He didn't say anything like that about you.'

Maurice gave a sniggering laugh.

'Your Mr Browne! That's funny! I must tell everybody that. Your Mr Browne!'

Jane stopped, her eyes shining with temper.

'He is My-Mr Browne. He told me to call him that. Do you know, I think you're exactly like Colin in the beginning of *The Secret Garden* and goodness knows I couldn't say worse of anybody.'

They had reached studio twelve. Maurice marched in, but over his shoulder he whispered so the teacher and his mother would not hear:

'And I know why they let you play Mary. You're exactly like she was when the children in India christened her "Mistress Mary quite contrary".'

That, for everybody working on *The Secret Garden*, was the beginning of the bad patch. Maurice was quite right when he said he was made much nicer in the film script than he was in the book. In the film script the bad cousin, who wanted Colin to die because he hoped some day to inherit Colin's father's money, was giving him medicines to make him ill, and Colin was not the spoilt little horror Frances Hodgson Burnett intended him to be, but a nice boy who was too weak and delicate to struggle against his wicked doctor cousin. He did have the screaming attack in the scene Jane had done in her test where she scolded him, but even that was not because he wanted smacking but because he was in pain. Had Ursula Gidden played Mary both children would have been nicer

than they were in the beginning of the book, but because Jane
was acting Mary her Mr Browne was letting her be the real
Mary, the sour, crabbed, bad-tempered little girl that in the
beginning of the story nobody liked. That was all right for a
day or two but, of course, quite soon there were sequences
where Colin and Mary should have begun to make friends.
That was hopeless. Maurice, who really could act, was delight-
ful in the scenes, but Jane, who could not, went on speaking
to Colin exactly as she went on feeling about Maurice. Her
Mr Browne cajoled, beseeched, almost prayed. Mr Phelps
tried to help. Miss Steiman worked with Jane on inflexions
for hours. Nobody could understand why she could not look

pleasant, and smile, and say simple lines like 'The moor is the most beautiful place. Thousands of little creatures live on it. All busy making nests and holes and burrows and chippering or singing or squeaking to each other.' Miss Steiman swore Jane could say the lines charmingly, with shining eyes, as if she could see the moor and the little creatures who lived on it, but she did not when Mr Browne wanted her to. What nobody knew except Jane was what Maurice did to her. While he was acting he looked like an angel, but the moment the cameras stopped turning and the lights were out he whispered things like, 'Now you're for it.' 'Look how depressed everybody is.' 'I should think you're the worst girl Mr Browne — your Mr Browne — ever had to direct,' or, just as they were starting a scene, 'Even the camera crew have given up hope. They say you stink, which is the worst thing a camera crew can say.' Then, on the words, 'Silence everybody', there he would be, looking angelic.

Poor Bee suffered terribly. Mrs Norstrum was as kind as she could be, but Mrs Norstrum had been in and out of studios since Shirley was four, and she couldn't pretend that anybody was pleased with Jane. In fact she knew that the studio gossip was that Mr Browne was losing heart, and it was possible even now he would postpone production. Jane's Mr Browne was as nice to Bee as he could be but that was not very nice because he was feeling desperate. The cast were kind, and the crew working on the picture were kind, but Bee could see it was just the kindness of people who were sorry for her. The worst thing was Bee did not know what to say to Jane. She knew that days were being wasted because Jane could not get her scenes right, but she could not blame Jane. After all, Jane had never said she could act; it was her Mr Browne who had given her the part. It was quite natural really that Jane should not be able to act; it would have been surprising if she could. She thought it was a mistake to talk about Jane's studio troubles at home; it couldn't help poor Jane, and it would perhaps spoil everybody else's good time, and Jane, looking savage, never suggested anything was wrong.

Everybody else's good time was one reason why Bee did not even tell John she was worried. He was so happy and was writing well. Rachel appeared to be enjoying her dancing lessons, and Tim, though he had not yet appeared in Hiram's Hour, was practising for it, and seemed in radiant spirits. Even Aunt Cora was cheerful. She was enjoying having her housework done for her, and, because she was getting rested-up, had fewer nervous spells, and gave herself over to what she really enjoyed – parties. It was almost Thanksgiving and she was planning a big party for that, and Christmas was not far ahead, and for that she had the most elaborate schemes, which kept her busy and happy for hours. Peaseblossom was living in a dream-come-true world. She had always wanted to travel and now John had the car she was seeing California. They were leaving long expeditions until after Christmas, but already they had been up the mountains, to old Spanish missions along the coast and to orange and lemon estates. Peaseblossom was a person who was determined not to waste her travelling opportunities. Wherever she went she took her camera, a notebook and three reference books; one on the birds of California, one on the flowers, trees and shrubs and one on animals, and whenever the children were near she tried to educate them.

Because John and Bee were always going to parties in the evenings with Aunt Cora, and because the Californian sun had given Bee's cheeks colour, and Californian food was making her fatter, at first John did not notice how worried she was. Then one Saturday he did notice and from that minute would not let any time pass before he knew everything.

'You can't think how dreadful I feel,' Bee explained. 'You said it would do Jane good to shine, but you ought to see what's happening, poor scrap.'

'Does she say anything about the part to you?'

'Not a word. Only that she hates Maurice Tuesday.'

'What's the boy really like? I've only heard Jane's view.'

'I don't know. I must say he seems a conceited little horror, but he certainly can act. I don't think it's his fault he's like he is. I simply can't stand Mrs Tuesday. I never speak to her more than I can help. She's a really silly woman. The boy's father's dead and the moment the war started she rushed across the Atlantic to stay with some unfortunate Americans, who must have been driven mad by her. She thinks Maurice is perfect and never stops talking about him, and I'm so ashamed because she's English.'

John thought for a bit.

'Stop worrying. I'm sorry for the Bee Bee Film Company, and Jane's Mr Browne, but it was their idea and not ours that they should sign Jane on; if she's no good that's their funeral. What we've got to worry about is Jane. I hoped this film was going to give her a chance to shine, but if it's going to mean that after all the excitement she's thrown out, she's got to see the situation straight. She must understand that to us she's our Jane, and we don't care a bit if she never acts the wretched Mary. Thank goodness tomorrow's Sunday. I shall take her out and have a good talk with her.'

Jane was surprised and pleased when John said he was taking her for a drive, but a little suspicious. Everybody liked going for Sunday drives and it was a bit queer she was going on her own. It was particularly queer that the others did not make a fuss. Jane did not know that John had seen first Rachel and then Tim and asked them not to argue. Tim was quite willing. Some time ago Mr Antonio had said, 'There come'a da Sunday you no'a go out with your Papa, then you come'a to us and eat'a da ravioli,' and Mrs Antonio nodded and smiled. 'You play'a da hymns while I cook'a da food.' Tim had no idea what ravioli was but he was sure he would like it, and if John wanted to go alone with Jane, then this was the Sunday for it.

Rachel was not so easy to handle. Three dancing lessons a

week, even though she enjoyed them, did not alter the fact that she was leading a routine school-room life while Jane went lioning off every day to the studio. If on top of that Jane was to have special treats on Sunday it really was too much.

'But, Dad, why only Jane?'

John did not like tale-telling, but he thought he could trust Rachel.

'I think she's bitten off more than she can chew up at the studio and I want to find out.'

'You mean she mightn't play Mary after all?'

'Your mother thinks that could happen.'

Rachel had an awful wrestle with her voice not to let it sound pleased. Inside she could not help being pleased. Jane had been so cocky and difficult and, in Rachel's opinion, an awful snub like that was just what she needed.

'Goodness!'

John held her by the shoulders.

'And if that happens you've got to be nice. You and Tim have been the lucky ones when talents were handed out. If Jane loses this part she's going to take it hard.'

'I'll be as nice as I can, but she's not been a bit nice to me since she had that contract.'

John gave her a kiss.

'I dare say you've put up with a lot, but we may find old Jane has been up against it ever since she went to the studio. Anyway, you say nothing about my taking her for this drive, and next week you and I will have a jaunt.'

'Just us?'

'Just us. We'll go out to lunch.'

Sunday was a lovely day. The sunshine at its most golden. John and Jane drove to a place on the Pacific coast called Santa Barbara. It was lovely, built like a town in Spain, with white houses in beautiful gardens, and bougainvillaea tumbling over white walls. They ate gorgeous Mexican food called tortillas, which were hot and made a very full feeling after eating. When they were pleasantly full and contented John drove the car out of Santa Barbara and parked it by the ocean, and suggested that they lie on the sand and that Jane should tell him all about *The Secret Garden*.

Perhaps it was feeling fat with tortillas, or perhaps because John truly did not think anybody's life was ruined if at the age of ten they did not after all play Mary, but at last Jane found herself able to pour out her misery.

On the whole, allowing for a certain Jane-ishness, she was quite fair, and she did tell the whole story; what she had hoped and how things had turned out, and how, in spite of everything, she still wanted to be Mary and would mind most dreadfully if the part was taken away.

John lay on his back and smoked his pipe all the time she was talking. When she had quite finished he sat up.

'Then you haven't seen David Doe since the shooting began?'

'No. I don't meet him while we're doing interiors.'

'Do you know where he lives?'

'Sort of. Why?'

'Because we're going right off now to call on him. I expect he's acted lots of times with people he didn't like, and he's probably got a way of dealing with the situation. Anyway, let's ask; I feel I shall like David.'

Jane got up. Her face happy for the first time for weeks.

'Could we? Could we really go and see him? Oh, Dad, what a marvellous idea! He knows how to tame anything. I believe he'd even know how to tame that awful Maurice.'

It was not difficult to find David's home. The neighbourhood children were playing around and, of course, they could point out where he lived. Mrs Doe answered the door. She was more than thin, she was gaunt, with sticking-out face bones which threw shadows and made her seem even gaunter than she really was. Looking at her you could tell life had not been easy for the Does. She looked as if she had tried so hard, and worked such long hours, that she was like a spring wound so tight it could not unwind, and you felt, however easy the rest of Mrs Doe's life was, she would never be able to sit still and relax. Mrs Doe was evidently used to visitors. She took the arrival of John and Jane as a matter of course and asked them out to the porch.

On the porch Mr Doe was reading the paper and Gardner, the eldest boy, a book. David was repairing a rabbit hutch. Mrs Doe had evidently been mending because her mending basket, piled high with Mr Doe's and the boys' clothes, was beside a rocking chair. John apologized to Mr Doe for disturbing him on a Sunday afternoon, but Mr Doe said it was not disturbing him at all. He threw down his paper. At once a little breeze caught it and blew the sheets across the backyard. Jane and the two boys rushed after the sheets to pick them up. An American Sunday newspaper takes a lot of collecting for it has more pages to it than a whole week's copies of a daily paper anywhere else in the world. While Jane was picking the paper up John got a chance to tell the Does why they had come. It was easier when Jane was not listening as he could say bluntly that he believed she was no earthly good, but she still wanted to play the part, and that she thought she could still do it if only she could get over not liking Maurice Tuesday. Because Jane was not there, Mr Doe, in his gentle, drawling voice, told John that he knew things were going badly; that they had been warned the picture might not be made after all.

Jane came back to the porch, her arms full of papers.

'We're not allowed to criticize things in America because we're visitors and haven't been here long enough to know, but I must say I do wonder why Americans want so much Sunday paper. In our house Aunt Cora takes two, and Bella, her cook, one and by Sunday evening everything's simply covered with paper.'

Mrs Doe looked at Jane with a soft expression on her queer, hard face. She knew from Jane's voice that what she wanted to say was, 'It's an idiotic waste printing all that', and Mrs Doe had all her life been a person who had wanted to say that ways of doing things were idiotic. She had been too busy since she married Mr Doe to say anything much, but she still felt that way, and liked the look of Jane, and even the rather truculent Jane-ish way in which she spoke. She took the papers from her, folded them and laid them down. She said to Mr Doe:

'Pa, Jane'll come in the kitchen and help me fix something to eat. You and the boys stop right where you are.'

Mrs Doe had a lovely kitchen. Full of little tins painted bright scarlet. Like Bella's kitchen it had all sorts of gadgets in it you never found in English kitchens; special crushers to crush ice and things like that. Mrs Doe said it was lucky Jane had come that day as she had a strawberry shortcake for supper, and as she was there they would eat it right now. It was a lovely looking cake with whipped cream and strawberries on it. Mrs Doe fixed things very like ice cream sodas for Jane and the boys. She took milk and ice cream from the ice box and beat them together with some strawberry jam. She said it was a special drink David was fond of, and she hoped Jane would like it too. While she was setting the cake and fixing the milk shakes she had switched on the coffee machine. While the coffee was making she talked. At first Jane thought she was talking just ordinarily. She told Jane about herself. How she had always planned to do things. Always wanted to start something and go places, but she never had. Pa – which was what she called Mr Doe – did all right as a truck driver, but life was hard raising two boys and there was never money to spare. Then her eldest boy, Gardner, turned out the spitting image of her. He wanted to do things and go places, and that was hard for he wanted expensive books and instruments, and even though, of course, he was aiming to work his way through college, that would cost money. Then David got into movies, and Pa was guardian to him, which meant he had a little more money, and someone nearby had just the instruments and books Gardner needed, and how he was all set to go to college when the time came. She turned to Jane to be sure she was listening, and that was when Jane felt that this story was on purpose somehow. Had David ever told Jane about his chipmunk?

'The one he was playing his pipe to when the men from the Bee Bee film unit first found him?'

Mrs Doe nodded. That was him. Nippie, David called him. Quite a little boy he had been when he first found him, and Nippie hadn't been more than a few days old. David had brought Nippie up in the house to start with, and at the beginning Mrs Doe had hated the little thing. There was something about that chipmunk that made her shudder. Nippie – though Jane mustn't tell David she had said so – was just about the meanest chipmunk in the world. Always good with David but when he wasn't there he stole things, he upset things and, worst of all, he did everything just to be annoying. Mrs Doe could see he hated her and wanted to anger her. Of course as he was David's pet, she never touched him, never complained about him, and at last she found out how to fix him.

Jane sprawled across the kitchen table. David's chipmunk and Maurice were by then the same person.

'How did you?'

The coffee was boiling. Mrs Doe poured it into a coffee pot. She smiled as she remembered Nippie. She said there was nothing that kind of no-good, stuck-up chipmunk hated more than not being noticed. It had come to her one day that if she acted as if he wasn't there maybe he would find it wasn't such fun trying to upset her. There's no fun in upsetting people if the people you've upset don't act upset. It worked wonderfully. Nippie couldn't understand at first. Not being spoken to. Not being pushed off things. Just nothing. There he was

229

like a child trying to attract attention, but he never got any notice taken. When he was bigger and David took him out to the woods he was a different chipmunk. Why, right to the day he died, which was just before David came to Hollywood, he never came near the house without looking in at her. Real neighbourly he became.

Jane sprawled even farther across the table. Mrs Doe moved about so fast that she wanted, if necessary, to be able to catch hold of her and hold her attention.

'Do you know Maurice Tuesday?'

Mrs Doe was at the ice box pouring cream into a jug.

'David never says much, but he's spoken of him.'

Jane knew from Mrs Doe's voice that whatever David had said it was not very complimentary, and she was glad; she was certain nobody as nice as David could like Maurice; still, it was satisfying to be sure.

'But David's chipmunk couldn't speak. You only had to watch him. I have to listen to that awful Maurice, saying things just so that I'll do Mary all wrong.'

'What's words? Sounds as though he acted mighty like David's chipmunk.'

Jane began to have an idea. Her eyes shone.

'What's a chipmunk like?'

'Little sort of squirrel.'

Jane's eyes shone more than ever.

'Maurice is a chipmunk. Just a mean, no-good, stuck-up chipmunk. I'll watch him just like you watched Nippie, but as chipmunks can't talk if he says things I just shan't hear him. I'll make a face like I was thinking of other things. He'll be so cross.'

'Madder than a hornet.' Mrs Doe picked up the tray. 'Come on.'

Jane was just following her when she thought of something.

'How did you look at the chipmunk? Like this?' She put on her worst proud expression.

'No. I smiled. Just kept on smiling. Acting as if nobody could feel happier.'

'I couldn't keep smiling and looking like somebody who couldn't feel happier when I'm with Maurice. Nobody could.'

Mrs Doe led the way back to the porch.

'I was glad I had. If you think rightly, it was that chipmunk took us out here, and it's that chipmunk'll see Gardner through college.'

Driving home so full of strawberry shortcake and strawberry milk shakes she could hardly bend Jane told John all about David's chipmunk, and how Maurice was a chipmunk.

'I'm beginning to see him. I've never seen a chipmunk, but this chipmunk has fair fur and blue eyes, and he skips about and I don't pay any attention, just smile and look pleased, and when he speaks it's just as if he never had, for chipmunks can't.'

John had been talking to David and Mr Doe while Jane was in the kitchen, and he'd heard that Jane's refusal to do anything but scowl at Maurice was part of the trouble.

'I'm glad you smile. It's nothing to do with me; I don't care if you are Mary or not, but if you want to be you've got to look as though you were getting to like Maurice.'

Jane considered that.

'So I will. Chipmunks are sort of squirrels. Nobody could help liking a squirrel. I believe Mrs Doe almost couldn't help liking Nippie. Anyway, she's glad now about him because David's brother Gardner's going through college, and in a way Nippie helped, being there when the Bee Bee film unit came.'

'And you're going to be glad of Maurice, because you'll be Mary because of him?'

Jane stuck her chin in the air.

'I'm never going to be glad of Maurice, but I'm going to be glad I tamed him. Because I shall; you'll see.'

CHAPTER 21

'NO-GOOD CHIPMUNK'

JOHN did not tell Bee exactly what Mrs Doe had told Jane partly because Maurice was Jane's problem, and if she wanted Bee to know how she was handling it she would tell her herself; but mostly because if Jane's plan for taming Maurice was a failure, and John was very afraid it would be, it was going to be difficult for Bee if people complained that Jane was behaving queerly and she knew the reason for the queerness. She could hardly say 'It's because Jane thinks Maurice is a fairfurred, blue-eyed, mean, no-good, stuck-up chipmunk,' but her face might show that she knew the reason and that would be awkward. So John just said that Jane had a new way of tackling the problem and Bee, who felt more embarrassed every day amongst the whisperings at the studio, said she was thankful to hear it, and she did hope it would settle things quickly one way or the other, because it was no fun for anybody as things were.

Jane's Mr Browne had spent an awful Sunday. Till late on Saturday night he had sat hunched up in a velvet arm-chair in the studio movie theatre watching rushes of the film so far made. In the first little bit, right up to the sequence where Mary started to like Colin a little and sit by his bed and tell him about the garden and the moor, he kept muttering, 'It's good.' 'It's right.' From then onward he ran his fingers through his hair till it stood on end, as if he had just come out of his bath, and as sequence followed sequence he groaned, first to himself but finally out loud.

On Sunday he spoke to nobody. He went for a long drive up into the mountains with just Hyde Park for company, and he thought and thought and could not make up his mind. He came home just as the sun was setting. He sat on his porch and looked at the telephone. Should he ring Benjamin Bettelheimer? Should he say, 'Let's call the picture off'? Should he? He looked questioningly at Hyde Park.

'What'll I do? Give it a few more days? Give your tail a wag if the answer's "yes".' Hyde Park got up. He went to his bowl and had a long drink of water. Jane's Mr Browne smiled for the first time that day. Then he too got up. 'Have a drink? Maybe you're right at that.' He mixed himself a drink called an 'old-fashioned'. He brought it back to his chair and sat down. As he sat Hyde Park thumped his tail three times on the floor.

At first nobody at the Bee Bee studios believed in what seemed a miracle. There was no one to give a hint of improved times. Jane was no better in school. Miss Barnabas was patient and long-suffering but there was beginning to be a weary note in her voice when she said the name 'Jane Winter'. Miss Steiman was conscientious and did her duty by Jane's inflexions, but she told everybody it would be a weight off her mind the moment she heard that shooting had been stopped on *The Secret Garden*, for that little Winter child just wore her to a shoe-string. The only people who did notice that Jane seemed different were the woman from Mrs Gates' wardrobe who dressed her and the hairdresser. Jane hated the dressing-up part of filming, and never had got used to her frilled pants, and she loathed having somebody endlessly doing things to her hair. On that Monday after meeting the Does she was full of her thoughts. Her eyes shone as she let her mind wrap Maurice in fair fur and give him a tail. She was so busy doing this that she never noticed she was being dressed in her frilled pants and petticoat, not conscious of the frock put over her head. She didn't feel the hairdresser and her curling tongs. When Mr Phelps came for her the hairdresser looked at the dresser and both their faces asked 'What's cooking?'

233

The scene was the one where Mrs Medlock brought the bad doctor cousin in to Colin and they found him and Mary laughing together having just found out that they must be cousins. A dreadful scene from the point of view of Jane's Mr Browne and Mr Phelps and nearly every person working on the picture. In the book Frances Hodgson Burnett had said that Colin and Mary made as much noise as if they were two ordinary healthy ten-year-olds, and not a sickly boy who was not expected to live and a 'hard little un-loving girl'. Maurice would be fine, everybody knew that, but what about Jane? This was the moment when she had to be gay and show she really liked Maurice.

Jane's Mr Browne told Jane exactly what he wanted. He had not the faintest hope of getting what he wanted in spite of Hyde Park's faith in her, but there was nothing about the way he spoke to show what his inside feelings were.

The first shot that afternoon was of Mary looking at the door out of which the actress who played Martha had just gone. Actually Martha had gone out of that door when they were shooting the picture on Saturday, but films are made going on from one day to the other and even Jane had got used to it. Maurice, as Colin, had said to Martha in a very grand way, because even though the part of Colin had been changed in the film he was still a badly brought up boy, 'What I want is your duty. Now go away.' Monday's shooting started with Colin in bed and Mary sitting by his bed looking at him in a very interested way. Maurice had to say:

'Why do you look at me like that? What are you thinking about?'

In the picture Mary was thinking how queer he was. Just like a boy rajah she had once met in India. What Jane was thinking was, 'How queer. I'm not pretending any more. He is a fair-furred, stuck-up chipmunk.'

Movies are made with a long shot, a two-shot and a close-up of each person, each taken separately with rearranging of

ights, cameras, sound and so on. After the first shot Maurice
aid:

'Take that silly look off your silly face. First because
hey've stopped shooting, and secondly because nobody's
othering how you look. They're going to give up this picture.
You're no good.'

Nibble, nibble at his nut, thought Jane, if it's nuts chipmunks eat. I don't hear anything, nothing at all. Aren't
chipmunks interesting!

When the photographers took the next shot a sort of
stunned breathlessness came over everybody. Mr Browne
looked at Mr Phelps. Mr Phelps looked at Mr Browne's secretary. The camera crew made faces at each other. The
lighting men nearly dropped off the cat walks. The ground

electricians made silent, whistling sounds and all the people standing about nudged each other. Two shots had been taken and neither needed taking again. In both Jane's expression was exactly right.

'Bijabbers and begorrah!' Mr Phelps said.

Jane's Mr Browne shook his head. His guess was it was a bit of luck and trouble would start again when she had to speak. But it didn't. Maurice could not think what had happened. He whispered every annoying thing he could think of, but it had no effect on Jane. Whether they were shooting or not she went on staring at him with an amused, interested face and said nothing at all.

Jane's lines, carefully rehearsed by Miss Steiman, were:

'I am thinking two things. The first one is you're like a rajah, they speak like you do. The other is how different you are from Dickon.'

Jane enjoyed herself. She had never seen a rajah so it was easy to say it and mean a chipmunk, which she had not seen either. As for his being different from Dickon, that came naturally. Dickon, who was David. Her eyes shone and her lines came out, not just as Miss Steiman had coached her to say them, but exactly right.

When the day's work was over and Jane and Bee had left the studio someone called out, 'A miracle. A dog-gone miracle!'

Jane's Mr Browne, who looked as though he had just got over having bad influenza, said to his secretary:

'Make a note for me. Order a can of liver for Hyde Park. That dog's sure got sense.'

CHAPTER 22

THANKSGIVING

THANKSGIVING was a lovely day. It was the day when American families met to keep Thanksgiving together. You would have thought that in Aunt Cora's house there was no need for anybody extra to come for Thanksgiving because she had her brother and his family with her already, but Aunt Cora was a great person for parties. In her funny, whiney voice, which sounded as if she could never enjoy anything, she would say, 'I could just do with a wonderful time.' So on Thanksgiving evening she planned an especially gorgeous cocktail party, which kept her busy for days beforehand decorating the house with horns of plenty with flowers and fruit pouring out of them, all of which she made herself.

The party was a great success, and this time not only Jane was made a fuss of but Tim. Over and over again Aunt Cora's whine rose over all the other voices. 'This is my nephew, Tim. You must listen to him next week. He's playing the piano in Hiram's Hour.'

Jane, in her yellow musliny frock that Aunt Cora had bought her for the first party, was fussed over by Aunt Cora and Aunt Cora's friends, but this time she behaved differently. She was polite all right and she remembered about American girls curtsying when she was introduced to people, but she did not look half as smug and pleased with herself as at the last party. Rachel, in one of Posy's frocks, was not having much attention paid to her; some of the guests congratulated Aunt Cora on her prettiness, but they were all busy talking to each other and to the rest of the family, so Rachel had plenty of time to notice Jane and be surprised about her.

'How queer,' she thought, 'now she really is acting Mary and they're pleased with her, she's nicer instead of worse.' What she did not know was a conversation Jane had with Mr Phelps the day before.

It was between shots. Jane's lessons were done, and she was blowing bubbles with Shirley; not ordinary soap bubbles but of exciting plastic stuff, so that when they were blown she could hold them in her hands. Mr Phelps came up to her.

'Come on, Jane. We're ready for you.' He took her by the hand and led her to the set. On the way he said, 'Sitting there playing with Shirely 'deed I wouldn't have known you for the child I was fetching all these last weeks.'

Jane knew just what he meant, only, of course, Mr Phelps did not know why she was doing so much better.

'I like it now. I like it especially now we're using the garden.'

Mr Phelps stopped and looked at her.

'That's not the reason and you know it. I'm wondering what's made you decide to behave yourself.'

Maurice being a chipmunk was Jane's secret; nobody in the studio was ever going to know that. She wanted to change the subject and she remembered a way of doing so.

'You said if I asked you some day you would tell me something I'd like to hear.'

'I did too, and now I'll tell you. You're the spittin' image of that spalpeen Mary, and though Ursula is the best child actress I ever saw, if you go on as you're doing you'll be better as Mary than she could ever be.'

'Why?'

Mr Phelps shrugged his shoulders.

'You're contrary and she was contrary, but that's not the half of it. Maurice is contrary, and he could make the Statue of Liberty cry. I was saying last week it must be something in the blood, you and Maurice both being English. That there wasn't a pin to put between you when it came to conceit and

238

contrariness; now I'm not so sure. There's times when you can be as nice as Ursula or Shirley Norstrum, maybe even as David.'

Jane turned scarlet.

'I'm not a bit like Maurice.'

'Everybody thinks it. Too good to know anybody. Puffed up like a toad over nothing.'

Jane for once was silenced. Was that what everybody was thinking? She was not like Maurice. She would not be like Maurice.

'It's not true; I'm not the smallest, tiny bit like Maurice.'

'We'll see. Myself I don't believe you are but everybody else does.' Mr Phelps lowered his voice. 'It's not long you'll be with us. Why not show everybody they've made a mistake, it's a darling child you are.'

They were on the edge of the set.

'Like David?'

He nodded.

'Like David.'

It was very difficult for Jane to change much. Nothing, not even being thought to be like Maurice, could alter her Jane-ishness; that was part of her, but she did notice what was worst in Maurice and tried to be the opposite. So when Aunt Cora's friends said, 'My! So you're playing little Ursula Gidden's part! I'll say that's something!' before she answered Jane thought of Maurice, not as a chipmunk but as himself thinking he was too wonderful to live, and she was careful how she replied and said sensible things, such as, 'It's because I'm like Mary in the book they've let me act her,' with the result that Aunt Cora's friends said to each other, 'That little Jane is just the nicest child.'

When the party was over Aunt Cora laid herself flat on a sofa while everybody cleared up. She said giving a party was fun but what it did to her nerves was nobody's business. Because it was Thanksgiving the children were being allowed to stay up and eat fried chicken for supper. As they tidied up the living-room they looked at Aunt Cora and wondered more than ever how she could be John's sister.

While Bella was getting supper the family went for a short walk up the street. The air was full of the queer, spicy smell which trees and plants seemed to give out in California. The sky was blazing with stars. The ocean rolled in with a gentle swish, swash. The tree frogs raised their nightly hymn. John stood still.

'Listen and smell. It's all so different from home and so exciting. We'll never forget our first Thanksgiving, will we?'

As he spoke it was as if wild gayness grabbed them all. California was exciting. It was different. It was queer. In a minute they were playing follow-my-leader up the street. John leading. Then Tim. Then Rachel. Then Peaseblossom. Then Jane and, last, Bee. John did the silliest, maddest things and, as well as they could, they all copied him, and as they skipped, hopped and jumped they sang a new version of 'California Here I Come', John making up the words as they went along:

> 'California here we come,
> Not at all where we started from,
> Where bowers of flowers bloom in the moon
>   on Thanksgiving in the evening,
> Tree frogs sing and everything.
> Dear old Bella said, "Don't be late,"
> That's why we can hardly wait,
> Fried chicken on a golden plate,
> California here we come.'

CHAPTER 23

CHRISTMAS

THE moment Thanksgiving was over Christmas began. Christmas in Los Angeles was quite different from Christmas in London. Of course its being lovely summery weather made it feel unchristmassy, but it was not only that; it was that everything was so grand. The shops decorated early and by Christmas the decorations were terrific. As well all the main streets were lovely with Christmas trees and coloured lights. In every shop there was a Father Christmas, and also chimes of bells, carol singing, models of reindeer that could do everything but breathe; in fact so much was going on that Tim said, 'Just walking and looking makes me feel peculiar, like that time I had too many ices and saw spots everywhere.'

One day there was a procession as long as the Lord Mayor's show. It was made up of platforms on wheels called floats. In front was Father Christmas on a gorgeous sledge drawn by his reindeer, and behind came characters from the nursery rhymes and fairy tales. John took Rachel and Tim down early to see it, and a kind man invited them into his store and let them hang out of a window on the second floor, so they saw beautifully.

Aunt Cora worked so hard getting ready for Christmas that she had a nervous spell which lasted from Thanksgiving to Christmas Eve, which was awkward as it meant everybody should have been especially quiet and tactful, which was impossible just before Christmas. It was particularly difficult, apart from Christmas, for nice things were happening to all of them. The grown-ups were making more friends every day, and there were endless parties to which, as John had the car, they could accept invitations without waiting to see how Aunt Cora's nerves felt. Manoff let Rachel come to another of his rehearsals, and again he spoke to her, only this time he said that after Christmas she might come to his Saturday mornings. Jane was beginning to enjoy life at the studio, even the school part. To put a crown on happiness, Tim's piano arrived. With so much to sing about how could the Winters remember to whisper and tiptoe?

Jane's enjoying herself at the studio came gradually. She had begun liking the work better since the first day she had turned Maurice into a chipmunk, and it had helped that soon after that the shooting began in which Mary and Dickon met in the secret garden. For Jane just being on the set with David made her day. He had only to put his pipe to his mouth and Mickey to flutter from a tree on to his shoulder for magic to happen, just as it had at her film test. The painted garden disappeared, and a real garden took its place. The great studio lights vanished and she was hot in real sunlight. It was not nearly Christmas in Hollywood but springtime in Yorkshire. It was not queer these things should seem true because the most important part was true. In the early garden sequences only Mickey was used, but David's pipe was real, and Jane knew it was not only Mickey that pipe had tamed but every kind of creature. That pipe! If only she had a pipe like that! If only she could learn the magic way to play it.

'If I could learn even a little bit of piping,' she told Rachel 'I believe I could have every cat and dog in London sitting in Saxon Crescent.'

Rachel, when Jane said this, had not been listening carefully as she was going through a set of dancing steps in her mind, but at that description of what a pipe could do she attended at once.

'Goodness! Well, if ever David does teach you to play a pipe, and tells you where to buy one, do learn other thing

242

besides bringing animals to you. I expect he's got a go-away-again tune he could teach you, and you'll have to know it. Just think of every cat and dog in London in Saxon Crescent all at the same time.'

On top of liking working with David there was another reason why Jane was enjoying those sequences which had both Colin and Dickon in them. Mickey was nicer to her every day, even sitting on her hands and taking crumbs from her, but he cut Maurice dead.

'Imagine,' Jane said to Bee, 'how awful Maurice must be when a robin scorns him, in front of everybody.'

Bee did not allow that sort of talk.

'Nonsense. Of course Mickey doesn't scorn him; it's just he doesn't know him very well.'

Jane had been called to the set, so she risked saying something she was not allowed to say.

'Oh, yeah?'

The queerest thing was happening to Jane; she, who had never liked a great many people, was beginning to like nearly everybody at the Bee Bee studios. Not, of course, Maurice, and not Miss Steiman. She would not have been likely to get on any better with Mrs Gates, for she thought clothes fitting a ghastly bore and would not try and help by standing still, but fortunately for poor Mrs Gates and her staff Jane's clothes fittings were finished with, for her things were ready. The unlucky Miss Steiman still coached her. Rumours reached her that everybody working on *The Secret Garden* was beginning to get on with Jane, and it astonished her. She still thought her the most unpleasant and exhausting child she had ever coached. Actually so would anybody who had to teach Jane inflexions. Learning how to say a line brought out all that was worst in her. She thought she said the lines perfectly all right without anybody's interference, and that that was what she thought stuck out all over her when she came to be coached. Miss Steiman tried to believe that all children were sweet really, however they might appear to behave, and she did believe, no matter what the provocation, that she should remain sweet and gentle herself, but day after day, when Jane had gone, she had to take two aspirins, and if anybody saw her take them she would moan, 'I'm just worn away. That little Jane Winter doesn't improve any.'

Unbelievably Jane was even beginning to like the studio school. It happened all in one day. Miss Barnabas would never be Jane's favourite person, but she stopped minding about her the day the school began to like her.

Every week one pupil was chosen to give a short talk to the rest of the school. Jane was told that she was to give a talk on London. She looked very disobliging when she heard the news, for giving a talk meant extra preparation, for an ill-prepared talk got you into trouble. One thing Jane had never been was shy, so when the time came for her talk she got up unconcernedly but terribly black-doggish. She told the school about the things she liked best. Kensington Gardens, where she took Chewing-gum; Madame Tussaud's, especially the chamber of horrors; the zoo; changing the guard at Buckingham Palace; going by a river steamer to Hampton Court and the Tower of London. Behind her mind, as she talked, she was thinking, 'I know they think nothing's as good as their old America, but I'm English, and I'm going to stand up for it.' As a matter of fact nobody was thinking anything like that at all. Most of the school would have found it fun doing the things Jane told them about, and envied her for having done them, so there was no need for her to be truculent. Luckily it was not truculence everybody heard in her voice; they did not know what it was they heard but they found it funny. In fact, so funny that they laughed at almost everything she said, but it was nice laughing. After that Jane was considered not the sourest, most bad-tempered girl in the school, but the funniest. When the teacher asked her question everybody waited hopefully for her answer, bein sure she would make them laugh, and they were not often disappointed. Jane could not see what there was to laugh at, and was entirely herself, and answered most questions as she always had done, with her chin in the air in an I-thought-everybody-knew-that voice, but of course she could not help liking the school and all the teachers better, for everybody being so nice was changing her. Not quickly, for she had known herself the plain, untalented Winter for so long that it took a lot of being popular to make her forget it; nor did she forget that the people at the studio had never seen Rachel or Tim, and if they had they might wonder why she had the sort of face she had. Then, too, she could not fool herself about talent. Although she was doing quite all right now in *The Secret Garden* her Mr Browne still had to work very much harder to get her right than to get anybody else in the cast right; even Mickey was less trouble. Never once had she got the respect and admiration she had hoped for. She was, in the Bee Bee school, of less importance than most of the pupils; they were nearly all under contract; many had played leading parts, and she was only to be in that one picture as a stopgap because Ursula Gidden was ill. Still, in spite of things not happening the way she wished, little by little Jane was not the Jane who came to California.

'Of course I only see her properly on Sundays,' Tim said to Rachel, 'but Jane's different. I haven't had a real fight with her for simply ages.'

Tim's piano came the week after his first radio show, which was like putting whipped cream on top of an already iced cake, for Tim enjoyed every second of Hiram's Hour. Mr Hiram P. Sneltzworther had said his announcer was just the funniest man, and Tim could not have agreed with him more. The things the announcer thought funny were just the things Tim thought funny, and finding the same things funny is a very short cut to being friends. The announcer, whose name was Brent, liked funny things to happen as well as to be said.

He roared with laughter when the seat fell out of the chair somebody was going to sit on, or a toy snake jumped out of the piano as the player opened it; and Tim laughed even louder, which was difficult, so of course, after the very first broadcast, they were conspirators, planning wilder and better jokes for Hiram's next Hour. Oddly enough, as well as being perfect about jokes, Brent loved music. Tim had found this out at his first rehearsal; he played several pieces of music for him to choose from, and found discussing music with him was like discussing it with Mr Brown. Brent told Tim not to spend his money buying music, Hiram's Hour would get him any he wanted.

'I hope my piano comes soon, then,' Tim said.

'What piano?' Brent asked.

Tim explained everything. How the Lord had fixed the Antonios' drug store piano; how sensible a choice Tim had thought the Antonios were because of the Sunday pictures; how Bella had said that the Lord would arrange for renting a piano, and how surprised he had been at Mr Hiram P. Sneltzworther being chosen. When he said this Tim remembered his manners.

'It's not that I didn't like Mr Hiram P. Sneltzworther awfully, but I didn't expect the person who fixed the renting of the piano to look like him. Though he's got a very nice face of its own sort, I didn't expect the Lord to send someone in a big car.'

Brent said Tim needn't apologize, he quite saw what he meant; that Mr Hiram P. Sneltzworther was not a type you'd pick right away as coming the way Tim figured he had come; still, you never could tell and he surely was sent to fix renting a piano and what were they waiting for? They would go out and choose the one to rent right away.

John drove Tim back from his rehearsal and was the first to hear the good news that the piano was on its way. He was not pleased.

246

'But, Tim, your aunt won't let it inside the house.'

Tim patted John's knee.

'Don't worry, Dad. Bella said when the Lord sent my piano he'd fix it with Aunt Cora where it was to be set down.'

But John did worry and so did Bee; they worried far into the night when they should have been asleep; but they need not have done, because Bella was quite right. As soon as Tim came back from his rehearsal he had rushed to tell her about his piano, so the next morning when she brought Aunt Cora her breakfast tray she stood by the bed, her old, wrinkled face looking serious. She explained the piano was coming and was not put off by squeaks and moans of horror from Aunt Cora.

'It's no manner of use yo' fussin' and frettin'. That piano's sure coming right into this house, and all there's fo' you to say is where it's to set.'

Aunt Cora, though she would never have owned it, was scared of annoying Bella in case she went away, for she could not imagine her home without old Bella in it. As well, though this, of course, she did not tell Bella, at her Thanksgiving party quite a lot of the guests had said when they heard about Hiram's Hour it was a pity there was no piano in the house so that they could hear Tim play. So, though her voice whined more than usual and she kept her eyes shut while she spoke, she said:

'Clear that chiffonier out of the living-room; the piano can stand in its place. Now go away and leave me. The thought of that piano's got me so low I don't know how I'll get up to go shopping.'

Bella did not care what Aunt Cora thought her reason was for giving in, for she knew the real reason. She hurried downstairs to Tim so fast that she arrived at the bottom breathless. Her eyes were rolling so that the whites showed. She clasped her hands.

'Ah has said time and again the Lord would fix it and he's sure fixed it.'

As soon as the piano arrived and was sitting in the living-room Tim rushed off to tell his news to the Antonios. Although the Antonios would stop getting money in their money-box when Tim stopped playing in their drug store they were as pleased at Tim's news as if he had brought them a present. They both threw all the parts of them that would lift upwards. Hands, shoulders, eyes and eyebrows. Mrs Antonio said:

'I burn'a da candle.' Then, overcome by what was really a miracle, 'I burn'a six candle.'

Mr Antonio kissed Tim on both cheeks.

'Da piano he come. You make'a da wonderful music.

Then he threw back his head and laughed till he was almost choking. 'And you kill'a da aunt.'

The great trouble about Christmas in America was that the grandness needed living up to. At home the children had presents and stockings and a Christmas tree, and each year they went to the carols at the Albert Hall, and to one of the shops to look round, but Christmas was something perfect in itself, and a grand way of keeping it was not part of it. But in America everybody gave everybody presents, and more than one present; it seemed to be almost a competition of giving.

'It's frightful,' Bee said to John. 'What on earth are we to do if all the people we know send us something? You know how generous Americans are and we can't live up to it, we haven't the money.'

John found a way out. It was not a very grand way, but it was something and the best they could do. He wrote a story. The train story only with a different finish, of the Winter family coming to America in the nineteenth century, travelling by wagon down the Santa Fé trail, finishing in Santa Monica as it must have been all that time ago. John found a printer and had his story done up as a sort of Christmas-card present.

The children could not do anything like that, but they too did not want to be the only ones not giving in such an orgy of giving, and they all had people they wanted to give to. From an English point of view they had quite a lot of money to spend. Since Jane had been working and Bee got a salary to look after her they all had regular pocket money; as well there was Tim's money-box money. As he had his piano and his music he shared that out between them. He said:

'We did all say we'd earn money. Bella said it meant chores for the neighbours, but we didn't know then about Jane's movie and my radio, but we've earned it just the same and I'd really rather share it for it will be all our shame if we miss giving an American a Christmas present who ought to have one.'

It was difficult for Rachel to take her share of Tim's money nicely. She was the only one not earning, and there was no chance at the moment she ever would, for with lessons, and dancing practice and dancing lessons, and going out in the afternoons, she never had a second to earn money doing chores, nor, quite truthfully, did she fancy doing chores while Jane, as she thought, lioned it in pictures, and Tim in a radio show. So she took her share, trying not to look as off-handish as she felt, and really she was very glad to have the money for her list of people who might be going to give her presents and so ought to have one back grew every day.

To add to the excitement cards began to arrive from England. Rachel had dozens from the Academy, and John and Bee had so many they did not know where to put them down. Jane was the luckiest of all. Dr Smith had not sent her a card; instead he had taken Chewing-gum to one of those places where they take sheets of little photos. Chewing-gum photographed beautifully; there were two sheets and each photograph, except one where he had moved slightly, was perfect. Jane was so pleased with them that at first she could not get her words out; at last she gasped:

'It's him! It's him! It's as if he was here.'

She was so thrilled that she could not part with the photographs; she even took them with her to the studio so she could look at them between shots.

'Show them to Shirley and everybody,' Bee suggested. 'They'll like to see them.'

But Jane would not. She could not explain but somehow the photographs of Chewing-gum were almost him, and she did not want people fingering them and talking about them; it would make him less real.

'I'll let David see them when I can get him alone, but nobody else. Chewing-gum's mine.'

Just before Christmas there was a little 'Secret Garden' party. Jane's Mr Browne made a speech wishing everybody a happy Christmas and then there was present giving. Jane had bought a book for Shirley and for David a set of tiny animals for his mantelpiece, but nothing for anybody else. She did not know that one day her Mr Browne had told everybody how he had met her through Hyde Park and the prize of the food parcel he had sent to Chewing-gum when she got the part. A few of the cast had asked her about Chewing-gum and she had told them how his parcel had arrived very grandly by air.

'And Doctor Smith laid all the tins out in a row and let Chewing-gum choose for himself which he would eat first, and do you know what he chose? Something called Finest Liver Inc., which was very clever of him for he never had liver in his whole life unless it was when he was a tiny puppy and belonged to an American soldier.'

It was a startled Jane who, when the present giving started, found herself holding a sheaf of envelopes. One, excluding David and Jane's Mr Browne, from everybody working on the picture, even one from Maurice.

'Open them,' said Bee. 'It's cards, I think. You must go and thank everybody.'

But it was not only cards. Inside each card was a slip of paper and on each bit of paper was 'Food parcel sent to Chewing-gum' and the name of the firm and the date the parcel was posted.

Jane sat surrounded by envelopes, the cards in her lap, the slips about the parcels on her hands.

Bee was overcome by everybody's kindness.

'How wonderful, darling! Just think, there must be enough food to keep Chewing-gum in luxury for years and years! Run and thank them all.' Jane got up. Her eyes were not shining. She looked at her most black-doggish. She went into her dressing-room. Bee followed her. 'Jane, what is the matter? You're behaving abominably. Scowling like that when everybody's been so good to you.'

'Can I have your sewing scissors?'

'What for?'

Jane was bent over the photos of Chewing-gum.

'Ssh, I'm counting.' Then, after a minute, 'There's just enough to give one to everybody. Maurice can have the one where he's moved.'

Nobody thanks for presents in a more pleased way than Americans. As Jane went round thanking and delivering the photographs she might have been giving away diamonds, everybody had such lovely things to say, and they all said them differently. Even Maurice, who could not see Chewing-gum clearly in his photo, caught something of the American manner, and managed to sound as if a photograph of Chewing-gum was one of his best Christmas presents, and he added that he seemed a handsome dog.

'Which he couldn't have said anything else,' Jane told Bee, 'because it's true.'

Bee thought Jane had behaved very well and, to tell the truth, it had surprised her.

'It was nice giving the photos; everybody's very pleased.'

Jane looked at her worst.

'So they ought to be. They are the loveliest photographs any of them ever saw.'

Christmas day was quite perfect. All the Christmas things happened only much more and much grander than usual. The children had stockings just bulging with presents. After church everybody drank egg-nog, which was the proper drink for Christmas morning in America. There was a glorious Christmas dinner in the middle of the day, with everything that should be there and lots extra. In the afternoon John took the family out in the car to deliver special presents. The first was Tim's for the Antonios. He had bought them scented candles to burn in front of their best picture. The Antonios were terribly pleased and kissed Tim on both cheeks, and gave him an enormous box of chocolates, and as the family drove away stood outside their drug store waving.

'Make'a da good Christmas. Have'a da good time.'

The family did not drive up to the Fossils' front door as Bee said they must not be asked in or they would be late and annoy Aunt Cora, so Tim was sent with Rachel's parcel. In it was a needlebook she had made for Nana, a calendar for Aunt Sylvia and for Posy something Rachel thought lovely, and which had cost much more than anybody else's present — a little pair of silver ballet shoes on a brooch.

To Jane's great disappointment there was nobody at home at the Does'. She had hoped to see David. It had worried her that only he and her Mr Browne had not given her presents. It was not that she wanted a present from David but he said so little, and it's difficult to know if a person is liking you when they don't talk to you. If he had given her a present it would have been a sign he liked her enough to bother, and that might mean, before the picture was finished, he would like her enough to teach her his magic. Jane left her present for David on the empty porch; as she got back into the car it seemed as if some of the shimmer of happiness that covered the day had gone.

At Aunt Cora's the house was full of people. There was a huge Christmas tree in the living-room blazing with lights, and round it were more parcels than it seemed possible could be meant for one house. All the family had gorgeous things but each of the children had one present which was so perfect it made all the others seem unimportant. Rachel had a huge box from Posy. In it was the special black tunic and tights Manoff liked his pupils to wear, and one pair of new ballet shoes and one pair of worn ones. On the worn ones was written, 'I wore these the first time I danced the Sugar-Plum Fairy. Hope they bring you luck. Love, Posy'. As she undid her other parcels Rachel's heart felt as if it were singing.

'Posy's shoes! A pair she's actually danced in! Oh, lucky, lucky me!'

Tim had a huge box from Brent. Goodness knows where

253

Brent had found it but what was in that box might have been invented especially for him and Tim. There was not a practical joke missing. Sham lighted cigarettes with burns to lay under them. Pools of indiarubber ink to lay beside an overturned ink-pot. Things that lifted plates. Things that squeaked and grunted and jumped. They were all there. Tim was spellbound by such a multiplicity of jokes.

'Look, Mum! I can do something new every day the rest of the time I'm here.'

Even on Christmas day Bee could remember that those sort of jokes every day might not be a riot with Aunt Cora.

'Wonderful, darling. Do you think tomorrow you and I might look at each one separately and decide to do what when?'

Jane thought her most beautiful present was the first she opened. It was a lovely little wrist-watch. On the card with it was written 'From Hyde Park and myself with best wishes. Your Mr Browne'. But presently she opened a parcel which made her forget there were any other presents in the world. It was a plain cardboard box with none of the grand American fixings of massed bows and flowers. Inside was something done up in brown paper. Inside that was an exact duplicate of David's reed pipe. On a piece of paper David had written, 'Happy Christmas. I'll teach you to play this. David'.

The evening finished with carols. Tim played and everybody stood round his piano. On the top of the piano, where he could keep his eye on it, was Brent's trick box. Rachel had her arms hugged to her and inside them were Posy's old shoes. Jane, wearing her wrist-watch, held the box with her pipe. As Tim crashed out the opening chords of 'O, come all ye faithful' everybody's eyes were bright, even Aunt Cora's, but nobody's eyes shone quite so shiningly as Jane's.

CHAPTER 24

ELLA

THERE is often a grumpy nothing-nice-will-ever-happen-again feeling after Christmas. The Winters usually had severe attacks of this, but this year so much was going on they missed even a touch of it. Even Rachel remained gay long after Christmas. Her dancing lessons stopped for a while round Christmas, but there were Manoff's Saturdays. To Rachel, Manoff's dancing mornings were so exciting that all the rest of Saturday after them she went round in a sort of daze. She tried to tell her family what it was like.

'Of course most of it's much too difficult for me, but just being there is simply superb. I get into a corner for bar practice. I think there's a shadow there and Monsieur Manoff won't see me, but anyway he wouldn't tell me anything; I'm only there because Posy asked him. When we do centre work you just can't believe what it's like. Manoff shows us steps, three or four at a time, some of them terribly difficult. When he does fast ones it's like fireworks just going off, and when he does slow ones it all slides together as if it was water coming out of a tap.'

'Splendid, dear,' said Peaseblossom. 'Wonderful chance for you; up the Winters!'

Rachel shook her head.

'It's a wonderful chance but you ought to see Posy dancing me at a Manoff Saturday. She did it last Sunday. Nana, Aunt Sylvia and Pauline laughed so much tears ran all down their faces. I tried to laugh too, but actually I felt rather wormish. But when Posy finished, Pauline told her to do her imitation of the first time she danced in front of Manoff. Posy – she would, she's that sort – went uninvited on to the stage where Manoff's company was dancing in London, and she made him see her dance. It's awfully funny as she does it; she gives herself directions in broken English and then she makes her feet try and catch up with the directions, but I expect it wasn't like that really. I can't imagine her in the learning stage.'

For Tim there was no question of Christmas grumpiness. There was that absorbing box of tricks and there was Hiram's Hour, with Brent and more tricks. In spite of John's, Bee's and Peaseblossom's efforts Tim managed to work three tricks on Aunt Cora. The ink on her desk, a cat's miaow from under the cushion of her chair when she sat down, and a snake in her bath. The last was so realistic that Aunt Cora had hysterics and had to go to bed for the rest of the day with not only a nervous but a dizzy spell. The hysterics caused such confusion that even Bella was cross, and Tim could see he had gone too far. He knew for certain he had gone too far when John told him he was a pestiferous little horror, and one more trick on Aunt Cora and he would burn the whole box of jokes. Tim knew that John was like Peaseblossom; if he said a certain punishment would follow a certain crime it would follow all right, so he said:

'Don't fuss, Dad. I won't do any more to her. As a matter of fact, I won't even do one in a room where she could go. But I wish I hadn't an aunt who's like that.'

The Secret Garden was getting on. The painted garden was changed from a bare wintry garden, with only the noses of the bulbs showing, to a garden blazing with flowers. In some films the director is very careless about the right trees and flowers for the place where the picture is supposed to be but not Jane's Mr Browne. All the proper things followed each other. First there had been snowdrops, crocuses, winter aconites, and scyllas sticking up through the grass under bare winter trees. Then they were changed and daffodils, jonquils, and narcissi began to replace them. Not in a sudden, startling way but a few more were put in every day so that people, seeing the picture, could watch the garden coming alive. With the daffodils a slight green fuzz was put on the trees, and this was slowly changed to buds, and then to buds unfolding into tiny leaves. As Mary, instructed by Dickon, cut back dead branches and tangles of ivy lovely hidden things appeared, as they would in a real garden. Early flowering fruit trees and forsythia, and the petals of these were arranged to drop, and as they dropped other flowering things were shown in bud. Lilac, may, and chestnut. With the coming of the leaves the green men of the picture crew became busy. Of course, even in a painted garden, three children could not play and work under trees without the shadows thrown by branches and leaves showing on their clothes and faces. Naturally the right shadows would not come from painted trees in an artificial garden under an artificial sun, but the green men made that right. They fixed the flickering shadows as artificial breezes blew, and they also fixed a kind of pattern of shadows of leaves and branches through which could be seen the ghost of Colin's mother, who was always in the garden now that Colin was there. Jane still thought it absolutely idiotic to have the ghost of Colin's mother hanging about, but there was so much that was nice going on that she never actually said how silly she thought it, which was lucky for nobody wanted to know what Jane thought.

Immediately after Christmas David started to teach Jane to play her pipes. Hearing the little, soft, calling music David's pipes made, Jane thought that after a few lessons she could make the same sounds, but not a bit of it. To play pipes needs patience and a certain natural ability. Jane had neither. If it had not been David who was teaching her, and the beginning of her being an animal trainer which would come from learning, Jane would have lost her temper at her very first lesson. She was clumsy with the pipes and, instead of David's magic tune, dreary squawks came out of them. It was the most difficult thing Jane had ever done to go on trying hard, and looking fairly pleasant at the same time. But somehow she managed it, for she thought that David would think somebody who lost her temper at pipe lessons not worth teaching. As usual when anything was going wrong, she kept it to herself. She said to Rachel:

'You just couldn't think how easy it is. Of course I can only practise between shots and Mickey isn't there, but if he was he'd fly straight to me.'

Rachel spoke to Bee about this.

'I do think, Mum, you ought to ask David to teach Jane go-away as well as come-to-me tunes on those pipes. Just think what Saxon Crescent is going to be like if she plays her pipes there. Full of cats, dogs, pigeons, sparrows and, I expect, seagulls.'

Bee was surprised.

'I will, darling, if I get a chance, but I'm amazed she's supposed to be learning fast for she makes the most ghastly noises; I spend my time apologizing about it.'

The picture had reached the stage where Colin was able to walk down the steps into the garden with only a little help from Mary and Dickon. Because it was a film, the secret that he was getting stronger was not so well kept as it was in the book. The wicked doctor cousin was getting more and more suspicious and frightened, and was planning ways of killing Colin. Jane's Mr Browne was directing the picture in such a way that the people who saw the film were supposed to feel the only times that Colin was really safe was in the secret garden. A scene had been shot by what was supposed to be Lake Como in Italy. It was a scene taken almost entirely from the book. Colin's father was sitting by the edge of the lake and he dropped off to sleep. Then he had a dream. Colin's mother appeared out of a mist over the water. She called out 'Archie. Archie,' which was Colin's father's name, and he got up and answered 'Lilias. Lilias,' which was her name. 'Where are you?' and she, fading as she spoke, whispered, 'In the garden. In the garden.' Then Colin's father woke up to find the postman had brought him a letter from Dickon's mother. A letter asking him to come home. After that there were a whole lot of scenes of horses galloping through the night and Mr Craven straining forward always saying 'Faster. Faster.'

Meanwhile none of this excitement showed in the garden. They had long ago passed the scene when old Ben Weatherstaff had found out that the children were making the secret garden their own garden, and they had passed the scene where Dickon's mother had visited them, the one which made her write the letter to Colin's father. They had played several sequences where they picnicked off the food Dickon's mother sent so as to fool the wicked doctor cousin that Colin was still too ill to eat a decent meal, but they had not shot any scenes where Dickon brought the creatures he had tamed on the moor into the garden. Jane's Mr Browne had kept that for the end, when the garden had come properly alive, and there was plenty of cover for the creatures to run into, and leaves on the trees for shelter for the birds.

One day when David and Jane had done all their lessons in the morning, and had an almost free afternoon, for they were shooting what Jane called 'sloppy bits', which were scenes between Colin and the ghost of his mother, David said, in the middle of a pipe lesson:

'Reckon that's better.'

Jane was overwhelmed at what, from David, was terrific praise.

'Do you really reckon it was? Oh, I am glad.'

David turned his pipes round and round. When he spoke again his slow words seemed more pushed out of him than usual.

'Tomorrow they're shooting most of my creatures.'

'In the garden?'

David had a worried look.

'Yes.'

Jane's eyes shone.

'How gorgeous! I've done that scene with Miss Steiman and I thought it was only Mickey was there.'

David was not listening to Jane but following his own thoughts.

'Bob'll be all right but the rest aren't fixed good for meeting folks; I'm feared they'll be scared.'

'You mean they won't even work with you?'

'Alone they would, but I can't be every place.'

Jane gazed at David, hardly believing what she heard.

'You mean you want me to help you with them? You'd let me help?'

David nodded.

'So they're not scared.'

As always when David was using his creatures in the picture, he had them on the set well before the shooting began to get them settled down. In this scene Colin had already been helped down the steps and was sitting on the grass and Mary was gardening. As Jane's Mr Browne had planned the picture Dickon brought a baby lamb to show Colin, and was to give it to him to hold, while he sat under a tree and piped until presently a little fox, four rabbits, Bob the squirrel of course, Mickey and, as well, a crow and a cock pheasant were sitting round or on him. Nobody interfered with David or his arrangements for his creatures for he alone knew what was best for them, so when he told Mr Phelps he wanted Jane to be on the set early Mr Phelps, though surprised, passed on the message to Bee.

To Jane the time spent in the garden with David and his creatures before the shooting began was something she was to remember all her life. It was the slowness and gentleness of everything that was so odd, and it was even odder that she, who hated slowness, wished that the time would go on for ever. David had an almost new lamb in his arms which he stroked all the while he was talking. He spoke even more slowly and

softly than usual. He said the lamb was called Ella and was
terribly scared, so he would give her to Jane in a minute so
as to get her accustomed to strange people holding her.
Presently he did just that. First he told Jane to pick up a
feeding bottle of milk which was under a painted rose bush.
Then to sit down and he would put Ella in her arms. Jane
hardly breathed as Ella's little soft, helpless body was laid on
her lap. Would she stay? Would she? For a moment it looked
as though she would not. She gave a terrified start. 'Stroke
her,' David said. 'Stroke her then give her the bottle.' Jane
stroked and whispered loving words, then very gently she

lifted the bottle and put the teat into Ella's mouth. For a second nothing happened, then Ella gave a wriggle to make herself more cosy, and began to suck. Jane dare not speak but she looked at David and her eyes would have told him Ella had settled down even if he had not been able to see she had for himself.

David began to talk again. It was the sort of introducing talk he had done at her test. He said that somewhere about were old friends of Jane's that she had met in the place on the lot where they lived. Andy, the cock pheasant, four of the rabbits, Joe, Arthur, Mary and Ann. Pedro, the fox; Jack, the crow and, as well of course, Mickey and Bob. Then he began to pipe and what happened was real magic. Mickey, of course, came first. Then two little eyes twinkled from behind a clump of tulips and Bob hopped out. David stopped piping for a moment and threw a handful of food towards Jane. Then he piped again and one by one the four rabbits were out nibbling; then, very shyly, the baby fox crept out from behind a peach tree and crawled up to David. Then, with an I'm-not-afraid-of-anybody caw, Jack, the crow, flew from a lilac bush on to David's shoulder and, as if encouraged by Jack, Andy, the pheasant, hopped on to the path and stood still, gazing at David with his head on one side. Jane went on stroking Ella and hoping and hoping just one of the creatures would come near her.

'If they do,' she thought, 'I'm helping David and I'm beginning to be part of taming them,' and in her mind she added Chewing-gum to the group. Not the Chewing-gum she knew, who was not obedient and inclined to chase any bird he saw, but a new Chewing-gum who sat down beside her and looked at Ella with worshipping eyes.

Presently Bob had eaten all the nuts near him and he skipped towards Jane. He looked at her thoughtfully: was this the girl he knew? Yes, of course it was. Why, he had met her not only in his cage but in this very garden. As if she were not there he picked up a nut that was almost touching her knee. Two of the rabbits, Joe and Ann, seeing how little fussed Bob was had a word with each other. Jane could imagine what they were saying. 'That's the girl David's brought along to see us. That's a good-looking lettuce beside her. Let's have a nibble.'

Jane's Mr Browne's voice came from somewhere behind David.

'Can you get rid of them without frightening them? Then we'll get cracking.'

David got rid of his creatures by getting up and taking Ella from Jane and wandering off with her down the garden. As he went the animals scuttled and the birds flew after him.

Jane's Mr Browne took Jane and Maurice through their scenes. The sequence was that Dickon, having wheeled Colin into the garden, had gone to fetch his creatures. Mary, with her rake, was weeding, and as she weeded she talked to Colin sitting on the grass beside her. They were discussing the magic in the garden, which was not only bringing the garden alive but making Colin's legs strong so that he could walk. That sequence finished as Dickon's pipe was heard, and was the beginning of the scenes with the creatures in them.

Maurice, as usual, did his scenes with Jane faultlessly, and Jane was better than usual; she was so eager to get to the scenes with David, and going to enjoy them so much, that she could almost be nice to Maurice without thinking of him as a chipmunk. All the same, the time it took to take the first shots bored her dreadfully, and she needed nobody to tell her to look up with a face shining with pleasure when at last she heard David's pipe.

Maurice was told not to move. Jane was to take a few steps towards David. In the first scene with the creatures only Ella was used. While Jane's Mr Browne was explaining to Maurice what he wanted him to do, and what he wanted him to feel, David whispered to Jane that it should be all right.

Full of the milk Jane had given her Ella had gone to sleep, and most likely would not know that she had been in Maurice's arms. Jane looked at Ella. 'Lucky Maurice,' she thought. 'It would be him who has to hold her.'

It was decided not to disturb Ella by rehearsing her. David pretended to give her to Maurice, and Maurice pretended to take her, but the real giving and taking waited till the cameras were rolling.

Jane had nothing to do in that scene except look interested, which was no trouble at all because she was. Her eyes on Ella she watched David cross to Maurice and very softly put her in his arms. Ella was either a very light sleeper or she was not as fast asleep as David thought, for the second Maurice touched her she opened her eyes, and on seeing him leapt out of his arms and out of the picture. Jane's Mr Browne said quietly, 'Cut', they would start the scene again. They started it four times but it was no good, Ella just would not be touched by Maurice. It was a new experience for Jane to see a scene being shot over and over again because somebody not herself was doing it wrong.

'I bet Maurice blames Ella,' she thought. 'But I know just how Ella feels and I don't blame her at all.'

Presently the lights were switched off and Jane's Mr Browne and David had a long talk. At the end Mr Phelps came up to Jane.

'David's after thinking the lamb'll come to you. Mr Browne'll try it that way.'

Another rehearsal took place. This time they went back to the scene which finished with David's pipe. As Jane heard the notes she had to drop her rake and go and sit on the grass beside Colin, while Colin said his line, 'It's Dickon. Oh, I hope the creatures will like me.'

That scene went badly. Maurice was furious that Jane was to hold Ella.

'Come on, Maurice,' Jane's Mr Browne said. 'You said

those lines all right at the first take. Now all the life's gone out of them.'

Maurice made an effort and after a few tries, because he really was a good actor, he got the lines fairly right, but never as well as he had the first time. The moment the lights were switched off he ran to his mother, his face scarlet with temper.

'Talk to Mr Browne, Mummy. I'm the star of this picture. People will like to see me holding a lamb. It will make a lovely still. I won't have that Jane hold her. It's my scene. Mine. Mine. Mine.'

Mrs Tuesday went to Jane's Mr Browne.

'Little Maurice is upset. He was so looking forward to cuddling the lamb; besides, it would have made a sweetly pretty still. I do hope you won't disappoint him; he is such a highly-strung little boy and so easily upset.'

Jane's Mr Browne was used to Mrs Tuesday. In every picture there was some place where she thought Maurice had not enough to do, and so might be upset. When he could, because Maurice was important to the studio, Mr Browne gave in to her, but not, of course, if it spoilt his picture. This time he couldn't give in because nobody could make Ella do what she didn't want to do. He explained this to Mrs Tuesday, but Mrs Tuesday was not satisfied.

'I shall have a talk with Mr Bettelheimer. My boy's the most wonderful little boy Bee Bee studios have ever had under contract and I won't have him slighted.'

Jane's Mr Browne told Mr Phelps to call Jane and Maurice on to the set.

'I guess Mrs Tuesday needn't worry any,' he said. 'My bet is Ella won't go to Jane either. In which case we won't have the lamb in the picture.'

Jane had said nothing since she had been told she was to hold Ella. The hairdresser fiddled with her hair and the make-up woman mopped her face with a tissue, but she never opened her mouth. She stood with her eyes shut clasping her pipe. When Bee asked if anything was wrong she only shook her head, and Bee supposed she was playing some game. But it was not a game. Jane was using her will. Over and over again she was repeating in her head, 'If Ella comes to me I've begun to learn magic. She's got to come to me. She's got to. She's got to.'

There were no words in the first scene with Ella. As David came slowly towards her Jane could hear her own heart beating. Ella was not asleep and David was stroking her. David came nearer and nearer. The cameras were rolling. The lights blazing down on the garden. Then David was beside her. He knelt and gave her Ella. For a second it was certain Ella would not stay. Then Jane, stroking her gently, whispered a line that was not in the script, 'Stay with me, darling. Stay with me.'

Jane's Mr Browne said 'Cut', and mopped his forehead. Mr Phelps grinned.

'The little spalpeen! If you make pictures for the next fifty years you'll never get anything more natural than that.' He broke off. 'Begorrah, what's happening?'

What was happening was Maurice was having a screaming attack. As the cameras stopped rolling he threw himself on the ground and kicked and howled.

Because Maurice had hysterics the other shots with Ella and the creatures had to wait until the next day. As they finished early and John would not call for them until six Bee took Jane home in a taxi. Jane was so quiet Bee asked if anything was wrong. Jane looked at her, her eyes shining as if large lamps were behind them.

'Nothing. It's been the most beautiful day of my whole life. I had all that time with David's creatures and none of them minded me. Ella lay in my arms, but I never thought I'd hold her in the picture.'

Bee had felt very awkward while Maurice had hysterics. She had kept out of Mrs Tuesday's way, but Mrs Norstrum had shaken her head and said it was unlucky, that Mrs Tuesday might go on being upset for days.

'I'm rather sorry about that, darling. It's nearly the end of the picture and we don't want Mrs Tuesday or Maurice upset.'

Jane gave a pleased wriggle.

'I do. When he screamed was the most beautiful part of the most beautiful day.'

CHAPTER 25

TIM'S BIRTHDAY

Aunt Cora gave a party for Tim's birthday. There was a very good treasure hunt, and various games with prizes, and a magnificent tea with a great pink and white cake with Tim's name on the top and nine pink candles. The children Aunt Cora invited were very birthday-minded; though hardly any of them had known Tim till that afternoon each of them brought him a present, done up in the beautiful American way with gay-coloured papers and enormous ribbon bows, and very nice presents they were; as well, when he cut his cake they all sang 'Happy birthday to you'.

At six o'clock the mothers and fathers of the children, as well as lots of other grown-up people, arrived for drinks. To begin with that part of the party was all right. Posy came, which pleased Rachel, and though of course Tim had to hand round everybody was nice and said, 'Happy birthday, Tim,' and lots of them had brought him presents, mostly boxes of chocolates, which they called candy, again done up too beautifully for words. Then suddenly Mrs Tuesday and Maurice arrived and the Winters were forgotten.

Mrs Tuesday seldom took Maurice to a party as she thought that people appreciated more their enormous good luck in meeting him if they only saw him as a special treat. Tim and Rachel stood in a corner watching Maurice being introduced to people by Aunt Cora. Rachel was filled with unwilling admiration.

'Of course he's an awful show-off, but I must say he does it well.'

Tim sighed.

'I do wish Aunt Cora wasn't here. I'd do one of my best jokes on him.'

Rachel glanced at him anxiously.

'You do remember you absolutely promised.'

'I know I did, but it's not breaking my promise to wish Aunt Cora wasn't here. It isn't often I agree with Jane about anything, but I do about him.'

Bee, with Jane, had been driven from the studio in Maurice's car. She came up to them and kissed Tim.

'Had a good party, darling?'

'It was, but it isn't improved since that Maurice came.'

Bee looked round anxiously to see Mrs Tuesday wasn't about.

'Don't you start that, Tim. We've enough trouble with Jane. He's all right really.'

Tim looked reproachfully after Bee.

'It's sad what things even the best mother can say.'

Jane, in the yellow muslin Aunt Cora gave her, looking as if Peaseblossom had brushed and washed her very fast, joined them. She had a very Jane-ish expression.

'I hope you're enjoying having him here. Isn't he awful? I had to drive home in his car sitting by him; luckily Mrs Tuesday kept on talk, talk, talk so I didn't have to say anything, which was a good thing for if I had I would only have said, "What a pity you couldn't hold Ella, Maurice".'

A group of people were gathered round Mrs Tuesday. Sentences flowed across to the children.

'Such a wonderful actor. . .' 'My, you must be proud. . .' 'He's so cute. . .'

When Mrs Tuesday spoke about her son her voice was awed and reverent.

'He is rather special, though of course a terrible responsibility. I don't look upon him as my son, but as a child who belongs to the world and has been entrusted to me to bring up.'

The Winters turned away their heads and made faces to show what they thought. Tim made a sound like somebody going to be sick.

John joined the group round Mrs Tuesday to see if anybody wanted a drink. One of Aunt Cora's friends laid a hand on his arm. There was a twinkle in his eye.

'Why, Mr Winter, you must hear what Mrs Tuesday's telling us about Maurice.'

Being a party John had to be polite. The children saw him, as he looked at Mrs Tuesday, push his face into an interested, polite shape.

'Poor Dad,' Rachel whispered. 'What a shame! He doesn't want to hear about him.'

Jane gave a pleased wriggle.

'I'm glad he's got to. I'm glad he should know all I ever said about Maurice is absolutely true.'

Mrs Tuesday was looking earnestly at John.

'I was saying he was not an ordinary boy, Mr Winter. Why, sometimes, when I've watched him working on a picture, I've said to myself, he can't be real; he just can't be; he's too special. And what the studio think! You'd never believe! Why, Mr Benjamin Bettelheimer himself said to me, "Take care of that boy of yours, Mrs Tuesday, he's too clever to live." Those were his very words.'

Jane nudged Rachel.

'I bet they weren't. I bet she's made that up.'

The guests turned to look at Maurice. He was surrounded by the 'darling children'. The children who had been so nice all the afternoon had, from the Winters' standards, slipped badly. They had all brought autograph albums or had pieces of paper for Maurice to sign. Still they had been nice so Tim forgave them.

'I expect they want his autograph for a swop.'

John, whose polite face had only just held out while Mrs Tuesday was talking, took advantage of everybody looking at Maurice to move away. He came to the children.

'What are you bunched together here for? Hop it and get some plates and hand round. And you'd better go and wash, Tim; your fingers must be sticky and I expect any minute now your aunt will want you to play.'

Jane put a hand in John's and tugged at his arm to make him lean down to her.

'Isn't he worse even than I told you?'

John laughed.

'I'll give you he's unlucky in his mother. The poor kid hasn't a chance.'

Tim did not mind the rest of the party because he was at the piano and, though nobody listened much, he did not care for he was always happy at a piano, and, anyway, it was far nicer playing than handing round food and being polite.

When everybody seemed to have gone Aunt Cora said would the family give the living-room a bit of a tidy up as she hated to see it mussed up. She would do it herself only she was just fit to drop, and if Tim would excuse her from his birthday supper she would go right up to bed, or she'd surely wake with one of her nervous spells.

As soon as Aunt Cora was safely upstairs Rachel burst out:

'Stop tidying. Posy hasn't gone, she's in the kitchen talking to Bella. She danced Mrs Tuesday for me in the hall when she was saying good-bye and I said she must dance her for you.'

Only Rachel had seen Posy's dancing imitations. She danced Mrs Tuesday so that nobody could miss who she was being. Everybody laughed so much they ached. Tim and Jane had to lie on the floor, and they all had to stuff things in their mouths so Aunt Cora wouldn't hear. Once Posy started her dancing imitations it was difficult to stop her. She danced Maurice, a funny, strutting little dance with a fixed smile on her face and her eyes turned to the sky. She danced Bella trying to watch the party and cook Tim's birthday supper at the same time. Finally, without saying who she was dancing, she danced Aunt Cora, too tired to lift her feet, her hands stretching out for food and then being snatched back as she remembered her diet, and all the time smiling and bowing to her guests. It was the best of all. John whooped and hiccuped with laughter and the tears streamed down his cheeks. Bee had to hold her hands as well as her handkerchief over her mouth to hold back the sound of her laughing from Aunt Cora, and the children rolled on the floor. Only Peaseblossom did not enjoy it. She had thought Posy dancing Mrs Tuesday in bad taste because Mrs Tuesday had been a guest and she had tried to bring the children up never to criticize guests, but she thought dancing Aunt Cora like that terrible.

'Very clever I know, but we mustn't forget how good she's been to us; that's not our way, is it?'

Rachel could see in Posy's eye that in another minute she would dance Peaseblossom, but luckily the door opened and Bella's old, beaming face looked in.

'Yo' supper's on the table an' seein' Miss Cora don't feel so good I fixed her place for you, Miss Posy.'

After Tim's birthday it was frightening how fast the time passed. One minute their leaving seemed weeks away, and the next boxes were being packed, and on John's writing-table were piles of labels with *Mauretania* on them, or W or Cabin Class.

Photographs taken when the family had visited the studio arrived. They were all good, but there was one of Rachel that the family were a little startled by. Rachel had worn one of the prettier of Posy's frocks, and had brushed her hair loose and tied a ribbon round it, a style which was becoming to her, but otherwise she was just her usual self. The photograph was really what is called 'a speaking likeness' only somehow Rachel looked not just pretty but downright lovely.

'Goodness!' Tim said. 'You look like a movie star.'

Peaseblossom made disapproving, clicking noises.

'Tch! Tch! Very nice just for once, but I prefer you with two sensible plaits.'

Jane thought Rachel looked marvellous. She had seen lots of stills of herself and she never looked like that. But she was not jealous. After all, there was the still of her holding Ella, which she would not have exchanged to look like Rachel or anyone else. All the same, her tongue could not twist itself round nice words.

'It reminds me of pictures of Maurice.'

Bee was delighted with the photograph. In her mind she had already framed it and put it on a table in the drawing-room in Saxon Crescent.

273

'They say we can have some more. We must get some for friends at home, and the grannies must each have one.'

John said:

'And Mrs Bones. And you should send one to Madame Fidolia, Rachel. She'll like it for her office.'

Rachel, from the moment she had seen the photograph, had her own idea about it. She would give it to Posy. Posy would not want a photograph of her. Why should she? But Posy might see her differently if she saw that photograph, and she might show it to Monsieur Manoff. Now that she attended the Manoff Saturdays the only way Manoff saw her was with her hair in a net, the way he made all his dancers wear their hair when practising, and, though it was useful to show the line of the neck, nobody could say it was becoming. He might have forgotten how she could look with her hair loose. Seeing that photograph, if only, only Posy showed it to him, might be the final thing to make him say to her, 'You will come to me and I will make you a great artiste.'

Another thing that happened was hearing the first of Tim's records. John, Peaseblossom, Rachel and Tim went to the recording studio to hear it. On one side Tim had played his beloved 'Jardin sous la pluie' and on the other Mendelssohn's 'Rondo Capriccio'. Everybody, including the people who had made the record, thought it good, but Tim was critical of the Debussy. He did not like anything about it. On the other hand he approved sufficiently of the Mendelssohn to have a record sent as a present to Mr Brown, and to order one for Brent.

Now that their time was so short they were all worrying about good-bye presents. Fortunately there was rather a good still taken at the studio of Jane surrounded by all the family which, if put in a grand silver frame, would be splendid for John and Bee to give Bella.

'And I can give the Antonios my records,' Tim said. 'They could go in the juke box and they'd make money out of them.'

But a present from John and Bee to Bella, and one from Tim to the Antonios only touched the edge of the present giving that had got to happen. For Bee, John and Peaseblossom there were masses of Aunt Cora's friends who had been terribly good to them, especially two sets who, in these last weeks, had taken them for trips, one to the Grand Canyon and another to Palm Springs. Then, of course, there was Aunt Cora. Though she might whine and have nervous spells she had been a wonderful hostess, and as well had to work towards the end, for when John, Bee and Peaseblossom went away for two week-ends it was she who took Jane to the studio and arranged about taxis for Rachel's dancing on Saturday, and she also had Jane and Tim on her hands the whole of two Sundays, which was no rest cure. She had said when John told her about the second week-end, 'My! I know they mean no harm, but having them about all day gets me so nervous! I just don't know if I'm standing up or lying down. If only Rachel did not spend her Sundays with that Miss Fozzle she might help. My! Just thinking of Sunday gives me a dizzy spell.' All the same she had taken on the week-ends, so she was certainly deserving of something pretty startling as a present.

For Rachel there were a tremendous number of presents to consider. Almost every Sunday she had spent with the Fossils, and Aunt Sylvia and Nana, as well as Posy, had been wonderful to her. Then there was Madame Donna and a lot of the girls in her school and, of course, Monsieur Manoff.

'What on earth does a person give somebody like Monsieur Manoff?' Rachel moaned to Jane.

As usual they were talking in bed.

'I'd wait. If he's going to ask you to stay and learn from him you needn't give him anything.'

'What are you going to give people? Like your Mr Browne and Mr Phelps and all those? And Shirley and David and everybody?'

It was dark for Peaseblossom had drawn the curtains, so Rachel could not see Jane's chin stick out, but she could hear the tone of her voice.

'I've made my arrangements.'

Rachel was used to Jane so she turned over.

'If you don't want to tell me I won't waste time asking. I'll go to sleep.'

But Jane did not go to sleep. It was not true she had made her arrangements. She lay staring into the blackness, planning and planning.

CHAPTER 26

LAST THINGS

JANE had the first good-byes to say. The shooting of *The Secret Garden* finished quite a time before she left for England. It was funny, after being the most important thing in her life, the film began to fade away like the Cheshire cat's smile in *Alice in Wonderland*. There were last scenes to shoot, some retakes, and then it was over. The good-byes Jane had to say, at the end of the last day's shooting which concerned her, were not the real studio good-byes. They were to the camera, lighting, and microphone crews, the wardrobe, the make-up and all the other people working on the mechanics of the film. She had not to say good-bye to Maurice, Shirley or David, for she was still attending the studio school, nor to her Mr Browne nor Mr Phelps. She would see them when she said her real good-byes on the day before they sailed home, the day when all the family were to see the picture, not the finished picture audiences all over the world would see, but good enough to tell how the finished version would look. It was for that real good-bye day that Jane was making plans.

Tim was the first to say good-bye to great friends. It was his last Hiram's Hour and Brent made quite an occasion of it. As well as playing the piano Tim had to say good-bye to the listeners. Because it was Tim's last performance John, Aunt Cora, Peaseblossom, Rachel and lots of Aunt Cora's friends were given seats for the show, but from Tim's point of view it was a poor evening. It started off all right with Brent pretending he had sniffed laughing gas, and there were jokes and tricks to follow which promised well, but somehow nothing went quite right. The truth was neither Tim nor Brent felt very funny. Tim hated to say good-bye to Brent and Brent to Tim. Luckily the audience did not seem to mind, and seemed to enjoy Brent making a serious speech saying good-bye as much as saying something funny. He called Tim 'this little guy', and said he was going to miss him so much, he figured he would have to go to England one day to visit him. After the show there was a kind of party in a dressing-room for everybody who had been in a Hiram's Hour programme with Tim, and as well Mr Hiram P. Sneltzworther came. Tim gave the presents he had brought. He had wanted to give tricks, but had not been able to find new ones, so he had to buy sensible things instead. He bought pencils with their names printed on them for the gentlemen who sang the advertisements for the second-hand cars, and for Brent he had something he would have liked himself – a magnificent fountain pen.

Everybody drank Tim's health after that and then Brent held up a hand for silence. He said that he would value his pen all his life, just as he knew the singing boys would their pencils, and they wanted Tim to have something he would value all his life. He was too young yet to use the gift they had chosen for him, but they hoped he would grow up to enjoy it. He then unfastened a leather case, and there was a magnificent silver cigarette box, with Tim's name and the date and nice things written on the top. Tim thought it was a beautiful box, but inside him he wished they had chosen something else; it was such a long time before he would be allowed to smoke. Brent and the singing gentlemen came forward with their cigarette cases open. Brent said:

'Maybe you won't use these yourself right away, but you'll feel kind of mean if you haven't cigarettes to offer your pals.'

Tim took one cigarette from each case. A little button thing opened the cigarette box. He pressed it. The lid shot up and then the marvel happened. Although it really was a cigarette box it was a musical box as well. As Tim opened it it played, tinklingly but charmingly, 'The Last Rose of Summer'.

Tim was enchanted; he thought it was the best present he had ever been given, even better than Brent's trick box that he had for Christmas. Visions of the number of people he could fool with a box like that dashed about in his head.

'I shan't pack it. I shall carry it in my hand all the way to London. I shall say to people on the train and on the *Mauretania*, "Would you like a cigarette?" Can't you see their faces when it plays!'

John had been having a drink with Mr Hiram P. Sneltzworther. He laid a hand on Tim's shoulder.

'It's your bedtime. Thank everybody and come along.' Then he looked at Brent. 'I don't believe you've improved my journey home. I expect I shall hear those six tunes a great many times before we get to London.'

Tim clutched the box to him. His face was pink he was so proud of it.

'You will.'

Rachel had to say the next good-bye. It was the last Manoff Saturday. On Saturdays, when she got up, she dressed in the tunic and tights Posy had given her, and John drove her to her class with just a coat over them. Because it was good-bye Saturday she felt quite emotional as she pulled on her tights.

'I can't bear it if I never wear these again.'

Jane was never very good-tempered in the mornings.

'Why wouldn't you wear them again? Posy gave them to you.'

Rachel smoothed a wrinkle on her leg.

'They won't feel the same anywhere else. Oh, Jane, if only Mr Manoff would say "You will stay with me and I will make you into a beautiful artiste", like he said to Posy.'

Jane gasped.

'Stay here! All alone when we go home. You couldn't.'

'I could.' Rachel crossed to the dressing-table. Then she gave a squeak. 'Goodness, a spot on my nose! Does it show dreadfully?'

Jane joined Rachel and had a look at her nose.

'Not terribly. I mean it sticks out like spots do. I do hope Peaseblossom doesn't say we're having too many good-bye parties when she sees it.'

Rachel put on her tunic.

'If I'd known it would give me spots I wouldn't have eaten anything extra, even at a party. To think my whole future might be ruined by a spot on the nose.'

After the class Rachel was to have more good-byes to say. She was to go home with Posy and say good-bye to the Fossil household. Her arms were full of good-bye parcels when she got into the car. John said:

'Mrs Father Christmas this morning?'

'Tell me truthfully, Dad. If I was a person you didn't know what's the first thing you'd notice about me today?'

John had heard Peaseblossom on the spot at breakfast.

'I shouldn't notice that spot if that's what you were thinking about.'

'Wouldn't you? Oh, I'm glad! It feels terrible to me.'

In three weeks Manoff was taking his ballet to dance in Chicago. He had not had a proper ballet company since he had come to America as a refugee from Czechoslovakia, which was before the Second World War. He had given lessons all the time, and worked hard himself, but he had not danced regularly in public, and he had been forced to let his great find, Posy, earn her living dancing in pictures. Now he was not only starting again with a big company and new ballets, but he was to have his dream of showing Posy to the world. All these things made him nervous, and rather bad-tempered. Rachel, working at the bar in the corner she had chosen because she thought she did not show there, could feel that the dancers, men and women working round her, were sort of strung up and scared. Presently Monsieur Manoff said they would now do centre practice. They would start with Posy's *pas de deux* with himself in his ballet about birds and go on to the *corps de ballet*'s entrance.

The *pas de deux* was so lovely that Rachel thought of nothing else while Manoff and Posy were dancing, in fact she had to scurry into the back row for the birds' entrance. Suddenly Monsieur Manoff stamped and help up his hand.

'Stop. Stop. It is as if heavy turkeys were in a farmyard. There is no delicacy, no charm. Little friend of Posy's at the back, you are as a little bird. Dance the steps to show these stupids how it should be.'

Rachel forgot to be nervous. They were charming steps for her, and she felt like a bird. As she finished Manoff beckoned her to him. Trembling at the honour Rachel curtsied, murmuring, 'Maître'. He took her hands and pulled her upright. He smiled at her.

'You have talent. You have a future.'

The rest of the morning for Rachel passed in a dream. It had happened. She was no longer the family failure. It didn't matter that she had not been chosen from Madame Donna's pupils to dance in *Pirouette*. It did not matter that Jane was lioning it at the Bee Bee studios. It did not matter that Tim was making a name for himself in Hiram's Hour. The greatest glory that could happen to a dancer was going to happen to her as once it had happened to Posy. Monsieur Manoff was going to ask her to stay with him and to say he would make her into a great artiste. He had not said it yet because he did not know it was her last Saturday, but he would directly he knew. The glory of it! The glory!

It was difficult to get near Monsieur Manoff after the class, so many people wanted to speak to him. It was Posy who arranged it. She led Rachel forward.

'Rachel wants to say good-bye, Maître. She leaves for England next week. She's brought you a present.'

Monsieur Manoff evidently liked presents. He was terribly pleased with his, which was a piece of good glass. He stared at

it so long that Rachel thought he had forgotten she was still there. Presently he looked at her.

'Thank you. I will value this, and when I look at it I shall say, "How is the little friend of Posy's getting on?" And some day I shall not need to wonder, I shall read of you in the papers. Yes? Good-bye, my child, and good luck.'

It was not Posy who saw something was wrong with Rachel, it was her adopted sister Pauline. Rachel had not seen much of Pauline, who was starring in a picture and very busy. That Saturday she had an afternoon off. After lunch she put an arm round Rachel.

'I've hardly seen you, and now it's "good-bye". Come for a walk round the garden.' As soon as they were out of earshot of the household she said, 'What's up?'

It was surprising how easy somebody as important as Pauline was to talk to. In no time she was hearing everything. Jane in the pictures, Tim in Hiram's Hour.

'You can't think how awful it's made me feel. You see, in England I was the one who was going to do something. Monsieur Manoff did ask Posy to come to him in Czechoslovakia, so he just might have asked me to join his company here. If he had it would have been such a compliment I'd never have felt a worm again whatever Jane and Tim did.'

They were by the pool. Pauline sat on the edge and took off her shoes and dabbled her feet in the water.

'I wouldn't fuss about it if I were you. His company was made up before you came here. When he had Posy over it was to join his school. Now he has a ballet and he's going to tour it's different.' She kicked up a spray of water. 'I've often found that things happening the way you don't expect them to turn out is the best way.'

'But nothing's happening to me at all.'

'That's what you think. You remember I told you I wanted more than anything to be a great actress; a stage one, I mean. I don't think I'd ever have let Garnie sign a contract for me to come here only the day I got the offer was the same day Posy saw Manoff. We'd no money so I said I'd go to Hollywood so that Posy could go with Nana to Czechoslovakia.'

'But it must be wonderful to be a film star.'

'I'd much rather act on a stage before an audience. But that's what I mean. I came here because of paying for Posy, but in the end it's going to give me what I want. After this picture I'm going to play Juliet in New York, and later on perhaps in London. Juliet! I'm so happy I can't tell you.'

Rachel was glad Pauline was so happy but she could not

283

see how Pauline acting Juliet could possibly mean things were turning out the best way for herself. She could hear the conversations. 'And Jane played Mary in *The Secret Garden*.' 'And Tim was a great success on the air.' 'Rachel? Oh, she went on with her dancing lessons.'

'I don't mean I haven't learnt a good deal from Monsieur Manoff because I have, and Dad says he hasn't lost faith in my future, but, seeing how the others have done, sometimes I do.'

It was horrible for Rachel saying good-bye to the Fossils. Dear, fat Nana had been so kind. Aunt Sylvia so welcoming and Posy had been the most important part of her being in California. Rachel gave her presents with a lump in her throat. For Nana one of the nicest of the photographs taken at the Bee Bee studios, in a good frame.

'I thought you might like it because of me wearing that frock of Posy's you altered.'

Nana was very pleased.

'And nothing could be nicer. I liked that one you gave to Posy, that she's sent to that Madame Fidolia, but I like this better. Less fanciful; I have never cared for fancifulness in my children.'

Rachel tried not to show that Posy giving away the photograph she had given her made her feel even lower than she felt already; but she did show it. Posy kissed her.

'I knew you'd never show it to Madame, but she ought to see it so I sent it. And I knew you'd never tell how pleased Manoff was with you so I told her.'

Rachel had flowers for Aunt Sylvia and Pauline, and a book on The Royal Ballet for Posy. Everybody was pleased. They put her into the taxi they had ordered and waved good-bye. When Rachel knew they could not see her she put her face into her hands to hold back crying. 'Oh, I do feel miserable – Monsieur Manoff didn't ask me to stay and now he never will – Posy can say what she likes but she gave my

284

photograph away because she didn't want it, and I don't see why she should, I'm nobody. It's all over. I'm going back to London. Oh, goodness, if only, only, one little nice thing people could talk about had happened to me!'

CHAPTER 27

GOOD-BYE TO THE STUDIO

IT was a pity, but Jane drove to her last day at the studio in a bad temper. First of all her plans had been upset. Her idea had been to drive to the lot just before school finished and say good-bye to everybody, and then, which she had already arranged, have lunch at the same table in the commissary with David. After lunch David was to take her to say good-bye to his creatures, and then the family were coming with Aunt Cora to see the film.

Bee and Miss Barnabas upset these arrangements. Miss Barnabas had told Bee not to take Jane away from her school one day before she need. That with all the good-byes Bee would have to say and last things to do it would maybe help to have one of the children out of the house. It had been a help, because with the packing to do Peaseblossom could not give the attention to Rachel's and Tim's lessons she thought necessary, and though she could trust Rachel up to a point to see that she and Tim worked by themselves, it was very unlikely Rachel could manage Jane. It had suited from another point of view. Aunt Cora liked going to the studio, and liked lunching in the commissary, so, on the last days after shooting stopped, Aunt Cora fetched Jane from school and they lunched on the lot before they drove home, which meant Aunt Cora was out of the house as well as Jane.

'Such a splendid arrangement!' Peaseblossom said to Bee. 'It is so much easier not to seem to be making a mess, and taking up Bella's time, when Cora isn't there to watch us pack.'

John drove Jane to school that last morning and saw she was angry.

'What's the trouble?'

Jane was shocked that she could have a father so dead to what was fair that he had to ask a question like that.

'Would you like to be pushed off to lessons on a day when Tim's been allowed to spend the morning saying good-bye to the Antonios, and Rachel's gone with Aunt Cora to buy food for the cocktail party?'

'I see your point, but let's be fair; nobody knew you didn't want to go. We thought you'd like a chance to say good-bye to them all, especially David.'

'Of course I want to. But I meant just to come in when lessons were over; and another thing, when a person is giving good-bye presents that person should choose who has them.'

John did not pretend he did not know what Jane was talking about. Bee had come to him some time ago about Jane's presents. 'We can leave the studio people,' she had said, 'to Jane, but we must see she gives something really nice to Miss Barnabas and Miss Steiman; they've been terribly kind and I'm sure Jane hasn't always been easy.' John had agreed with Bee and a beautifully bound book of poetry and a dozen lovely handkerchiefs had been bought.

'So that person should if that person could be trusted to say thank you properly to people who have been good to her.'

Jane stuck her chin in the air.

'I've written in the book and I'll say polite things to Miss Steiman.' She lowered her voice. 'But inside I'll be thinking I hope she needs these handkerchiefs soon because she gets an awful cold.'

'You're a little horror. I can't imagine how I came to have such a daughter. For goodness' sake don't spoil our last day, and do try and leave a good impression behind. We don't want everybody in the Bee Bee studios in the future saying, "As cross-looking as that English child, Jane Winter".'

Miss Steiman was relaxing and deep breathing before the day's work when Jane walked in. Between her deep breaths she was thinking how wonderful it was she would never have to teach that little Jane Winter inflexions again. Jane disapproved of the way Americans did up parcels. Not because she did not think coloured paper and big bows pretty, she did, but Peaseblossom had said, 'We must never go back to brown paper and string again, must we?' and that sort of statement made her think the opposite. Jane was carrying Miss Steiman's parcel as if it smelt. She had learned what she was to say by heart, but the way she said it was not a credit to Miss Steiman's training in inflexions, for there were none at all and no pauses either.

'I've come to say good-bye and to thank you for taking so much trouble with me and to give you these to remember me by.' Then, in quite a different voice because what she was thinking got the better of her, 'Mum chose them and paid for them. I didn't.'

Miss Steiman needed very little to make her feel good. Jane being polite, Jane bringing her a present was quite enough to make her sure that her belief that all children were sweet really was right. She kissed her.

'Now, isn't that kind. Oh, Jane, what perfectly beautiful handkerchiefs! Every time I use one I'll surely think of you.'

Jane gave Miss Barnabas her book before school. She had written, under Bee's instruction, 'To Miss Barnabas to say thank you. Jane Winter'. Miss Barnabas said thank you and kissed Jane, but she broke off lessons a few minutes early to say a proper thank-you and good-bye. She made a little speech. She showed the school her book and said she was going to treasure it. She did not say Jane had been a model pupil or anything like that, because she couldn't, but she did say that they had enjoyed having Jane with them, and it was important that they should because Jane was English, and if they hadn't enjoyed having her they might have thought that

when the chance came to visit Britain they wouldn't go because
they had known a Britisher whom they did not like and judged
all British children by her.

'Which I hope Maurice is listening to,' Jane thought, 'for
nobody could want to visit the place he came from.'

After Miss Barnabas had finished speaking all the pupils
came to say good-bye. Jane for once was embarrassed; they
were all so nice, and almost all of them had brought her a
present, so nice that Jane by herself thought of the right way
to say thank-you. She asked them to put their names and
addresses on a piece of paper and she promised to send each
of them post cards of London when she got home. Even as
she made the offer she could see that she was not going to
like carrying it out. She saw herself at the table in the dining-
room at Saxon Crescent writing post card after post card until
her hand ached.

Jane said a proper good-bye to Mrs Norstrum and Shirley.
She had brought Shirley a new plastic bubble blowing outfit
because she had used up so much of Shirley's. Shirley had
for Jane a lovely book full of pictures of Los Angeles. Jane
and Shirley had seen each other every day while *The Secret
Garden* was being made and they had said all the things they
had to say, and knew each other well. Saying an official
good-bye seemed silly. So they just smiled at each other. Mrs
Norstrum was the one who said things. She gave Jane a
parcel for Bee. She said she had always thought English people
were stiff, and knowing Bee had shown her that lots of them
were just as homely as Americans. She did not say she was
sorry to say good-bye to Jane, because she was a straight-
forward person who did not say things just for pretence, and
quite honestly she thought it was better Shirley should stand-
in for Ursula Gidden, who was always nicely behaved and
never made trouble in the studio, but she did say they would
always remember Jane, which was true.

Jane had not meant to say an especial good-bye to Maurice

but she had to because Aunt Cora was talking to Mrs Tuesday when Jane, her arms full of presents, came out of the schoolroom. It was a short good-bye. Jane said:

'Do you want a post card sent you from London?'

'No.'

Jane nodded.

'I thought you wouldn't. Good-bye.'

As they walked to the commissary Aunt Cora gushed about the charm of Maurice and Mrs Tuesday. Luckily Jane was not attending. 'Thank goodness he didn't want a post card,' she thought. 'I'd have hated to think of a nice piece of London on the mantelpiece of that no-good, stuck-up chipmunk.'

Lunch in the commissary was awkward. Aunt Cora did all the talking; Mr Doe was still made shy by her and only said, 'Yes, ma'am. No, ma'am.' Jane was glad when it was over and she and David, with Mr Doe and Aunt Cora far behind, were on their way to the place where the creatures lived.

David opened the gate into his little zoo.

'I brought them all up to say good-bye.'

'Ella?'

'Sure I've brought Ella.'

It was like making the scenes with David in the picture only better, because there were no cameras or lights to scare the creatures. David opened the doors of their pens and cages and laid food about. There was no need for the pipe playing; this was ordinary; this was only old David. Mickey came first closely followed by Bob. Then Pedro streaked out and lay like a dog at David's feet. Then, as though Pedro was not a fox, Ella came dancing after him, not the little new Ella who had been in Jane's arms, but a longer-legged but still enchanting Ella. Then out came Joe, Arthur, Mary and Ann, the rabbits, tearing at a lettuce which lay almost on Jane's feet, but paying no more attention to her feet than they would if they had been two tree stumps. Andy, the pheasant, strutted along and presently flew on to one of David's knees, and immediately, as if to say 'What's this? He's as fond of me as he is of you,' Jack, the crow, flew on to David's other knee. As well there were creatures Jane had met in David's sort of zoo, but not in the picture: more rabbits, the other squirrels and the pony. It was perfect. Sitting there on a box Jane forgot everything. That today was the last day. That she was on a studio lot. Even that she had never been grand in the way she wanted to be, and that so far nobody had asked her to stay on and make more pictures.

What seemed a pause in time was broken by Aunt Cora. Her whining voice rang through the zoo.

'Jane. Jane. You really must hurry. They're showing the picture in just a quarter of an hour.'

At Aunt Cora's voice all the creatures disappeared back into their cages and pens. Jane's eyes blazed.

'She's frightened them. She frightened them away. I could kill her.'

David had not moved.

'They'll come back.'

'By you playing your pipe? Oh, David, before I go will you tell me something? Is my pipe playing good enough for me to be a tamer yet? Is it?'

David took, as usual, a long time answering.

'Taming wild creatures isn't just piping; it's how you feel. They know that.'

'But they like me. Ella sat in my arms when she wouldn't look at Maurice, and Bob likes me and Mickey and all of them.'

David nodded.

'They like you.'

'So I can start taming creatures myself when I get home, especially Chewing-gum? I want to start with him doing tricks.'

'I don't know nothing about tricks, but I wouldn't trouble a grown dog; he'd think it kind of mean.'

'But I've been learning my pipe specially for him. Don't you think I could train him? Don't you?'

'Maybe. Don't rush at it. Start with a little bird. I figure little birds like piping.'

Aunt Cora's voice whined again.

'Jane. Jane. Will you come. You can't keep everybody waiting.'

Jane got up.

'I'm sending you a book on bird watching from England. Dad says you'll like that. Good-bye.'

David felt in his pocket. He brought out a small parcel. His words seemed more difficult and pushed out than usual.

'Good-bye. It's fine having known you.'

Jane stumped ahead of Aunt Cora. She felt miserable and she was not going to let Aunt Cora know it. She hated saying good-bye to David and his creatures. She wished he had been more certain about her being a trainer. It was a come-down, after hoping that, starting with Chewing-gum, she would have a troupe of performing dogs so good they would get a contract for Bertram Mills' circus, to follow David's suggestion and start with one small bird. All the same, inside her she knew he was right, and she knew that was what she would try to do. Bee and Peaseblossom did not know it but she had hidden her pipe and meant to practise it all the way to England. She stopped being miserable. She could see herself sitting on the wall of Saxon Crescent playing her pipe and as she piped the bird would come. Then another bird. Then another. Then the whole Crescent would be full of birds and people would say . . .

'Jane,' said Aunt Cora, 'come and walk with me. It's downright rude rushing ahead that way. What's that you're holding?'

Jane looked at her hand. David's present. It had no ribbon or grand paper, just a bit of newspaper round it and an elastic band. She took off the band and the paper. Aunt Cora peered at what Jane was holding.

'What's that?'

'A chipmunk. I wouldn't wonder if David carved it himself. It's a no-good, stuck-up chipmunk. I shall keep it always.'

Although the children had known from the first time they went to a theatre that they must not say one word at a public entertainment, or they would not visit one again for a year, both Rachel and Tim let out faint squeaks when they first saw Jane on the screen. It was, of course, the scene in the railway carriage. They had been rather bored by the beginning of the film. They liked film stories that stuck to the book story. They did not mind hearing the welcome the Cravens got from the incredible number of servants waiting in the hall, but after that they thought the further the story went from the book the more of a bore it was. There were such a lot of parties, and eating and drinking and riding horses, and they detested the sloppy scenes in the garden, which was not secret then but Mrs Craven's garden full of roses. When Mrs Craven sat on the bough of the apple tree which was afterwards to break, and talked about how lovely it was going to be to have a baby son called Colin, they nudged Jane to show they were thinking it wasn't going to be nice at all. They really only began to enjoy the film when the bough broke. Tim forgot himself and whispered, 'Good', which got him a little kick and an awful frown from John.

Jane in the railway carriage, except for wearing heavy-looking mourning, was very like a black-doggish Jane anywhere, only Jane never spoke to anyone in the voice Jane as Mary used to Annie Street as Mrs Medlock. She had, of course, pretended Annie Street was Mrs Gates and had spoken in the grand way she would have liked to have spoken to Mrs Gates, only luckily never had. But after that scene in the railway carriage a funny thing happened, not only to her family but to Jane herself; Jane ceased to be Jane and was Mary. The story showing in front of them had taken hold of them all. Even in the scene with Ella nobody nudged Jane;

it was not Jane who was holding Ella, it was Mary. It was not Jane who was growing nicer every minute, it was Mary.

Of course the film affected them all differently. Tim clapped when the wicked doctor cousin left Misselthwaite Manor for ever. John was interested, of course, in the way the story was told. Peaseblossom, Bee and Aunt Cora cried off and on all the time. Rachel, forgetting all about Jane, was caring for nothing but Colin. Although she knew the book she kept saying in her head, 'Let him walk. Let him walk. Make his father come back quickly before that awful man kills him.' To Jane it was the garden. Though she knew it was a painted garden; though she had said the lines over until she yawned, entranced she watched the garden come alive. She forgot Dickon was David; he was only Dickon to her, the boy who could show how to bring a garden alive; could teach Mary how to make creatures obey him.

It was a bewildered, blinking Winter family who found themselves, when the lights went up, in the grandly fitted private cinema of Bee Bee Films Incorporated. Jane's Mr Browne said:

'Well? What do you think of her?'

Bee mopped her eyes.

'That poor Mrs Craven only meeting her boy when she was a ghost.'

Peaseblossom blew her nose.

'Very affecting. What a wonderful improvement nature made in the characters of those two children.'

Tim knelt on his seat.

'I'm glad that awful doctor got sent away. I hope he starved.'

Rachel got up.

'Colin could walk. He could walk as well as anybody at the end.'

Aunt Cora powdered her nose, which was shiny from crying.

'That Maurice Tuesday is certainly a wonderful little actor.'

That brought all the family back from the story. They turned to Jane.

'You were good, darling,' said Bee. 'I forgot it was you.'

Rachel looked puzzled.

'Do you know, so did I.'

Tim sighed.

'So did I, and I liked Jane better when she was Mary.'

John laughed.

'You did marvels with her, Browne. Come along, kids, we mustn't keep Jane's Mr Browne and Mr Phelps hanging about, they're busy men.'

Mr Phelps said good-bye to Jane in the cinema. He gave her a kiss and an envelope.

'There's a four-leafed clover on a brooch in there to bring you luck. I'll not be forgetting you.' He pointed to his neck. 'You'll see I'm wearing the tie you gave me. Good-byé, you little spalpeen, it's a trouble you've been but one I'd not have been missing.'

Jane's Mr Browne took her hand. They walked together through the lot.

'Sorry it's over?'

Jane looked round at the now familiar streets, studios and offices.

'Sort of.' She looked up at her Mr Browne. 'You see, I'm nobody at home. I know to you I wasn't much here, but I was to the others.'

'But you wouldn't like this life.'

'I might if I acted always with David and the creatures.'

'That wouldn't happen. You'd go from picture to picture, maybe without playing with him again.'

'All the same, I'd like to have been asked to stay. I'd like just once to have been really important.'

'In what way?'

'Any way so Rachel and Tim could see I was important. I'm not sure how. I suppose people bowing and flowers . . .' She was not certain what she did want so she broke off. 'I've got a present for you.'

Jane's Mr Browne was the right person to give a present to. He didn't wait until he got home to undo it. He undid it right there in the middle of the lot. It was a good present. A drinking bowl for Hyde Park. Jane had had it specially painted for him. On one side was written 'Hyde Park' and on the other 'No bad fish'. Jane's Mr Browne seemed pleased. He lifted her chin and looked at her.

'Thank you. Hyde Park will surely value that. Good-bye, little friend. Watch out for the mail van. Neither Hyde Park nor I are going to forget you.'

CHAPTER 28

CALIFORNIA, HERE WE GO

TIME seemed as if it were running through a sieve. The family were no sooner back from the Bee Bee studios than they were rushing upstairs to change for Aunt Cora's good-bye cocktail party. Peaseblossom, perhaps because she had cried so much at *The Secret Garden*, seemed to feel it was time she stiffened up. She was in her most ordering-about mood.

'Now hang up these clothes ready to travel in tomorrow, and don't forget, girls, these best dresses are to be packed, in the paper I have left ready, the moment you take them off.'

Both Rachel and Jane hated to be told things twice, and they already knew about packing the party dresses, but only Jane argued.

'All right, we know.'

'And don't let me hear that tone, Jane. Because you were good in the film that's no reason for rudeness at home. That's not the Winters' way, is it?'

Jane scowled as the door shut behind Peaseblossom.

'I know what's the matter with her. She's thinking of the *Mauretania* and being seasick. If she tells me once more to pack anything I shall say "When we get on the *Mauretania*, Peaseblossom, dear, think of chocolate creams floating in hot castor oil."'

Rachel had her frock over her head. Muffled groans came before she got out at the other end of it.

'I wish you hadn't said that. I've been saying and saying to myself that nobody can feel sick if they eat a strawberry ice, but I'm not sure enough to be able to think of chocolate creams in hot castor oil safely.'

There were shouts from downstairs. Jane opened the door.

'Is Rachel there? Come down, Rachel, I want you.'

'What is it?'

Rachel, scrabbling at the buttons on her frock, hurried down the stairs. John was holding a cable. Jane hung over the landing rail to hear what the fuss was about. Had Monsieur Manoff asked Rachel to stay after all?

Rachel read the cable out loud.

'Please cable date arrive London Stop Glinken seen Rachel's photograph and heard Manoff's views on her work wishes see her immediately with view engaging her good dancing role new production Fidolia.'

Rachel's hands shook so much with excitement she could hardly hold the cable.

'Oh, Dad! Oh, Dad!'

John took the cable from her.

'Don't shake it to pieces. I've got to answer it.' He put an arm round her. 'I told you I refused to despair of your career.'

'But you said you felt it in your bones it would happen here and it never has.'

'Hasn't it? Where are we now? Isn't that the Pacific Ocean outside? Aren't those mountains in California?'

Rachel had to hug herself with both arms.

'I'm so happy I hurt.'

John gave her a kiss.

'That's good. It was your turn for a break. Good dancing role! Imagine how proud we're all going to be on your first night.'

Jane went back into her bedroom. John and Rachel had not looked up. They did not know she had heard. 'How proud we're all going to be.' She scowled at the labelled luggage. 'I suppose they'll forget I was once nearly a film star. Well, fairly nearly one. They'll talk, talk, talk about Rachel's dancing and Tim's piano, and Peaseblossom will say,

"We may not all be equally talented but we can all be equally nice people."' Then Jane remembered her pipe. She opened a drawer. Yes, right at the back under the lining paper was a lump. Let them wait. She would show them. She might start with only one small bird, but in the end she would have . . .

Peaseblossom opened the door.

'Not dressed yet, Jane? Let me do you up, the guests will be arriving soon. What were you dreaming about? Chewing-gum?'

Jane was still half in her day-dream.

'Partly him, but mostly lions, tigers, elephants and giraffes. Did you ever see an absolutely tame giraffe in a circus, Peaseblossom.'

'No, dear.'

Jane spoke with superb confidence.

'You will.'

Aunt Cora's good-bye cocktail party was the biggest success of all her cocktail parties. Everybody that Bee, John and Peaseblossom had made friends with came to it, and they nearly all brought good-bye presents. The children handed round. Everybody told Jane that they would surely go and see *The Secret Garden*, and Tim that Hiram's Hour would not be the same without him, and Rachel, her face shining with being so pleased, did not mind at all, because when she was asked if she was sorry to be leaving she was able to say, 'In a way, of course, but, you see, I'm probably going back to a theatre engagement. A good dancing part in a new show.' As she repeated the sentence over and over to different guests she felt better and better. 'It's as if I'd shrunk in the wash,' she thought, 'and was getting starched back to my proper size.'

Tim, after a time, gave up hanging round and went to the piano. He was feeling very gay. He was sorry to leave California, but he longed to travel on the Chief and *Mauretania* again. He felt much too gay to play ordinary music, so instead he played things people could sing. Presently all the guests were standing round the piano, roaring at the top of their voices. Tim finished in grand style with 'The Battle Hymn of the Republic'. John and Bee thought it polite of him to have finished with that, and the guests' voices rose louder than ever as they sang 'Glory, glory Hallelujah', but Tim had not played for politeness, nor for anybody in the living-room; he was playing very loud so that it would reach the kitchen where Bella would be singing, swaying to and fro, her eyes rolling, for that was her favourite hymn.

When everybody had gone there was present giving. After much thought the whole family had combined on a cocktail shaker and glasses to go with it for Aunt Cora, for, after all, giving parties was her favourite thing. Aunt Cora was so pleased with her present and so exhausted by her long day, and the emotion of saying good-bye, that she had the beginnings of a nervous spell and had to go up to bed quickly so that she would be fit to drive them the next day in the borrowed station wagon to their train.

When Aunt Cora had gone to bed the family went to the kitchen and gave Bella her presents. A vase from Rachel; a china dog from Jane; one of his records from Tim; and the family group in the silver frame from the grown-ups. Although, of course, they would see Bella again in the morning it was the proper good-bye and everybody felt miserable. Tears trickled down Bella's wrinkled black cheeks.

'I sho' hates to see yo' go. I couldn't hate it more if yo' was my own family.'

Bee took her hands.

'And we hate to leave you, Bella. You've been part of the family for six whole months.'

As they would have plenty of time to sleep on the train the children were allowed to take a last evening walk. John looked up at the stars.

'I shall remember the nights in California; more even than I shall remember the sun.

'It's the smell,' said Jane. 'It smells Californianish.'

Rachel sniffed, then shook her head.

'It isn't. It's it being warm that's so Californianish, as if the sun was still out only not showing.'

Tim was scornful.

'You aren't listening. It's the tree frogs; they're the most Californianish thing of all. I shall hear ker-up, ker-up for ever and ever.'

Suddenly they were playing follow-my-leader up the street just as they had at Thanksgiving. John leading. Then Rachel. Then Tim. Then Peaseblossom. Then Jane and, last, Bee. They sang their final and silliest version of 'California Here I Come'. John made it up as they jumped and skipped along:

> 'California here we go,
>   Right back where we started fro'.
> Where bowers of flowers bloom in the sun
>   every summer at dawning.
> Birdies sing and everything,
> Old Chewing-gum said, "Don't be late,"
> Be sure I can hardly wait,
> Open up dear London gate,
> Saxon Crescent here we come.'

The same railroad station. The same train. Even the same coach, with dear Joe, his black face spread into a wide, recognizing grin; but it was so different from their arrival. Nothing was strange now, and instead of just Aunt Cora there were a crowd of people to see them off. Posy had rushed down to say that she had heard from Madame and good luck about the job. The Antonios were there to see the last of Tim. They had brought everything they could think of that he would like from their drug store, and seemed to mind terribly that he was going away. Mrs Antonio was crying.

'You take'a da good care. I burn'a da candle, I burn'a ten candle.'

Mr Antonio tried to smile but he seemed to mind too much to do it very well.

'I hate'a da train. I hate'a da good-bye.'

There were heaps of friends to say good-bye to Pease-blossom, Bee and John and, as if they had not done enough yesterday, they had brought even more good-bye presents. Aunt Cora would have enjoyed the fuss only she did not care for being mixed up with the Antonios; also she had a feeling Posy noticed this and thought it funny, which was true. With little steps she was dancing for Rachel an impression of Aunt Cora not liking the Antonios.

They were told to get on the train. Joe pulled up the steps. The family leant forward, waving and shouting. The train made American train noises. They were off.

Jane had been squeezed to the back of the family. There was nobody to see her off. She had not expected anybody, but it seemed mean she was the only one without a special friend. Of course David wasn't a railway station sort of person, but it would have been grand if he had marched down the platform, with Mickey on one shoulder and Bob on the other and perhaps Pedro walking behind.

'Now,' said Peaseblossom, 'we must settle ourselves. You three children . . .'

Joe was standing by them, an enormous box tied with wide satin bows in his arms.

'Miss Jane Winter?'

Jane was so surprised she could hardly untie the bows. She took the lid off the box. Inside, on top of sheets of green paper, was a card. 'Best Wishes and Bon Voyage from the Directors of Bee Bee Films Incorporated.' She pulled back the layers of paper. For a moment there was complete silence. Then Rachel said:

'Orchids! Real, film star flowers.'

302

Tim gaped into the box.

'Hundreds of them!'

They looked with respect at Jane. Rachel said:

'This is the grandest thing that's ever happened to us.'

Tim nodded.

'Most likely the grandest thing that will ever happen to a Winter.'